Pra

TENDERFOOT

By

Mary E. Trimble

May E Trimble

Tenderfoot

Copyright © 2009 by Mary E. Trimble

ISBN: 978-0615831954

The major event in this book is non-fiction; some of the characters are real and some are fictional.

Originally published by Treble Heart Books 2010

Printed in the United States of America

Cover design by Bruce Trimble
Front cover image by Bruce Trimble
Back cover image of Mount St. Helens courtesy USGS

Published by ShelterGraphics
Camano Island, WA

OTHER BOOKS BY MARY E. TRIMBLE

Tubob: Two Years in West Africa with the Peace Corps

McClellan's Bluff

Rosemount

This book is dedicated to my husband and best friend, Bruce Trimble, whose sense of humor, support and candid critiquing helped to make my dream come true. I am also grateful for the love and moral support of my children, Byron, Jeffrey, Bonnie and Robin.

Author's Note

*M*ount St. Helens, a perfect snow-white, cone-shaped mountain, was a favorite showpiece among Washingtonians for generations. A popular vacation spot, it boasted of beautiful lakes, challenging trails for hikers, with rustic vacation homes and resorts nestled on the shores of pristine Spirit Lake. Photographers came from across the country to capture the elegant symmetrical cone of "America's Fujiyama."

In early spring 1980, the first of many earthquakes threatened the tranquility of this majestic mountain and, on May 18, 1980, Mount St. Helens exploded in a violent eruption, blowing off the top 1,300 feet with five hundred times the force of the Hiroshima atomic blast. Within hours, the explosion destroyed 234 square miles of forest. Trees were either blasted away, snapped like pieces of straw, or scorched while standing, reducing one of the world's most superb mountain landscapes to a gray wasteland.

When Mount St. Helens first erupted, it sent a low-frequency shock wave straight up, which in turn reflected off several layers of the atmosphere and then bounced back to the ground in a large donut-shaped ring fifty to three hundred miles around the mountain. Thus, most people within fifty miles of the mountain did not hear the blast, yet it was heard as far away as Canada.

Fifty-seven people lost their lives as a result of this catastrophic eruption, though only about half those bodies were recovered. Most deaths were due to suffocation, others died from burns, or as a result of falling objects. Of the lives lost, a few were scientists, but most fatalities were sightseers who had been repeatedly warned to stay clear of the area. An estimated 7,000 deer, elk and bear, and untold thousands of birds and small animals also perished. The Toutle River grew so hot witnesses reported seeing fish jump out of the water to escape the heat.

A menacing plume of ash boiled 60,000 feet into the atmosphere as the mountain turned itself inside out. The heavy ash cloud swept eastward across the continent in three days, and circled the globe in seventeen days. In Yakima, Washington, 138 miles from Mount St. Helens, emergency crews removed an estimated 600,000 tons of ash from the business district and residential areas. The heavy ash flattened wheat fields and weighted down fruit trees. Agricultural losses in the Pacific Northwest totaled millions of dollars.

Extensive property damage affected many local residents. The blast and subsequent floods ruined or severely damaged more than three hundred homes, along with farm buildings and equipment. Hundreds of livestock were lost, either swept away in flood waters or buried in debris. Massive mudflows wiped out roads and bridges and for months afterward, extensive repair work was undertaken to regain use of the Columbia River and its tributaries.

Campers and loggers ten miles away from the blast zone heard an aftermath roar that one logger described as sounding "like a couple of big passenger jetliners coming through the woods." Within seconds, darkness covered the area and a terrific heat rolled in, burning people and trees within its path.

Tenderfoot is a work of fiction taking place during the months surrounding the Mount St. Helens eruption. The characters in this novel are fictitious, with the exception of Washington State Governor Dixy Lee Ray, Harry Truman, an old-timer who for fifty-four years ran the Mount St. Helens Lodge in the shadow of the mountain, and geologist David Johnson whose radio warning, "Vancouver, Vancouver, this is it," alerted the world of an eruption of unbelievable magnitude. Whenever possible the geological events leading to the eruption are factual as are descriptions of the aftermath. Although the characters have been fictionalized, various experiences of blast victims represent true accounts.

Chapter One

AS I SEE IT
Kevin Walsh
Clearwater News staff columnist

March 20, 1980. Mount St. Helens is grumbling, like an old man waking up from a long nap. University of Washington seismologists recorded an earthquake measuring 4.1 on the Richter scale about twenty miles from Mount St. Helens. They're speculating our "America's Fujiyama" may be in for a little action.

*L*ost again. Corrie's sweaty hands gripped the steering wheel, her stomach clenched. Sometimes it seemed to her that she'd spent the better part of her life lost. She wished she could think of it as an adventure, but it was un-settling, not knowing where she was. She'd turned off the highway to get a better look at this part of the country. Ranch country. She was more than ready to quit the city with its crazy traffic and congestion. And why not move? No one at home needed her attention now that her daughter Gwen was away at college. Actually, there was no one at home besides her Labrador retriever, Bo. She could do what she'd always wanted to do, write in the country, about the country, and observe first-hand this kind of life.

But, where to start? Even more important right now, where was she? If she could just find that highway again. Didn't they believe in street signs around here? There's a sign. Great. A sign with a cow, "400 Feet." She smiled, remembering. When they were kids, her older brother used to swear that "Pedestrian Crossing 50 Feet" meant twenty-five people. Using that logic, one hundred cows would be crossing ahead.

The road curved sharply with a bend in the river and suddenly a huge bunch of cows blocked the way. Big cows, little cows, brown cows, spotted cows. Corrie slammed on her brakes and at the same time noticed a guy on horseback signaling to her. What? She had her hands full trying to stop. A cow stepped right in her path and she turned sharply to avoid it and skidded to a stop, cross-wise on the road. She felt a soft bump on the passenger side. She could barely see anything through the dust she'd created screeching to a stop. Oh, my God! Did I hit that cow?

Corrie opened her door and was half way out when the guy on horseback yelled, "Get back in your car!" She quickly backed in and slammed the door.

Lowering the window, she started to lean out. "I'm so sorry—" Before she could finish her apology a cow stuck its huge head through the window, forcing her back. It slobbered on her arm and shoulder. "Eeew!"

The guy was right beside the car now, barking sharp commands. At the cow, hopefully. "Haw! Haw! Get away from there!"

The cow banged its head on either side of the window as it backed out, splattering more slobber on her arm and leg. The gooey stuff dripped a crooked stream down the inside of the car door. The air was filled with sounds of a horse's heavy breathing, creaking leather, jangling tack, the man's yelling and then a loud bellow from the cow echoed throughout the car. Corrie, realizing she'd been holding her breath, breathed deeply. The car reeked of cattle.

Another fellow, younger than the first, appeared on horseback, also yelling. "What's the holdup?"

The cowboy closest to her just shook his head. "Take 'em on over Chad. Where's Julie?"

Chad, pointed vaguely in another direction as he took over herding the cattle off the road. The cowboy closest to Corrie climbed off his horse and stepped over to the car, leading his horse. He shoved his big hat back and stooped to look into the car.

"Ma'am, are you all right?"

"I'm okay. Did I hurt that cow?"

"I don't think so, it wasn't much of a bump. You're driving too fast for these back roads, though. Didn't you see that cattle crossing sign?"

"Well, yes, I did, but–"

He waited.

She bit her lip. But what? I thought it would only be a hundred cows? I didn't think the sign meant today? This was awful. Telltale heat crept up her neck into her face.

She looked up into his face. Clear blue eyes waited expectantly. He glanced past her car and let out a sheer whistle, making her jump. He waved his arm with some kind of signal. Looking out the side window through the dust, Corrie could see the younger guy signal back. She was probably talking to the boss. He walked around her car, leading his horse, apparently looking for damage, then returned to her open window, and stood, waiting. He took off his hat and brushed it against his leg, raising road dust from both his hat and pants. The dust slowly drifted into her car.

"Ma'am, I've got to get back to work. Is there something I can do for you?"

"It seems I'm lost."

His eyes widened. "Lost?"

"I'm looking for the highway."

He pointed in the direction she had been headed. "At the end of this road, turn north and that road will take you right to the highway." He climbed back into the saddle with one smooth movement and backed his horse, giving her room to turn.

It took a few back and forth attempts to straighten out the car. Driving away slowly, her face burning with embarrassment, she glanced back in her rear-view mirror. He sat stone still, watching her. His horse jangled its head up and down, apparently anxious to get back to work. Once out of range, she reached back and fished out a towel from the back seat and wiped the thick goo from her arm, shoulder, her leg and the door. Yuk.

Okay, she was at the end of the road. North. Which way was north? She sat for a moment, trying to figure it out. Why couldn't he have just said left or right? She turned right.

She wound around, soon realizing she wasn't getting any closer to the highway. She hoped to find a spot to turn around when...oh, no, not again. Cattle milled on the road. Lots of cattle–more than last time. When the cattle spotted her car they spread out, soon surrounding her, rolling huge eyes in her direction. They bellowed constantly, low bellows from the big cows, with answering shrill bawling from the calves. A dog's demanding bark rose above the din of cattle noises. Finally, a blue-gray dog came into view and, despite herself, Corrie was impressed with the dog's ability to marshal the cows across the road, nipping at their heels to keep them moving.

She came to a full stop, but didn't open her door or window. She thought of honking but only fleetingly. The same man was purposefully riding toward her, his mouth a grim, straight line. She cringed.

He was talking to her. She couldn't hear, but could see his exasperation. Tentatively, she rolled down the window part-way.

"Ma'am, are you just trying to irritate me? What are you doing?"

"I'm trying to find the highway."

"I already told you how to get to the highway."

"Could you please tell me again?" She couldn't keep the frosty edge from her voice.

"Get yourself turned around, again, and when you get to that intersection where you turned right, turn left. That's north."

"Thank you." What more was there to say?

"You'll have to wait a few minutes while I get this stock off the road. This is the first of 'em and I have quite a few more coming. Just sit still."

"Okay." She felt like a reprimanded six-year old.

It was only March and you wouldn't think there would be so much road dust, but on this gravel, mostly dirt road, this many mingling cattle raised enough to cover her car. Corrie didn't dare run her windshield wipers, for fear of a stampede and this cowboy's wrath. She rolled the window closed in an attempt to keep the dust out of the car.

Corrie sat back and watched, fascinated despite her awkward predicament. The other cowboy, Chad, she remembered, caught up to them and, after glancing at her, rode behind her car and moved the cattle forward, then over to the side of the road. She unrolled the window a crack to hear the sounds of cattle moving, the protesting low grunts, interrupted by strident bellows answered by shrill bleats, apparently signals between mothers and calves, the shuffle and thud of hooves. The two cowboys whistled and yelled sharp commands. "Haw! Haw!"

A young girl, in her early teens perhaps, appeared from the direction the cattle were heading. She reined to a stop to watch the commotion and made a gesture that clearly meant, "What's going on?"

The younger cowboy rode near her and said something Corrie couldn't hear. The younger girl looked at the car and laughed, turned her mount around and started that strange high-pitched yipping noise, guiding the cattle away from the gate and into the pasture. The girl rode as though she were a part of the horse. They all did.

When the last of the cows lumbered across the road and into the pasture, the older cowboy closed the gate and waved her on. Again, with a lot of starts and stops, she managed to turn around. At least this time he didn't wait to watch her.

Finally finding the highway, she made her way back to the closest town, Clearwater. She needed to find a realtor, someone who knew her way around. And a car wash.

As Corrie drove down Clearwater's main street, she watched for a real estate sign. Ah, there was one, Clearwater Realty, a small office in a big old building with a shoe store on one side, a craft store on the other.

The bell jangled as she walked into an empty office. A woman came from the back, drying her hands on a paper towel. "Good morning."

Corrie introduced herself. "I'm from Seattle and am looking for a place to live temporarily."

The agent's warm smile put Corrie at ease. "Tell you what. I was just going over to Stella's for a cup of coffee. Why don't you join me and we'll see what we can figure out."

Jay-walking across the street, Corrie learned that the realtor, Nancy Abbot, had been in the real estate business for several years and lived in the area even longer. Corrie gripped her light jacket closed against the chilly early spring air. The restaurant hummed with the clatter of dishes, voices and laughter. A woman balancing a heavy tray of dirty dishes made her way back to the counter. The waitress glanced over her shoulder at a man who had apparently cracked a joke at her expense. "That'll cost you, Jake." She saw the two women. "Sit anywhere, Nancy, I'll be right with you."

The welcoming aroma of coffee, bacon and pancake syrup filled the air. The small room was stifling. Corrie slipped off her jacket.

Nancy, skilled at asking the right questions, ferreted out Corrie's mission within minutes. Before realizing it, she had told Nancy she was divorced, had a daughter in college, was now a full-time writer, and wanted to live in and write about the country. "I know it sounds strange. I've always been fascinated by country life, but I really know nothing about it."

Stella, the owner, hurried over to them, coffee pot and cups in hand, and filled their cups. They both declined to see a menu. "I guess just coffee for us," Nancy said.

The realtor turned to Corrie. "What kind of writing do you do?"

"I've been a travel writer for a number of years, but have recently published a novel." Nancy's expressive face showed her interest, so Corrie continued. "It is actually fiction, but based on a real family's story about their little girl who died of cancer. They not only lost their only child, they almost lost their marriage, too. It's a story about faith and hope."

"It sounds wonderful. I'd like to read it."

"The book is doing pretty well. It won the Pacific Northwest Book Award, which gave me a real boost." It was still hard to talk about herself in what seemed to her a boastful way. She had to get over that, her agent had told her often enough. She needed to be her own best fan.

"Do you have a place in mind, Nancy? I'm not real fussy, just a little cabin would be great. It's only temporary."

"Not really. If you were interested in buying a place, I could help you." Nancy flattened her lips together. "I wonder...."

Corrie leaned forward. "Yes?"

"I might know of a place, but I don't know if he'll consider it. Tell you what, let me make a phone call and see if I can set up an appointment for tomorrow morning. I won't be able to reach him until this evening. Where are you staying?"

"I stayed at the Clearwater Motel last night. Guess I'll check back in for another night or two."

"Okay. This isn't a sure thing at all, Corrie, but we'll see what we can figure out."

As she settled in the motel for another night, Corrie's optimism wasn't quite as keen as it had been. The realtor hadn't been all that encouraging. What a day this had been. Her face flushed with the memory of that embarrassing situation with the cowboy. She was out of her element here, that's for sure.

Chapter Two

AS I SEE IT
Kevin Walsh
Clearwater News staff columnist

March 21, 1980. Residents close to Mount St. Helens report persisting aftershocks following yesterday's earthquake. It's been 123 years since Mount St. Helens has given us anything but pleasure and spectacular views. The mountain has been a popular vacation spot with its pristine fishing lakes, rustic resorts and challenging destination for hikers. Staff photographer Al Helfens tells me photographers come to Mount St. Helens from all over the world to capture its elegant symmetrical cone. "Not many mountains are that perfect," Helfens claims.

*N*ancy called Corrie later that evening at the motel. "Now don't get your hopes up, but we can go look at that cabin tomorrow morning."

"Great." Corrie punched the air.

"I don't know how great you'll think it is when you see this place. Let me tell you a little bit about it. It's on my brother's ranch, about fifteen miles out of town. He's never rented it out, I just happened to think about it when you mentioned 'cabin.' His hired hand lived there for several years, but it's been empty for a long time now. It's probably filthy."

"I can clean it up. It sounds perfect."

"Well, not really. J, that's my brother, isn't that wild about renting it out. And really, Corrie, I'm sure it's a real mess. But let's give it a try. I don't have anything else I can think of right now. I'll pick you up at eight o'clock tomorrow morning, if that's okay. He'll wait for us, but he's really busy right now and we can't take too much of his time."

Corrie's heart pounded with excitement. She could hardly wait.

* * *

They rode to the ranch in the realtor's car. Corrie sat back and relaxed, relieved that she wasn't the one who had to find the place.

"Does your brother have a cattle ranch?"

"Yes. J has one of the largest ranches in the region now, about ten thousand acres. He's bought up a couple of neighboring ranches in recent years."

"Wow. That sounds big. Did you grow up on a ranch?"

Nancy nodded. "Near Randle, over by Mount St. Helens. Speaking of Mount St. Helens, did you hear that they're getting some rumbling over there?"

"I saw a little piece about it in the paper at breakfast this morning. I wonder if it will amount to anything?"

"Hard to say. It's so beautiful. The mountain is a perfect cone. Have you been there?"

"No, never. Tell me more about the ranch."

"I can tell you it's a lot of work. They're into calving now so it's pretty much round the clock."

"Does your brother have a family?

"He's a widower. He has a daughter, fourteen. And our nephew has been staying there. He used to come in the summers, but he graduated from high school last year and is working for J full-time."

"Just the three of them run that big ranch?"

"No. He has a hired hand. Moe's been with J for years; in fact, he worked for the previous owner."

Corrie, appreciating the luxury of not having to drive, admired the scenery. "I love these rolling hills. It's beautiful here."

"It really is. The hills change color with the seasons. Things are just beginning to green up. It's my favorite time of year. I always think of spring as the time of hope." They passed under the log arch. "Well, here we are. That's J's brand, the circle with "J" in the center."

Corrie couldn't help feeling like a little kid. It was all she could do to keep herself from jumping up and down on the seat.

"Now don't get your hopes up. I really don't know if he will go for this."

Corrie nodded, but she really couldn't imagine it not working out. It had to work out.

Nancy swung the car into the circular driveway near what appeared to be the back of the house. The yard was plain, but tidy. The house, half red brick and half wood siding, blended into its surroundings. "Tish, J's wife, used to have beautiful flower and vegetable gardens, but he just couldn't keep them up."

They stepped onto the back porch and Nancy knocked at the back door.

"Come in, Nan," a voice boomed out.

Nancy opened the door and stepped in, Corrie trailing after her. She stopped dead in her tracks. Oh, no. It was that cowboy! She could feel the heat of her face.

J's eyes widened. Nancy looked from one to the other. "What? Have you guys met?"

"Sort of," Corrie mumbled.

A reluctant smile crept along J's face. "I see you found the highway."

"Yes, finally. I've never been very good with directions."

"Taking them, or following them?"

"I mean, north, south. I get lost in strange places."

J smirked.

"How did that happen? I kept running into you."

"Or the cows."

"Well, yes. Was that cow okay?"

J shrugged. "No problem."

Nancy cleared her throat. "I'm feeling left out here."

Corrie and J spoke at once. Both stopped. Nancy looked from one to the other. "One at a time now."

J shrugged.

Corrie hesitated. "I was just looking around and got off the highway on to a side road and ran into...well, not actually.

"I think that's pretty accurate."

"I came across cattle crossing the road."

"Right after the cattle crossing sign."

She ignored him and looked straight at Nancy. "I asked for directions back to the highway and he said to turn north. I'm more comfortable with...you know...left or right."

Nancy nodded, as though all was clear now.

"But then," J prompted.

"But then, I guess I turned the wrong way and came across them again."

J turned to Nancy. "We were taking some of the herd to the Wagner place."

Nancy gave them both an indulgent smile. "Okay, let's talk about the cabin."

J shook his head. "Look, that place is a mess. I tried to call you back this morning, but I guess you'd already left. I don't think it would work out."

Nancy glanced at the kitchen clock. "We're already here. Let's just take a look at it."

J shrugged. "Be my guest. But I don't wanna hear how bad it looks."

Nancy opened the door and stood aside for Corrie. As she passed through, Corrie caught a glimpse of brother and sister exchanging glances. Sibling talk. Nancy put her hand on J's arm. "I know you're busy, J, we won't keep you. We'll just take a quick look and..."

J stepped out too. "I'll tag along." The blue heeler Corrie had seen with him yesterday trotted beside him.

Corrie wished J wouldn't come. How could they talk about the place with him right there? In any event, he made her nervous. They'd already gotten off to a rocky start.

The cabin was a short distance away from the house, on a little knoll. It looked like something from a museum, one of those original pioneer log cabins that a family of twelve had lived in. Two steps led to a sagging porch. Nancy tried to open the door. "It's locked?"

"No. Here, let me try." J shouldered her aside and with a shove, the door creaked open. A heavy, musty odor rolled out.

Nancy held her nose. "Oh, my."

"Hey," J shot back, "I don't want to hear about it."

Nancy glanced at Corrie. "Right. It's lovely, J."

He narrowed his eyes at his sister.

Corrie looked around. The place definitely held possibilities. "I'm surprised it has separate rooms. I expected only one room." The bedroom and bathroom were partitioned by framed wallboard.

"Yeah, I think that was a later improvement. The place didn't used to have running water, either. That little shed," he pointed to a small building a few feet away, "used to be an outhouse."

Thick dust covered every surface. Cobwebs darkened corners and windows. A sagging couch discouraged anyone from sitting on it. Suddenly a mouse scurried out of the corner by the couch and scampered out the door, the dog hot on its trail. Corrie blinked in surprise.

She walked over to what had been its nest and poked the fluffy pile with her toe. "Any more critters? The nest material looks like stuffing from the couch."

Corrie caught Nancy giving her brother a long look.

"Yeah, we'll have to set some traps. Mice probably wintered here."

Corrie walked past a wood stove that separated the kitchen area from the living room. An ancient electric range stood along one wall. "Does the stove work?"

J turned on a burner, creating a strong smell of burning dust. "Appears to."

Corrie opened the refrigerator door to nothing but a foul smell, rusty shelves and a moldy half-empty jar of mayonnaise. "How about the refrigerator?"

J reached behind the refrigerator and plugged it in. With a little cough, the motor came to life.

A quick glance told her all she needed to know about the bedroom. The only decent piece of furniture in the whole cabin was an oak dresser. Leading from the bedroom, the dinky bathroom needed lots of work. A new medicine cabinet would do wonders. She looked at her reflection through a mirror speckled with black marks from the ruined backing.

Corrie returned to the living room, where J and Nancy waited. "This would be perfect for me."

Clearly surprised, Nancy said, "Really?"

J, surprised too, stammered. "I don't know. I've never rented it out. I don't think you'd want to live here...."

"How much would you charge?"

J lifted his hat and ran his fingers through his hair. "I don't know. Hundred bucks. But I don't think—"

"That's more than fair. Maybe I could help out a bit. I really don't know much about ranching." Ha, what an understatement. "But I'd like to learn."

"Can you cook?"

"Cook? Of course I can cook, but that isn't what I want to do." It came out stronger than she'd intended.

J shook his head, then glanced at his sister before he looked back at Corrie. "Can you ride?"

"Yes, but just for fun and I haven't done it for a long time, but..."

"W-e-l-l, I just don't think—"

"Please. I'd love to give it a try."

J sighed with gusto and glanced at his sister, rubbing his jaw. "Okay. I don't think you'll be very comfortable out here, though. It still gets mighty cold at night."

Nancy, apparently remembering her role as realtor, chipped in. "What will she do with all this old furniture? Take it to the dump, I hope."

J blinked. "The furniture?"

"Yes, that lumpy davenport, that awful kitchen table and mismatched chairs, the sagging bed. The furniture."

"Yeah, they're pretty ratty."

"Literally," Nancy agreed. "Can you have Chad take it to the dump?"

J nodded.

"I think I could use the stove and refrigerator though." As long as they worked, Corrie didn't want to replace them for such a temporary stay. "I have furniture I can bring and..."

"I've got to get to work." J turned to leave. He obviously couldn't wait to leave.

"J, before you go, do I have your permission to do some...things?"

He stopped and turned around slowly. "Things? What kind of things?"

"Paint the walls, replace the medicine cabinet and mirror, put some kind of floor covering down? Maybe I could put that stuff between the logs?"

"Chinking. Do you know how to do that?

"No, but I'm sure they could tell me at the hardware store."

J hung his head. He clearly wished he were somewhere else. Another sigh. "Okay, paint and whatever else you want. I'll get Moe to do the chinking. That'll make his day."

"Thank you, J. I really appreciate this."

He nodded and whistled for his dog. "Julie. Let's go."

Oh, Julie was the dog. The other day she'd assumed it was the young girl.

After he was safely out of hearing, Corrie clapped her hands with glee. "Nancy, thank you. This is perfect."

Nancy rolled her eyes. "I don't know how perfect. You have a lot of work to do. Don't let them haul off that oak dresser. I gave it to J for the cabin but I'd like it back for my downstairs bedroom. Unless you could use it?"

"No. I won't need it. I have a bedroom set I plan to bring."

Corrie glanced around, mentally taking note of the things she needed. Nancy seemed in a hurry to leave, so she followed her out and closed the door, jerking it to make it close all the way.

Back at the motel, Corrie sat on her bed, head hung in thought. She and J hadn't gotten off to a great start. He really hadn't wanted to rent the cabin, that was obvious. She hoped she was doing the right thing. Could she be happy living here when she really didn't feel welcome?

Chapter Three

AS I SEE IT
Kevin Walsh
Clearwater News staff columnist

March 24, 1980. Seismologists are recording as many as 40 earthquakes an hour. Yesterday an earthquake sent avalanches rolling down Mount St. Helens' north face above Spirit Lake. Visitors are urged to stay away. A meeting has been called in Vancouver, WA for Tuesday March 25 for representatives from USGS, State Patrol and Washington State Department of Emergency Services.

Corrie flinched. Was that a bug crawling down her neck? It was! She squirmed, tried to reach under her tee-shirt. Now it was moving toward the front. She pulled the collar of her shirt out so she could see it. Nothing. All day, she'd been convinced she had bugs crawling inside her clothes, on her hair, in her shoes. Sweeping the log walls had disturbed whole generations of bugs of every description. Finally, that gruesome job was done.

She glanced at her watch, dusted it off so she could read it, and tried again. Five o'clock. Nothing appealed more to her at this moment than returning to the motel and taking a long hot shower.

A knock at the door made her jump. Corrie had left the door open to clear out the dust and to let in fresh air. An older man stood in the doorway. He glanced at her, then embarrassed, looked away.

Had he seen her look down her tee-shirt? She brushed her hair away from her sweaty face and attempted to look composed. "Yes?"

"J says you want that chinking done."

"You must be Moe." She sounded silly, even to herself.

He looked at her evenly. "I'm Moe. That chinking gotta be done inside and out."

"Okay, that'll be fine."

"It's gonna make a mess."

"That's okay, I'll clean it up. I appreciate..."

"I'll be back tomorrow, then." He turned and stomped down the steps.

Corrie stood at the doorway, watching him leave. A truck stopped and backed up to the cabin, swirling dust as it jerked to a stop. A young man climbed out. He called out, "Hey, Moe, can you give me a hand?"

He stepped up to the door and removed his cap. It seemed whenever she saw J, he was wearing the traditional wide brimmed cowboy hat, but this young fellow wore a baseball cap. His hair stuck out in the back. Hat hair, her brother called it.

Corrie smiled. "Hello, you're Chad, I gather." She had no intention of reminding him of their previous encounter. She could see the family resemblance, though he was a little shorter and much thinner than J. But he had the same clear blue eyes and that direct way of looking at a person.

"Yeah. My uncle says I need to clear out all this old furniture. Okay if I do it now?"

"Sure, the sooner the better. I've boxed up those dishes and some pots and pans. Maybe they should go to Goodwill, or someplace like that."

He shrugged. "Whatever."

Moe walked past her in the doorway and stood by the old couch. "Okay, ready?"

The two men carried out all the old furniture except for the oak dresser and the boxes, exchanging no words, only grunts and nods. They cleared the place in less than five minutes. Now it would be easier to clean. And paint. But first, a hot shower was calling her name. She returned to the motel, showered, and walked to Stella's for dinner.

The next day, while Moe chinked inside, she cleaned and painted the bathroom a light green. The metal shower stall would require two coats, but she'd have to do that another time.

Corrie tried to engage the older man in conversation. "I hear you've worked on the ranch a long time."

"Yep, long time."

The same young girl she had seen that horrible day when she mingled with the cattle rode by on horseback. Corrie considered stepping out and saying something, but held back. The girl looked over at the cabin, craning her neck, trying to see what was going on.

"Is that J's daughter?"

"Yep. That's her."

She finally gave up trying to carry on a conversation, for both their sakes. She wondered if he didn't like her, or was just shy. Probably irritated at having to do that messy job.

A few days later, before she left for Seattle, Corrie stood in the doorway and admired her little cabin. At last it was as clean as she could get it and the inside walls separating the rooms were freshly painted. Moe's chinking job looked wonderful making the log walls clean but rustic. She closed the door, noticing someone had fixed it so that it shut easily, and, with a sigh of relief, climbed into her car.

She'd already called her landlady to give notice that she would be moving out of the apartment. Since she'd sold what had been their family home, her belongings were either in the apartment or in storage. She'd have a little rearranging to do but it shouldn't take long. She figured two weeks, tops.

* * *

J looked out his kitchen window at the cabin. Before she'd left for Seattle, Corrie left a note saying she'd be back in a couple of weeks. During the time she'd been at the ranch, he'd only seen her from a distance as she was going to and from the cabin. A tenderfoot woman. What had he gotten himself into here? He didn't need more complications in his life.

Gretchen finished packing her lunch, topping it off by dropping an apple into the brown bag. "Bye, Dad. See you later."

"Okay, Honey. Have a good day at school." He returned her kiss on his cheek with one on her smooth forehead. "Be good."

"Oh, Dad, do I have to?"

He laughed.

"You look tired, Dad. Your calving season look."

"Yeah, I was up most of the night. One of the heifers had a rough time of it. She finally had a nice, big bull calf though."

"It took all night?"

"No, we were just finishing up with her when another one started in. Since I was already up I sent Moe home. He's getting too old for this all night stuff."

"I could stay home today and help."

"No way."

She sighed. "Well, I'd better get going then or I'll miss my bus." On rainy days or in the winter, someone took Gretchen to the road at the end of the long driveway, where J had built a little school bus waiting shed. But on nice days, she walked the distance.

J watched her leave. His little girl was growing up. He mentally braced himself for the years to come. They'd been on their own now for almost ten years. Gretchen was only four years old when

Tish died. What a nightmare year. Tish's heart condition left her barely able to take care of herself, let alone a little girl. Nancy had helped all she could, either coming out or taking Gretchen home with her. He couldn't have managed without his sister.

Actually, it was because of his sister's insistence on having this woman rent the cabin that he'd consented at all. It was hard to say no to Nancy after all she'd done for him, for all of them.

J sighed. But now, here he was, with someone else to worry about. This woman didn't know beans about ranching, cattle, couldn't even tell north from south.

He looked out the window again. It had been two weeks and two days since she left. "So where is she?"

* * *

Corrie and her brother, Dave, were finally on their way. Dave drove a U-Haul and Corrie, her small Datsun packed to the roof, followed close behind. Dave had taken off a couple days from work, just to help her settle in. Good old Dave. What a great brother. He had been a little surprised, even reluctant, with her announcement about her plans, but had agreed to help.

Corrie mentally ticked off the things on her "to do" list. They should lay the new tile on the kitchen and bathroom floors first. She sorted out the next tasks.

Moving was rarely fun, but this time it seemed exciting, a real change. Living in the country in a cabin would be such a departure from anything she had done. She turned off the radio, finding it a distraction with so much new going on in her life to think about.

She wished that she felt more welcomed at the ranch though. She couldn't help but feel like an intruder. Would she ever be a part of things?

Corrie had a huge regret. She'd forgotten to ask J if she could bring her dog. Twice she'd started to telephone him, but both times had hastily hung up, afraid he'd say no. Now the extra-large yellow lab sat in the little car's front seat, watching the scenery rush by, looking as though he was ready for an adventure, too. She reached over and gently tugged on his long soft ear. "You're going to love it there, Bo."

The dog turned to her, head cocked, trying to understand her words. His heavy tail thumped the seat.

Of course, she could bring her dog, she reasoned. She'd even had him with her in the apartment. It wasn't like the cabin was too fancy. When she went the first time, Bo had stayed with Dave. But he was her dog and they were a team. Corrie bit her lip. It was just the two of them. How could she have forgotten to ask if she could bring her dog? She hoped J wouldn't mind. Then, too, she hoped he wouldn't feel like she'd pulled a fast one, intentionally not mentioning having a dog.

* * *

J peered over the top of the morning paper as Chad slapped together sandwiches, slathering mayonnaise and mustard on each slice of bread. "Not so much mustard on mine." "Okay, I keep forgetting." Chad layered baloney and cheese slices on alternate pieces of bread. "Did you see that woman's moving in?" J dropped the paper and bolted from the table to the window above the sink. He watched as Corrie and a man carried in armloads of boxes. A big yellow lab pranced around them, getting in the way.

Chad joined him at the window. "That's a nice looking dog. So who's the guy?"

"I don't know. I said she could live here, I didn't agree to a couple moving in. And she didn't say anything about a dog." J's eyes narrowed at the activity.

"Lunch is ready."

"Yeah. Okay." He looked through the window again and steamed. "I don't think she's married and I can't have some unmarried couple living here. I won't expose Gretchen to a situation like that."

"Unc, sit down. Your sandwich is getting cold."

"I'll be right back. I'm gonna put a stop to this right now." He jammed on his hat and strode toward the cabin, the blue heeler close behind. His long legs quickly covered the distance.

The big dog rushed over to J and Julie, his thick tail swinging back and forth so rigorously his whole hindquarters swayed. He zeroed in on Julie first and dove his nose under her belly. She growled, showing her teeth, causing him to back up, looking horrified.

"Julie!" J commanded. She quieted immediately, but continued to eye this rude stranger, daring him to do that again.

Corrie caught up with Bo and grabbed his collar and held tight. "J, I forgot to tell you I have a dog. I hope it's all right." She loosened her grip and Bo bounded toward J, delight spreading across his large face as he mashed his nose in J's crotch. Julie, immediately alarmed, forced herself between J and this new threat.

"Bo! Oh, dear. I'm so sorry." She again grabbed her dog's collar. "He's really friendly, too friendly, I guess."

She looked so uncomfortable, J felt sorry for her. He nodded and reached down to let Bo smell his hand and then ran his thumb along the big dog's muzzle. Julie stiffened and growled deep in her throat. "It's okay, Julie, he's just a big friendly dog."

"I'll tie Bo up."

"No, don't do that. Just let them sort it out."

"But..."

"Let him go. It's okay."

Corrie released her hold and now Bo, more slowly this time, moved toward the blue heeler. He stood still, thick tail sticking straight out, while Julie smelled his important parts, then cautiously, he smelled hers. He held himself so stiffly, his legs trembled. He returned to Corrie's side and sat down.

J smiled. "There, that's settled." He glanced up and frowned as the man with Corrie returned from the cabin. "Look..."

Corrie smiled. "J, I'd like you to meet my brother, Dave Russell."

Relief surged through J. He pumped Dave's hand. "Here, let me help you with these things."

"No, thanks, J. Dave and I can handle it. What were you going to say?"

He shrugged and shook his head.

She glanced at the woodpile. "Thank you so much for the supply of firewood. That was thoughtful of you."

"You bet. There's a phone line to the place—you'll have to stop by the phone company to have it connected."

"Great, I'll do that."

Awkward moments filled the air. "Well, I'll get back to my lunch now."

His step was lighter as he returned to the house.

* * *

By the end of the day Corrie and Dave had laid the tile in the kitchen and bathroom, Dave installed new curtain rods at the three small windows and Corrie hung her freshly made curtains. The two of them carried in the furniture and arranged a throw rug in the center of the tiny living room.

Dave spent the night, sleeping on the sofa bed, and the next morning hooked up Corrie's computer and printer.

"Well Kiddo, you're all set. You be sure to call me if you need anything."

"I will, Dave. Thank you for everything."

"That fellow, J, seems pretty decent."

"I think he is, but I don't think he's wild about me being here."

Dave nodded, amusement dancing in his eyes. "He'll get used to you."

As she watched the U-Haul lumber down the driveway, Corrie felt a sense of loss. She wished Dave could have stayed another day and explored the place with her. She suddenly felt awkward. What had she been thinking, barging in on someone's home? She briefly considered jumping into her Datsun and chasing Dave down. But she didn't. She just stood motionless, watching curling dust trail the truck.

Chapter Four

AS I SEE IT
Kevin Walsh
Clearwater News staff columnist

April 2, 1980. The Forest Service has sealed off the mountain above the timberline and evacuated its ranger station on Pine Creek, which is dangerously situated in the path of an old volcanic mudflow south of the mountain.

In the meantime, interest is escalating within the scientific community. U.S. Geological Survey teams, including volcanic hazards people from Denver, are pouring into the Mount St. Helens area carrying metal suitcases packed with equipment. They report that as they approach the mountain, the ground quivers beneath their feet. That's true dedication for you.

Corrie turned the page of her book, trying to concentrate on the words. She shifted in her chair. Hadn't she already read this page? Here she was, all settled into this beautiful, peaceful country and she felt at odds. Bo, curled up on his rug by the door, watched her. He rose, circled his rug and flung himself back down with a deep sigh.

She looked up from the page she'd read at least twice. "Okay, you poor dog, let's do something."

The dog sprang to his feet, wagging his tail. She had seen a lot of coming and going in the small barn. Only an hour ago Chad had walked past her cabin and into the small building. She slipped on her jacket and ventured out. Was it okay for her to just go in there?

The door was set ajar and she pushed it open. Bo rushed past her to the nearest cow, barking a delighted greeting. The cow bawled alarm and stomped around the confined stall. Julie rushed forward with one commanding bark. J yelled to Bo, "Hey! Get away from there!" He glared at her. "Get him away from that cow."

Corrie rushed forward to grab Bo's collar. "I'm sorry. I thought..."

"Just keep him away from the stock," J snapped.

Moe's strained voice commanded J's attention. "Okay, I've got it."

Corrie tugged Bo's collar, commanding him to sit. She stood transfixed by the scene.

Moe, stripped to his tee-shirt, had his arm almost entirely into the huge cow, a light chain trailing out of the vaginal opening. J was at the cow's head, steadying it. At Moe's nod, Chad began to pull steadily on the chain. Corrie held her breath, fleetingly wondered if she should leave, but continued to stand, frozen in place.

"Hold it," Moe said. "Son of a bitch, here comes another contraction." The old man groaned softly and grimaced with pain as his arm was squeezed. "Okay, go ahead."

"Come on, you little shit," Moe gasped. "Okay. Here we go."

Moe quickly removed his arm and a little head popped free, and then, unbelievably fast, the whole slippery body emerged. The little calf lay on straw, sopping wet and limp. J released the cow's head; she turned and struggled to her little one to lick its nose, eyes and mouth. She nudged it and amazingly, the little fellow raised its head, stood on wobbly legs and made his way to her.

"That was wonderful. That's the first animal birth I've ever seen."

Chad looked up. "Really? Hang out around here and you'll see plenty."

Corrie, still hanging on to Bo, looked at J. "I'm sorry about Bo. Everything's just so new to him."

J's eyes softened. "He'll settle down, but you'll need to teach him not to rush at the stock." He walked to the next stall, where the cow Bo had disturbed munched on hay. "She'll be awhile yet. Let's check her in a couple of hours." He turned to leave.

Corrie mustered her courage. "Is there anything I can do to help?"

"You could clean up the supply room," Chad blurted before J could get out a word. J looked sharply at his nephew, his mouth a straight, thin line.

"I'd be glad to," Corrie chimed in before J had a chance to argue. J shrugged and left, blue heeler close behind. Bo tugged at his collar, eager to check out Julie. Corrie gave another commanding tug back, and Bo remained sitting. Corrie turned to Chad. "Would you show me what to do?"

They entered the large supply room, Bo closely in tow, where they found Moe washing his hands and arms. Moe gave Chad an amused look and nodded slightly. Corrie wondered if she would ever catch on to their silent language.

Moe wiped his wiry arms dry on a grimy towel. Although bent with age, the old man seemed vigorous and strong. Slipping on his old denim shirt, he reached into the pocket for a round tin of Copenhagen. He carefully placed a plug of tobacco between his lip and gum, put on his battered old hat, nodded briefly to Corrie and left.

The room seemed large for the small building. Counters ran along two walls, a double sink on one side. Branding irons, leather straps, rubber tubes, chains, and lengths of rope hung on pegs. Cupboards lined the walls; an open door revealed medical supplies. The room reeked of disinfectant. Bloody fingerprints smudged the refrigerator door.

Chad dumped a gooey chain into the sink. "Okay, see this disinfectant, Pavosol? You need to sterilize these instruments with it." Chad nodded toward the deep sink containing forceps, suction pump, and now the pulling chain. "Just rinse 'em off in running water and then soak them in this steel pan with the Pavosol. I just eye-ball it, but the ratio amounts are on the bottle." He showed her where to put the instruments after disinfecting them.

"All right. I'll do that. How about me cleaning these shelves and the other cupboards? Will that help?"

"If you want to, they sure need it. Some of this stuff was used last night, but I didn't have a chance to clean it up. I was going to get out here right after breakfast, before my uncle saw this mess, but then we got busy with that other heifer."

"I'm glad to help." She opened the smudged refrigerator door. "I'll wipe this down, too." She began filling a pail with hot water, adding a good dose of detergent.

Moe wandered into the supply room mid-morning.

"Hey, Moe." She was up to her elbows in soapy water, washing down cupboards. An electric space heater warmed the room and she had slipped off her coat and pushed up her sweatshirt sleeves.

Moe grunted a sort of greeting. He watched for a few moments, and then turned to leave.

"Moe, before you go..."

He stopped, his eyebrows raised in question.

"What should I do with these empty containers I found in the cupboards?" Corrie gestured toward several empty bottles and jars on the counter.

"If you don't find replacements, leave 'em out so we know to get more, otherwise toss 'em. Ask J what he wants to replace."

"Okay. What about the dirty towels?"

"Put 'em in this here pail." He nudged a plastic pail near the door with the toe of his old, cracked boot. "The next person what goes to the house will take 'em.'"

Corrie, invigorated with a worthwhile project, bent to her task, following Moe's instructions to the letter. Bo spent the time with her, snoozing on a discarded feed sack. Occasionally, he started to leave the supply room, but she called him back. "You stay with me. We don't need to get yelled at again."

Later, J returned to what Corrie later learned was the calving barn to check on the heifer. Bo immediately jumped up when he poked his head into the supply room.

"Bo!" Corrie said sharply. The big dog went from bounding to a slower gate mid-stride as he greeted Julie, then J. Julie gave him a wary glance, then stood between the big dog and her master.

"Get over it, Julie," J chided.

Corrie gave the last shelf a swipe with the sponge. "Hi, J. Would you look over these supplies and tell me which ones you want to replace?" She hoped she sounded reasonably capable.

J glanced around. "This is a big improvement. Thanks, Corrie."

She thrilled with his appreciation.

He quickly sorted through the dried up tubes, empty bottles and jars, tossing some in the trashcan.

"I'm going into town later this afternoon. Can I pick up these things for you?" Corrie hoped she didn't sound too eager.

"No...well...okay, if you don't mind. I can't get away right now."

Corrie pulled out a writing tablet and a stubby pencil from a drawer and stood poised, ready to take instructions.

J chuckled. "I've never had a secretary. Okay, besides replacing this stuff," he pointed to the empty containers on the counter, "get 600 cc's of Bose, 1200 cc's of 7-Way Clostridium...." He dictated a large order and told her where to find the vet's office in Clearwater. "Have him put it on my account."

Chad's irritated voice rang out. "You blockhead! Knock it off!"

J reached for a length of rope from a peg on the wall and stepped out of the supply room.

Chad whacked the cow on her thick neck. "She keeps kicking this little fellow aside, won't let him near her. I'm sure getting tired of this."

Corrie peeked out of the supply room to see another cow, apparently the one Chad had tended during the night, again kick at the calf, throwing it against the stall wall. The little calf lay there, stunned.

J slipped alongside the cow. "Time for a lesson in motherhood, I guess." He hobbled the cow so quickly Corrie couldn't even see how he had done it. "That'll stop her from kicking, at least. If she still won't let him near her, we'll have to put her in a chute so this little guy can eat. She'll catch on."

As J worked with the stock, Corrie observed him. He was certainly capable. But more than that, he held a certain attraction. Handsome, yes. He had obvious body strength, but strength of character, too. She sighed. Well, never mind, she thought. He was fun to watch, but she wasn't interested. Been there, done that, to use a tired cliché.

Suddenly J looked her way. Instinctively, she whirled around, back to the supply room. For Pete's sake! She must have looked so foolish, gawking like that. Turning away so abruptly made it even worse. Why couldn't she have simply nodded and smiled? She felt like an awkward teenager.

* * *

Corrie took Bo into town with her. She just couldn't trust that he'd behave on his own. Always willing to go, the big dog pressed his nose to the two-inch window opening she'd allowed. It was still early spring and chilly.

The veterinarian's office was easy enough to find with J's good directions. After filling the order, the vet showed surprise when she told him who the supplies were for. When she asked, he explained which ones needed refrigeration. "They should be okay in the car for awhile though, with this cool weather," he assured her.

On the same block, she found the Salvation Army and left the boxes of assorted dishes, pots and pans from the cabin.

She drove to Nancy's office and invited her to join her for a cup of coffee. As they settled in at Stella's, Corrie shared with the realtor her life so far at the ranch. Nancy nodded. "I'm impressed. But don't feel like you have to work all the time, Corrie. Just enjoy your new life. Aren't you cold out there at night?"

"A bit. I build up the fire before I go to bed and it stays pretty cozy. For the first time in my life I'm wearing socks at night though."

As they were leaving, Nancy turned to Corrie. "Do you play bridge?

"Absolutely. I love bridge."

"We need a substitute tomorrow night, at my house. Can you come?"

Corrie nodded. "I'd love to."

"Great. Seven-thirty. When you come, maybe you could bring that oak dresser, get it out of your way. Borrow J's truck. Have him or Chad load it into the truck though. It's really heavy."

"Ask to borrow J's truck? I don't know..."

"I'll call him tonight and mention it. It'll be fine."

Corrie shopped for groceries. Although she didn't go to a lot of work to cook just for herself, she bought staples and a few dinner items for the next week. She stopped at the hardware store and bought a shade for the single bare bulb that hung from the kitchen ceiling. The only other light in the cabin was from lamps she had brought.

Her final stop was the newspaper office, an older building at the edge of downtown. As Corrie completed a subscription order, she heard excited voices from the back room. A single voice boomed, "We've gotta get up there."

A large man emerged from the back room. He spotted Corrie at the counter and smiled. She smiled back.

"Have you heard about Mount St. Helens?" he asked. "They just had another big earthquake."

"A little bit, in the paper, in that column."

"That's my column. I'm Kevin Walsh." He extended a beefy hand. She shook it and introduced herself, briefly mentioning her situation.

Kevin nodded with interest. "A writer, huh? I'm getting a bunch together to go up to that mountain. Want to come? Should make good story fodder."

"Uh, well," she stammered. Is this what she wanted to do? Go to a mountain that's getting ready to blow up? Sure. Why not? "That sounds great. Thanks."

"We'll meet at Stella's for breakfast Saturday morning, around seven. We should get an early start. It's a long drive. See you then."

Corrie felt light-headed as she returned to her car. Within about an hour she'd made plans to play bridge and go to a mountain threatening to explode. And she'd thought life in the country would be slow-paced.

* * *

J met Moe in the calving barn. "Moe, take the night off. Chad and I'll manage."

The old man nodded. "Yer not going to get an argument from me."

J looked around, craning his neck toward the supply room. "She's not back yet?"

"Nope. I don't know what's taking her so long."

J wandered into the supply room. She sure did a good job cleaning the place. He smiled when he remembered catching her watching him. Deep within, something stirred. He slowly shook his head. Now wasn't a good time to start something like that. He had his hands full already with a teenage daughter and a busy ranch. He continued to stand in the middle of the room, appreciating its cleanliness. She might work out after all. As an extra hand.

Chapter Five

AS I SEE IT
Kevin Walsh
Clearwater News staff columnist

April 3, 1980. A new eruption occurred today sending a plume of ash thousands of feet into the atmosphere. The ash cloud blew as far as 150 miles away, south to Bend, OR. USGS experts say that harmonic tremors indicate that molten rock is moving further up from deep inside the volcano.

*B*ack from town, Corrie stopped at J's and knocked at the back door. Gretchen opened it and blinked surprise. "Hello. I'm Corrie. We haven't had a chance to meet."

"Yeah. I remember seeing you that day we were moving cattle."

Corrie felt her face getting warm. "Yes, well..." She heard J's voice in the background. "Gretchen, invite her to come in."

Wordlessly, Gretchen stood aside.

Corrie remained in place. She would not barge in.

"Come in," Gretchen mumbled.

"Thank you. I'll just be a minute. May I speak with your dad?"

"Dad, it's for you," Gretchen called, as though he were wanted on the telephone.

J appeared at the kitchen doorway, filling it, looking comfortable and less intimidating in his stocking feet. He glanced at Gretchen and questioned her with his eyes. She shrugged one slim shoulder.

"Hi, J. I picked up those items for you at the vet's. Here's the statement. I'll go ahead and put the things away in the calving barn.

"I'll be going out there right after dinner. I can take 'em."

"No, that's fine. I'll put them away. The vet told me which ones needed to be refrigerated. I'll take care of it."

J glanced at the coffee pot, which had just gurgled to a stop. "Would you like a cup of coffee? Got a fresh pot here."

Gretchen turned sharply from the counter where she was slicing carrots.

Corrie clearly got the message. Don't.

"No, thanks, I want to get back home, er, to the cabin." Darn! Why did she have to stammer? For now, it was her home. She turned to leave, but said over her shoulder, "It was nice meeting you, Gretchen."

No response. It was hard to say if Gretchen just didn't know what to say, or if the girl didn't share the sentiment. Out of the corner of her eye, Corrie could see J's glance toward his daughter.

"Yeah," Gretchen answered without enthusiasm.

Without breaking her stride, Corrie continued down the steps and out to her car. She drove to the calving barn, unloaded the supplies, put them away and returned to her cabin. Back in her cabin, she gathered paper and kindling to build a fire in the wood stove.

Add one more person to the unwelcoming party. Well, that's not quite true. She felt she'd made headway with Chad and Moe today, even J, with her offer to clean the supply room. But she couldn't do that the rest of her life. How else could she make herself useful?

* * *

With Corrie out of earshot, J turned to his daughter. "Gretchen, what was that all about?"

"What?"

"You were rude to Corrie. Why?"

Gretchen bent to her task as though slicing this particular carrot was the most important thing going on.

"Gretch?"

"Why does she have to be here anyway?" She slammed the paring knife to the cutting board and turned to glare at her dad.

Startled with her vehemence, J's mouth dropped open. He noticed tears puddling in his daughter's eyes. She swiped them away and turned back to the counter.

"Gretch." J's voice was soft, hesitant. "What is it?"

"We're doing just fine without her!"

"Honey, she's not here because of us. She's here because she wants to learn about ranching. She's a writer. She wants to learn, that's all."

"Why here? We're not the only ranch around."

"Because your Aunt Nancy suggested this place. Corrie stopped at her office, looking for a place to live, and Nancy remembered our old cabin. I even tried to talk them out of it."

J shook his head at his daughter's stiff, unyielding back. "I think Corrie's feeling a little out of place...."

"She is."

"Well, let's try to make her feel more welcome."

Gretchen shook her head.

"Hey, I won't put up with you being rude to her. Is that clear?"

Silence.

"Gretchen. Look at me."

She slowly turned, cautious now.

"All I'm asking is that you be polite. Just common courtesy. Okay?"

"Okay. But I'm not going out of my way to do it."

"I didn't ask you to."

"Fine."

"Fine." He grinned.

A reluctant smile tugged at her pinched face. "I'm not smiling."

"No, of course not."

Chad burst into the room. "When's dinner?"

Gretchen glared at him. "Have you ever thought of just walking into a room?"

Chad stared at her, then at J. "What'd I do?"
J shook his head, rolled his eyes. "Dinner in about a half hour, sooner if you help."

* * *

The next morning Corrie woke up wondering what she would do with the day. Until just recently, her day's activities had been dictated. When she worked at the office, any spare time was spent writing and trying to manage household chores, always feeling behind. Then, when staying at home to write full-time, she'd always had a feeling of impending deadlines. The move here to the ranch had been all consuming, for a time at least. But, now that she was here, what should she do? It was odd, unsettling even, to have nothing pressing to do. At least tonight, she had playing bridge to look forward to.

She rose, slipped on her warm, fuzzy robe and let Bo out, and lingered on the porch. Nothing happening that she could see. Yet, knowing what a busy time of year this was, according to Nancy, anyway, something must be going on.

She set her cabin in order, fed Bo, ate a quick breakfast and dressed. Then she set out to explore. Bo ran, putting himself in the lead. "Heel," she commanded more than once, not wanting him to race ahead.

This was Thursday. Gretchen would be at school. She felt relief with that, but then chagrin. Why should she care where the daughter of the rancher was? She'd always had good rapport with teenage girls, why did she feel so intimidated with this girl? Gretchen's obvious hostile attitude, that's why.

They arrived at the big faded red barn. No sounds from inside; she opened a large creaky door. Streaks of sunlight with dancing dust-motes shone on shining bales of hay. The barn appeared old, and for now at least, empty of livestock. Bo immediately set out to investigate and Corrie, relieved to not have to worry about him bothering stock, allowed him to explore. He snuffed and puffed his way around the hay bales, feed sacks and into the far corners of the stalls.

Corrie breathed in the pleasantly musty smell of hay, leather and horses. She stepped into the tack room, the source of the wonderful leather aroma, and smiled with delight at the sight of saddles lined up on a rail, bits and other tack on hooks. Tools apparently dealing with horses lay scattered on a small workbench. It had been years since she'd ridden, and even then someone else had saddled the horses for her.

Corrie wandered out of the tack room and felt eyes on her. She looked around. Bo stood stock still, staring upward, his tail straight out. She looked where he pointed. A cat, hunched on a beam, watched them. Its yellow eyes flickered between them. Apparently deciding neither was a threat, it began a loud purring. "You must be a barn cat." Corrie's voice echoed in the cavernous barn. "I'll bet you're not even a pet, you're a mouser. You're pretty though, a nice little calico."

She looked through a streaked, dusty window to a large split rail fenced corral where several horses gathered, munching at feed racks. Trees bunched at one corner, Ponderosa Pine and Russian Olive, she'd learned from Nancy. Shade from the trees no doubt brought comfort during hot summer days.

She stepped out a small door to the corral and stood under the lean-to attached to the back of the barn. The horses looked up, a couple of them advanced a few steps toward her. Bo rushed out but Corrie commanded him to come back and sit by her. He sat, but looked as though he were ready to spring. She held fast to his collar, just in case. Horses and dog stared at one another. Bo barked one single, sharp greeting.

"Bo, be still," she commanded. His tail swept the dusty ground, setting up a cloud behind him. A horse whickered, its ears pointed forward. Bo's tail quickened.

Corrie became aware of the sound of hooves coming her way. What should she do? Wait. Why do anything? It's probably okay to be here.

J and Chad appeared around the corner. "Here," Corrie said, "I'll open the gate for you."

Both nodded and rode in single-file. Bo greeted them, but with more restraint then before. He wagged his tail at Julie, but didn't overwhelm her with friendliness. She allowed him to smell her, then returned the compliment. Corrie breathed a sigh of relief.

"I hope it was all right for me to be here," she said to the men's backs as they unsaddled their horses.

J glanced at her and smiled. "Sure, it's fine."

"Ummm, J, do you think I could ride with you sometime? I'd love to see the ranch from more than just the road."

Chad chimed in. "I could take her, Uncle J."

J appeared to ignore Chad's offer. "I'll be riding out again tomorrow morning. You're welcome to come along."

"Okay, thanks." It occurred to her to ask what time, but she hesitated. She would just wait around until it happened.

She turned to leave, then remembered. "J, did Nancy call you last night?" She stopped with his questioning look, hoping he'd offer. No such luck. "About the truck? I'm playing bridge at her house and she suggested I bring that oak dresser when I come."

"Oh, that. Yeah, she called. No problem."

"Thanks, I'll pick it up around sixty-thirty. Let's go, Bo." She tapped the dog's back to get his attention away from J's boots.

* * *

Corrie dressed casually for bridge, slacks and a soft yellow sweater. She worried about borrowing J's truck. She'd had little experience driving some-one else's vehicle, let alone a truck. She couldn't help but feel it was an imposition, but there was no other way that she could see to get that dresser moved. At any rate, Nancy had suggested it, so it must be all right. With hesitant feet, she made her way to J's house.

She found him sweeping out the cab with a whiskbroom. The truck still dripped from the wash he had given it.

"You didn't have to do that. It was fine before."

"No problem. It gave me a good excuse to clean it up."

Gretchen stepped out on the porch. "Dad, dinner's ready." The girl glanced at Corrie but quickly averted her eyes.

J stopped his sweeping and looked up at Gretchen. "You guys go ahead. I'll be there in a few minutes." He watched Gretchen expectantly.

"Hi, Corrie," the girl said, with a bare trace of enthusiasm.

Corrie smiled at her. "Hi, Gretchen." She turned to J. "I'm sorry. This is your dinnertime. I..."

"That's okay. Get in, we'll go over and get that dresser."

He sat behind the wheel and she stepped up into the truck. "Do you know how to drive a stick?"

"Yes, I do. I have a gear shift on my Datsun."

"Adjust the mirrors to suit you, move the seat. Don't pay any attention to the four-wheel drive stuff. You won't need it."

"Okay, thanks."

They pulled up close to the porch and he lowered the tailgate. She opened the front door and for the first time since she'd moved in, he entered the cabin. He stood still, looking around.

"This looks nice, Corrie. Better than it's ever looked."

"Thanks, J. I love it here."

He turned to look at her, nodding, looking as though he were seeing something he'd missed before. His eyes softened, he swallowed. She inwardly squirmed. "The dresser's in the bedroom."

Without another word he walked into the small bedroom and tipped the dresser back, taking the heaviest, top end. She bent to pick up the other end.

"Be careful, it's heavy," he warned.

"I've got it."

They made their way down the two steps and J hefted his end onto the truck, then strode toward her and took the bottom of the dresser. He slid it into place next to the cab. With lengths of rope he pulled from behind the seat, he tied it securely in place. Corrie was mesmerized watching his hands expertly tie various knots to hold the dresser snug.

"Don't you try to take it out when you get there. Roger and Ronnie will carry it." He glanced up, waiting for her answer.

She continued watching his hands, wondering how he knew which kind of knot to use.

"Okay?"

She jolted. "Right."

"Do you know how to get there?"

"No, I don't. I forgot to ask." He probably thought she was hopeless.

"They live right on the main drag." He gave her the simple directions. "Turn north, that's right, at the stop light and it's on the west, left, side of the street. Big green house. You can't miss it." Was that a smirk?

"I'll find it," she said with confidence she didn't feel.

Corrie returned to the cabin to get her purse, then slid behind the wheel. The truck started with a rumble and she put it in gear. Luckily, it was pointed in the right direction so she didn't have to maneuver it while J watched.

* * *

As Corrie turned onto the long driveway, J watched. She had guts, doing these new things. Not every woman could change her life so drastically. From the looks of the cabin, he figured the house she left behind must have been nice. Yet, she'd made this dinky cabin into something special. He continued to stand, watching the dust settle after she'd passed. He wished he could have gone along with her. Sighing, he slowly walked back to the house and his waiting dinner.

Chapter Six

AS I SEE IT
Kevin Walsh
Clearwater News staff columnist

April 4, 1980. Dixie Lee Ray has declared a state of emergency and ordered the National Guard to control the growing hordes of sightseers. Time will tell how effective this order is. Personally, I don't think it's going to stop people from flocking to the mountain. Northwest people are like that. We want to be in on the action.

The truck wasn't difficult for Corrie to drive but its size took some getting used to. Compared to her small car, the truck took so much more space on the road and she worried about taking more than one lane. In town, Corrie easily found Nancy's house from J's directions.

Nancy opened the door as she drove up. "Corrie, I'm sorry I forgot to give you directions. J called and gave me a bad time about it."

"That's fine, Nancy. I had no trouble getting here." He'd probably warned Nancy to keep an eye out for her, knowing how directionally challenged she was.

Nancy called her husband and son away from television's nightly news. After introductions,

Nancy's husband, Roger, and their teenage son, Ronnie, immediately headed for J's truck to unload the dresser.

Their spacious home reflected Corrie's opinion of Nancy. Its warm colors and furniture groupings invited comfort and conversation. Corrie helped Nancy set up the living room for an evening of cards. Just as Nancy started to click off the television, the news commentator mentioned Mount St. Helens.

"We're hearing more every day about that mountain," Corrie observed.

"Yes, I'm glad we don't live as close as my brother, Rick. They live in Randle and his wife, Barbara, tells me they're getting rumblings on a regular basis."

"Wow. That would be unsettling." Corrie started to say she planned to visit the mountain Saturday, but the doorbell rang. Within minutes eight women organized themselves at the two card tables. She recognized Kim from the Clearwater News office. Nancy introduced Corrie to the friendly group and she immediately felt welcomed. Of course, knowing Nancy helped. Corrie sensed Nancy's popularity with this group.

Most of the ladies lived in town, but there was one rancher's wife, Marjorie, with whom Corrie hoped to discuss ranching some day soon. The group represented a typical cross-section of small town people with a banker, schoolteacher, librarian, a retired secretary, the newspaper receptionist, the rancher's wife and, realtor Nancy. Corrie substituted for a woman whose husband was critically ill. By the end of the evening she was assured she'd be invited back on a regular, though substitute, basis.

At the end of the evening, after the women trouped out, Corrie lingered. "Nancy, I had a wonderful evening. I didn't realize how much I'd missed the chatter of women. What a delightful group! Thank you for inviting me."

"We loved having you, Corrie. And you won some points, in more ways than one, with that small slam."

Corrie grinned. "That was fun."

"So, you know how to get home, right?"

Corrie imagined J had prompted this question. "I think so. I'll turn right where I turned left before and it's pretty much a straight shot from there, right?"

"But at the edge of town you make a left turn at the light, remember?"

"Oh, that's right."

Seeing Nancy's concerned look, Corrie laughed. "I'll be fine."

On the way to Nancy's, she'd turned the volume down on the radio so she could concentrate. Then as she headed out of town, she turned it up louder so she could listen. Country, of course. It was fun listening to other people's taste in music.

A right turn; then after awhile, the left. There, now it would be easy. What a great evening. She'd learned so much about these women, their joys and sorrows. What a difference between a gathering of women and a group of men, or even of mixed couples. Men seemed to talk of such surface things, never sharing feelings. Sports and jokes, maybe something as deep as investments. It was a relief to participate in girl-talk. She thought of her daughter, Gwen. They needed to set a date for a visit. She and Gwen could talk for hours.

She hadn't realized before how dark it was at night, especially with no streetlights. Her skin prickled. She had been on this road a long time. Too long. Had she missed J's driveway? Actually, she hadn't driven here at night before. J's house was so far back from the road, she probably wouldn't have seen the house lights, if he even had them on at this hour. She drove on, hoping she would come to it yet.

She passed an old run-down tavern on her left, Milo's, stuck way out there with no other stores except a gas station. Right, get your gas, get your beer, all in one stop. Wait a minute. She didn't remember seeing that place before. She had passed J's!

As soon as she could, though it was quite a way past the tavern, she turned off on another road, looking for room to turn around. Actually, that seemed like a pretty substantial road. It looked to her that it paralleled the highway. In any event, she couldn't find a place to turn that big truck around. That's all she'd need, to put J's truck in a ditch.

She drove on, dismayed when the road curved away from the highway. Finally, she found another smaller road where she could get turned around in the intersection. There was certainly no traffic to worry about. But then she couldn't find the place where she'd turned onto this road. It was so dark! There. Ummm. Left or right? She turned left, thinking this road would surely link up to the highway. It ended at a darkened ranch house. She could go to the door, wake up those people, and say she was lost and could they give her directions to J's. No. She'd work it out.

Every time she backed up the truck she feared she would back it into a ditch. She throat tightened, her heart pounded, her hands felt sweaty. Why? Why did she always get lost? She tried to read her watch, but it was too dark.

There! Finally, the highway. Or at least it looked like the highway. She had seen one truck go by. But which way should I turn now? She calculated the different turns she had made, trying to work it in reverse. She turned right, hopefully toward J's.

Her heart thudded when she again passed Milo's, still to her left. "Well, I've done it again. I'm still going the wrong way." This time she pulled into the tavern's parking lot to turn round. As she straightened the truck to drive onto the highway, the engine skipped a beat. And died.

"No." She tried to start it up again, but after several attempts feared she would run the battery down. It sounded like it was out of gas. She couldn't find the dome light switch in the dark, so she opened the door. The gas tank read full. She closed the door and sat in the dark truck for several minutes. She could go into that tavern and ask for help, but would that be a smart thing to do? This was a tavern, after all, and who knew how safe that would be?

She tried once more to start the truck, but with no success. She climbed out and locked the door. It wasn't really properly parked but people could drive around it.

At least this time she knew which way to walk. She wondered how far it would be. She'd been traveling along at a pretty good clip. It could be miles.

Oh-oh. She could hear loud voices coming from the tavern, then a motor starting. It sounded like a beater. She felt entirely out of her element way out here in the country, in the dark.

She stepped to the side of the road and into a ditch. Caught by surprise at its steepness, she slid to the bottom, scraping her hip and left hand, gravel and sand rattling past her to the bottom. Her right foot stepped into a thin layer of mud. She jerked her foot back, but the shoe stayed. She could barely make out her hand in front of her face, let alone find that shoe. She felt around, dragging her hand through the muck until she found it. She slipped it on, goo and all. It was more than mud—it was mixed with something with a strong smell. Drainage from fields. Yuk. The car swished by and she scrambled out of the ditch, filling her shoes with sand and gravel. She stopped to empty them and resumed her trek.

If another car came by she'd take her chances Her light shoes were not intended for walking and the wet one with its layer of grime chaffed at her foot. Shivering, she berated herself for not taking a coat. She trudged on. A sliver of a moon gave just enough light for her to see her watch. Twelve-twenty.

When she lived in the city, walking had been one of her favorite pastimes. She regularly walked around Green Lake in north Seattle. But not freezing to death or wearing muddy, flimsy shoes. Normally, she could walk a fourteen-minute mile, but she wasn't keeping her normal pace tonight. She hadn't a clue how far she'd walked, nor how far she had to go.

In the dim light, the fields looked like water. The same breeze that made her shiver made the fields look like waves. In the distance she could see a house with its lights on. Should she try to walk to it and ask for help? No. J's can't be much farther.

Had she passed J's again? Tears stung her eyes. She couldn't believe this. What would she tell J? That is, if she ever found his place again.

There! His arch. Corrie nearly fell to her knees, never so glad to see anything. There was still almost a mile to walk, but now, nearly home, she felt nothing but relief. That relief turned to aching feet though by the time she limped to her porch. She opened her door and Bo bounded out, nearly knocking her over.

"Okay, okay," she said, hobbling inside and fending off his exuberant greeting. Corrie left the door open so he could make a potty run. She pulled off her shoes, along with her socks, tugging at the muddy one stuck to her foot. Blisters had formed on the heel of the muddied foot. Bo came back inside and she closed the door and collapsed on the davenport, pulling the afghan over her. She should take a shower, get into bed. Yes, in a few minutes. She was barely aware of Bo, leaning on the davenport, settling in with a loud sigh.

* * *

Corrie awoke the next morning with a start. J's truck! Her mind whirled with explanations; they all sounded so lame. Her whole body felt lame. She apparently hadn't moved since crashing on the davenport the night before. She pushed back the afghan and struggled to her feet. Stiff legged, she made her way into the kitchen and glanced at the clock. Eight o'clock! She knew J and the others would have been up hours ago. She took a few swallows of cold coffee and rushed, as much as her sore body allowed, to dress and run a comb through her hair.

Then she remembered. They were supposed to go riding today. She slipped on her new riding boots, wincing with pain as she tugged them over her swollen, blistered feet. She glanced at her sore, scraped hand. She should put something on those cuts. Later.

Just as she opened her door and descended down her porch steps, she noticed J. From his purposeful walk she could tell he, they, had a problem.

She tried to smile, but could tell only a part of her face responded. "Hi, J."

He nodded, eyes wide.

"J, I had a problem with your truck last night."

"Problem? What kind of a problem?"

"Well, I'm not sure. I got lost and–"

"Lost? You got lost between town and here?"

"Well, yes. It was so dark and I, ah, I missed your driveway."

It was probably just as well he was speechless.

"Anyway, I finally got turned around but then your truck died. It's off the street," she added quickly, "and I locked it up."

He opened his mouth, but nothing came out.

"I'm pretty sure I can find it."

"Pretty sure?"

Finally, a word. "It's at Milo's Tavern."

"Milo's! You went that far?"

"Well, yes. Then I tried to get turned around but was afraid of getting stuck in a ditch and it was awhile before I could find my way back to the highway."

"This is all sounding familiar."

"But I did, I found it." She wished she didn't sound so defensive. "Your truck is in Milo's parking lot."

He nodded, probably wishing he understood. "What did it sound like when it died?"

"It...sort of sputtered, then quit. I tried a few times to start it, but I was afraid I'd run down the battery."

His face lit up. "I think you just ran out of gas."

"No, I checked the gauge and it said full."

"I think the truck was on auxiliary. I'm sorry, Corrie, I forgot to mention that to you."

"Auxiliary? What's that?"

"A spare gas tank. So how did you get home?"

"I walked."

"You walked? All the way from Milo's? What time did you get home?"

"I'm not sure, around two, I suppose."

"Why didn't you go into the bar and use their phone to call me?"

"Well, for one thing, I had your truck."

"We have lots of vehicles around here. I'm surprised someone didn't stop and give you a lift home."

"Only one car went by in all that time."

He looked at her expectantly.

"I hid, in the ditch. I didn't know if it would be safe."

His eyes traveled the length of her. He sighed, then shook his head.

Corrie swallowed. This was every bit as awful as she'd thought it would be. "Let's take my car and go get your truck. I'll get my keys."

She realized how inadequate her little Datsun was for a big man like J. He removed his hat but he still couldn't sit straight up. His knees almost touched his chin.

"It's so dark around here at night. I'm used to city streets and lights."

He grunted. "We're going to have to do something about your sense of direction. We can't have people and equipment strung out over the countryside."

"In Seattle I get lost sometimes, but there are always lots of people around to ask. Actually, it's how I manage to get around."

He shook his head and snorted.

"J, I'm sorry. I hope I didn't hurt your truck."

He chuckled. "I'm sure you didn't. I wish I'd told you about the spare gas tank. You should have had enough..."

"But I used a lot more gas, getting lost," she finished for him.

He laughed. "I guess you probably did." He pointed to the left side of the road. "You can start slowing down, there's Milo's."

"Oh!" she said, surprised. "I wasn't expecting it so quickly. It seemed a lot farther away last night." He leaned forward as she stomped on the brake to turn into the tavern's parking lot.

"I'll bet it did. I can't believe you walked all that way."

Corrie pulled up alongside the truck and handed J his keys. She got out of her car and walked to the truck, dreading that he wouldn't be able to start it either.

He slipped behind the wheel, turned a lever, and the truck's engine churned to life. "That was it. See this lever? Just turn it for the regular gas tank." His eyes softened as he searched her face. "It's okay, Corrie, you didn't know."

Maddening tears blurred her vision–relief and tiredness taking their toll. "I'm glad it's okay." She abruptly returned to her car. "I'll see you at the ranch."

He continued to sit in his truck, waiting for her, apparently.

She signaled him to go ahead. He declined, slowly shaking his head, signaling for her to go.

Her stomach clenched. He wants me to go first. What if I miss his place again?

She slowly pulled out. At least she turned the right way. Didn't she?

Every once in awhile she looked in the rear-view mirror. He steadily followed her, probably not wanting her to get lost. Again.

There. The arch! She triumphantly drove under it and made her way back to the cabin and parked her car. He had turned the truck and parked by the large barn. She hurried, as much as she could with her blistered foot, to catch up with him.

"Shall I join you today for that ride?"

"No. Not today. You're beat. You rest up. We'll do it another time." He turned and briskly made his way toward the barn.

Humiliated, she stared at his back and blinked back tears as she returned to her cabin. Bo, waiting on the porch, gave her his exuberant greeting and she absently patted his big head. She opened the door and glanced at the mirror she'd hung in the living room opposite the small window. An embarrassing bedraggled image stared back, eyes with dark smudges under them, not a speck of makeup, hair looking like she'd slept on it wrong. He's right. I'm beat. She headed straight for the bedroom, struggled out of her boots, jeans and shirt and gratefully sank onto her bed.

She was a fish out of water here. A city girl who couldn't even find her way on a straight piece of highway. She didn't know their ways; she didn't even think J liked her. He apparently didn't trust her enough to let her ride one of his horses. To him she was just something more to worry about. She drifted off to sleep, a total failure.

Chapter Seven

AS I SEE IT
Kevin Walsh
Clearwater News staff columnist

April 5, 1980. A team from Clearwater News visited Mount St. Helens for a first-hand account of recent activities. We found the north side ugly with streaks of black ash scarring the once pristine mountain. Other areas are untouched.

Local authorities are finding it difficult to keep people out of the area. The 8,000 miles of trails and logging roads can't all be guarded, though the main access roads are blocked.

*T*winges of guilt prickled J's conscience. He hoped he hadn't been rude to Corrie, but there was no way he would take responsibility for some-one as green as she was to ride a horse when she looked so beat. She hadn't said anything about it, but he could tell she favored one leg, probably sore from that long walk home. And he'd noticed her skinned up palm. He chuckled to himself, re-membering how his dad would have described her: Driven hard and put away wet.

Still, he didn't want to be rude. But, my God, they would have to do something about her sense of direction. It was so natural to him. Gretchen didn't seem to have a problem with directions. She certainly knew north from south, east from west. Out here though, you have to know these things or you'd get lost on the range.

Maybe this morning would be a good time to invite Corrie to ride with him.

"Dad?"

Gretchen stood by the toaster waiting to butter the next four slices that popped up. J scrambled eggs at the stove while Chad sat in a haze at the table. He'd been up much of the night; in fact, hadn't been to bed since two.

"Daaad! Hello!"

"Ummm? What, Gretch?

"Pam asked me to come over this afternoon. I'll do my homework and practice this morning, then go there after lunch. They've invited me to spend the night. Okay?"

J stirred the eggs absently.

"Dad! Okay?"

"Yeah, honey. That's fine. You riding over?"

"Yes. I'll be home sometime in the morning."

He finally focused on the conversation. "Right, and then you have some chores to do around here, like vacuum–"

"I know, I'll do all that on Sunday."

He nodded, and then glanced at his nephew. "Chad, try to knock off early today, get a good night's sleep. I'll work calving tonight."

Chad perked up when J placed the scrambled eggs in front of him. Gretchen placed a huge platter of toast on the table, along with a large jar of strawberry jam.

As they devoured breakfast, J's thoughts returned to Corrie. He'd watch for her this morning and ask if she wanted to go riding.

After breakfast, Gretchen automatically began cleaning up the kitchen, her chore on the weekends. J switched on the light in his office, just off the kitchen. He'd write a few checks and get the bills in the mail today. He could hear Chad's shower running full blast. That kid had been a lifesaver this year. He could do a man's work now.

Gretchen started her warm-ups at the piano. He was so grateful for her interest in music. She took after her mother in that regard. His daughter had taken lessons since she was about eight. He never had to remind her to practice. According to their agreement, she could have lessons as long as she practiced. Her relationship with Mrs. Williams, her piano teacher, was wonderful and Gretchen wouldn't dream of not being prepared for her music lesson. He stopped writing and cocked his head, listening. She really was getting good.

He sealed the last envelope and started for his truck to run the bills up to the mailbox. Chad joined him as they left the house. "That bald faced heifer is about ready, Unc. I'm gonna check on her now."

J nodded and held up the envelopes. "I'll be there as soon as I take these up to the mailbox." He heard Corrie's car starting up. Good. He'd talk to her now, see if she wanted to go riding.

Corrie slowed down as she passed them and rolled down her window. "Hi."

J stepped up to the car. "Hi, there."

"I'll see you guys later. I'll be gone until this evening sometime. I've left Bo outside today. I'm sure he'll be fine. See you!" She skirted around Chad and continued down the long driveway.

J watched the car, then shook his head with disgust.

Chad watched too. "What's the matter? Where's she going?"

"How would I know?" J snapped.

Chad's eyes widened. He opened his mouth to say something, apparently thought better of it, shrugged and turned toward the calving barn, muttering something J couldn't quite catch.

J lifted his hat, ran his fingers through his hair and jammed it back on. Where the hell is she going? He guessed that answered the riding question for today.

* * *

Corrie parked her car next to the Clearwater News van. She felt a mixture of excitement and hesitancy. And hunger, she realized as she stepped into Stella's and took in the heavy aroma of breakfast. She spotted Kevin's long arm waving at her from a large half-round booth. Corrie recognized Kim from the newspaper office and from playing bridge at Nancy's.

Kevin stood as she neared the table and allowed her to scoot onto the padded bench to sit next to Kim. He introduced her to Al, the Clearwater News photographer, Robert, the paper's editor, and Greg, a freelance writer and friend of Kevin's. A waitress poured coffee and Corrie ordered a strawberry waffle.

Apparently Kevin and Al's friendship dated back many years. Kevin seemed to be calling the shots on today's venture. Robert was along for the ride, as were she and Kim. Al, the photographer, didn't say anything during the entire breakfast except, "Pass the salt."

Robert showed interest in Corrie's profession. "A writer, huh? Bring your book by and we just might publish a review."

"Great. I'll do that."

When asked what she did before writing full-time, Corrie explained her previous work as a computer analyst. "I liked that job, but getting called in the middle of the night when a program "blew up," as they called it, got old. At quarter's end, I could count on having to get up during the night at least once and go to the office to straighten something out. It was a relief to just stay home and write."

"Yeah," Kevin agreed, "create your own nightmares." They all laughed at the truth to that.

As they stood to leave, Corrie heard a familiar voice. "What are you doing with this unsavory bunch? You guys look like you're up to no good!"

"Hi, Nancy." Corrie smiled at her friend. "Am I falling in with the wrong crowd?"

Kevin put his arm around Nancy's shoulder. "Hey, Nancy, join us. We're going up to Mount St. Helens. We've got room for one more in the van."

"No thanks. I'm showing property today. You guys be careful up there."

They trailed out to the van, packed with camera equipment in metal cases, leather briefcases, plus coats and boots. Corrie reached into her car and took out her warm coat and her steno pad, so she could take notes.

"I hope everyone has warm clothes," Robert said, "it's probably still pretty cold up there."

Corrie enjoyed the bantering among the friends along the way. Al rode "shotgun" as he called it and held a map of the Mount St. Helens area. The day was sunny, though still cool. As they approached White Pass, Corrie expressed surprise at the snow piled up alongside the road by snowplows. The road, however, was bare and dry.

"It's still only mid-April. There's probably snow at St. Helens, too," Kevin said.

"And God knows what else," Al muttered.

* * *

J heard the phone ringing as he approached the back porch steps. He quickened his step and reached for it. It was probably for Gretchen anyway. "Hello."

"J, hi."

"Hi, Nan, what's up?" He settled into a chair at the kitchen table.

"I'm going over to Randle tomorrow to pick up Mother and bring her over to stay with us for the week."

"Lucky you." Although Nancy and their mother got along pretty well, J often cringed at her outspokenness. He knew many of her comments were made out of concern for him. For years she had worried over his being "alone," without a woman to take care of him and Gretchen. He could never convince her they were doing all right.

"Yeah, well, we thought we'd come over and have coffee with you on her last day, when Rick and Barbara come to pick her up. We'll be by in the afternoon. Mother hasn't seen your place in a long time."

J sighed. "Okay."

"Try to contain your enthusiasm."

"Calving season isn't a good time for company, Nan."

"I know. But this is when she's coming. She wants to see Gretchen and Chad, too. It's been ages since she's seen them. We won't take a lot of your time. You fix the coffee and I'll bring cookies, okay?"

"Okay." It was just one damn thing after another around here.

"I saw Corrie this morning."

"Oh, yeah?" Despite himself, his voice lifted with interest.

"She and a bunch of people from the newspaper were on their way to Mount St. Helens."

"They what? I thought they were trying to keep people away from that mountain. Boy, those newspaper people frost me. Why is the press always the exception to the rule?" He suddenly stood and paced as far as the telephone cord allowed.

Nancy chuckled. "Well, bro, I dunno. But that's where she is today, in case you've wondered."

She chuckled again at his steamy silence. "See you Sunday."

"Yeah, right. Thanks for the warning."

He hung up, but kept his hand on the receiver. Why would Corrie do such a foolish thing? How did this even come about, meeting those newspaper people? She just got here! His brow creased. She'd better stay with the crowd. That'd be a hell of a place for her to get lost.

* * *

Up ahead the newspaper people noticed Spirit Lake Highway barricaded and guarded by State Patrol.

"Oops. Better turn around, quick," Al warned.

Kevin turned the van just before the barricade. "We'll take one of the logging roads south of Randle."

Although the road was bumpy and the passengers found themselves hanging on to whatever they could, this narrow track road was apparently free of entry restrictions.

Corrie was surprised it was so easy.

"They know people are doing it. But State Patrol and the Sheriff's Department can't be liable for every little road. It's all they can do to cover the main access roads," Robert explained. "Couldn't you get by the barricade as press?" Corrie asked.

Kevin nodded. "Probably, but it's just as well this way. Now we can go where we want. If you come in as press, they still want to restrict you."

The van, heavy with six people plus all their equipment, lugged as they began a steep climb. Kevin dropped to low gear. They stopped often for Al and Greg to take pictures while Kevin and Robert jotted down notes.

Corrie viewed the terrain with interest. Towering trees poked through several feet of snow, creating an exquisite beauty. As they rounded a bend, the menacing, scarred mountain, ringed with dirty black snow loomed. Black ash spit from the crater, darkening the sky.

Kim sucked in her breath. "Wow. Look at that. The last time I saw that mountain, it was a perfect cone, white and beautiful. Now look at it. It's dirty and ugly. I'm so glad I came with you guys. I would never have believed the change."

Kevin took a closer look with his binoculars. "Kind of creepy, huh?" He handed the binoculars to Corrie.

"Boy, I'll say." An uneasiness electrified the hairs on the back of her neck. A steady flow of steam laden with ash rose from the mountain.

Al, who had been hanging out the window snapping pictures, straightened himself back into his seat. "Are we going to Truman's place?"

Kevin nodded. "Might as well. We've come this far." He put the van in gear and headed for Spirit Lake.

Kevin caught Corrie's eye in the rear-view mirror. "The press isn't always welcomed at Truman's. Maybe we'll catch him on a good day."

"You've been here before?"

"Yeah. A few years ago, for a story. He's sort of a local legend. He can be real mean, but he's usually been nice to me. He's owned the lodge and fifty-four acres since the thirties, and I guess he has some bootlegging history. He originally came here to hide from the law. At one time he hid stills up here, too. He called his moonshine 'Panther Pee.'"

Al shook his head. "Makes me thirsty just thinking about it."

Kevin chuckled. "There's a funny story circulating about William O. Douglas, the Supreme Court Judge. He stopped by Spirit Lake Lodge and wanted to rent a cabin. Apparently he looked kind of scruffy and struck Harry Truman the wrong way. Truman kicked the old man off his property." Kevin braked to let a doe and her tiny spotted fawn cross the road. They all craned their necks to see the special sight. Kevin continued. "Anyway, some old boys nursing beers at the bar recognized Douglas and told Truman who he just kicked out. Truman chased after Douglas and convinced him to return. They've been good buddies since then."

Corrie laughed. "It's strange that Harry Truman bears the same name as our straight-laced former president. The name seems to be the only thing they have in common."

They swung into a small parking area, next to a pink 1956 Cadillac. "Well, here we are. Truman must be home, that's his Caddy. Let me test the waters, before we all go traipsing in. If he's in a bad mood we won't stay. I don't want us to get shot at."

"Geez," Robert said. "How old is he now?"

"In his eighties."

While Kevin made his way to the lodge, Corrie and Kim wandered around the grounds, now beyond rustic. The resort consisted of a run-down lodge and several sagging cabins. A weather-beaten boathouse stood at lake's edge.

Kim looked around with distaste. "This place gives me the creeps."

Corrie nodded. "The setting is beautiful though." Spirit Lake nestled unblemished between mountains, its clear water reflecting surrounding trees and steep bluffs. But beyond the lake, the ash-blackened face of the north side of Mount St. Helens gaped grotesquely, tarnishing the pristine view.

Corrie's thought turned to J. It'd be fun to get his impression of this place. She turned to Kim. "Do you know J McClure?"

Kim shook her head. "Nancy's brother? No, I don't. You're living on his ranch, right?"

"Yes. I just wondered if you knew him."

Kim scrutinized Corrie. "What's he like?"

"Oh, nice." She dropped the subject, but couldn't get his image out of her mind. He probably didn't even know how good-looking he was. Her heart had almost stopped when he approached her car that morning, smiling his great smile. For some reason, she couldn't get out of there fast enough. Did he wonder where she was going? She inwardly sighed. What difference does it make? She was through with that sort of thing.

Kevin stepped out the lodge door and motioned them to come in, Harry Truman at his heels. The old man looked rumpled, but happy enough to see them. When he spotted the photographers, he stepped in front of the Mount St. Helens Lodge sign as a background. Truman talked fast, making it hard to catch all he said. He peppered his language with swear words and spoke in a loud, raucous voice, waving arthritic hands to emphasize his points.

Corrie stood back by Al, watching the photographer handle his cameras with confidence and speed.

"I wonder if he talks this way around children." Corrie remembered reading Truman had held interviews with school children about the situation at the mountain. Al shot pictures as fast as Truman talked.

"Probably. I'm not sure he can turn it off. No wonder kids love him."

A string of cats jumped through a hole in the screen door and rubbed against the visitors' legs.

Corrie stepped from side to side, trying to avoid them. "What a gaggle of cats."

"You want a cat?" the old man shouted to her. "I got sixteen of 'em. Here, take one." The old man bent over, attempting to grab a scraggly black cat.

"No, thanks. I've got a big dog," Corrie answered cheerfully. She shuddered when a cat rubbed up against her.

"What, you don't like cats?" Al asked softly.

She stepped aside, trying to avoid a second cat's attempt to rub against her leg. "Not this many at one time."

Kevin brought Truman's attention back. "What do you plan to do, Harry, if the mountain blows?"

"I've been at the foot of this mountain for fifty-four years. I'm stayin' right here." He looked around the group with tired eyes. "Let's go in, I'll fix us some drinks."

"Here we go," Al muttered.

Truman fixed drinks all around, not bothering to ask anyone what they wanted. He poured a generous amount of Schenley's bourbon into smudged glasses, topping them with coke.

The strong drink made Corrie gasp. They all politely consumed what they could and chatted with Truman about his resort's popularity over the years. Finally, Kevin laid several dollar bills on the bar and reached over to pat the old man's stooped shoulder. "Well, buddy, we gotta go. See you next time."

They all trouped out. Corrie sighed with relief as they climbed into the van. Truman waved as they pulled out.

Robert wrote quick brief notes. Kevin only occasionally wrote something down. Corrie found her steno pad and briefly noted her impressions. Overwhelmed by all that she'd seen, she'd have to give more thought to explaining this strange place.

At one point they encountered a USGS scientist taking measurements. They pulled over to the side of the road, climbed out and introduced themselves. The scientist apparently didn't mind taking the time to answer questions. He introduced himself as Dave Johnston, and explained he was using a level to measure elevation changes between the instrument station and a stadia rod. "These changes in tilt show whether the mountain is expanding or subsiding."

As they spoke, Corrie felt tremors. Startled, she grabbed the arm of the closest person, who happened to be Kim. "Do you feel that?"

"You get used to it," Johnston assured her. "Remember, this is a live volcano. You have to expect activity."

But in the twenty-five minutes the series of tremors lasted, Corrie couldn't shake off her initial alarm. Should they even be here? Her chest tightened. Were they toying with danger?

Chapter Eight

AS I SEE IT
Kevin Walsh
Clearwater News staff columnist

April 6, 1980. A helicopter landed at Harry Truman's Spirit Lake Resort carrying NBC-TV crew who plans to film an interview for the Today Show. Truman has vowed he will not leave his home of 54 years at Spirit Lake, even though the resort lies in direct line with the north slope of the mountain, the site of most of the recent activity. Truman claims, "That mountain's part of Truman and Truman's part of that mountain."

A subdued group returned to Clearwater. As they neared the newspaper office, Robert said, "That old man is crazy. That run-down place of his isn't worth dying over."

Al nodded. "You wouldn't think so. If lava starts pouring out of that mountain, he's not going to be able to do much to save his place, anyway."

Kevin parked the van and they began to gather their belongings. "Tell you what, I'm not ready to call it a day. What say I call Joanne and we take a run out to the Roadside?"

Robert shook his head. "Boy, don't you ever quit? I'm beat."

"Same here," Greg agreed. "Anyway, my wife's waiting dinner for me."

"Yeah, I've got stuff to do at home," Kim said. "Thanks though."

"I'm in," Al said. "They have good burgers there, if you can put up with the noise."

Kevin turned to Corrie. "How about it, Corrie? Can you join us?"

Thoughts rushed through her mind. Did she really want to go to a tavern? They often looked so...tacky. But it didn't take long to come to a conclusion—hunger and companionship won out. "Sure, I'd love to go."

Kevin nodded toward the office. "I'll just step in and give Joanne a quick call. Let's take just the van. Parking's always a mess there."

As the van pulled into the parking lot, the vehicle vibrated with music pulsating from the tavern. "Sounds like Stampede's still here," Al said. "I wonder if it's ever occurred to them to turn down the volume."

"It's Saturday night so we may have to fight for a table," Kevin yelled above the din.

They found a spot for four at a long table littered with empty bottles, over-flowing ashtrays, and crumpled cigarette wrappers. Kevin signaled a waitress to bring a pitcher of beer. In seconds, the waitress left a bowl of pretzels, a pitcher of beer, mugs, and cleared up the mess immediately around them. When Joanne joined them, she and Corrie laughed, recognizing one another from bridge at Nancy's. As she had been at Nancy's,

Joanne was impeccably dressed. By contrast, Corrie felt grubby.

The smoky haze that filled the room took getting used to. Neon beer signs lined the walls, giving the room an eerie green glow.

They had no sooner ordered their hamburgers when a cowboy approached Corrie to dance. He merely tapped her on the shoulder and motioned with his hand. Her first inclination was to decline. She didn't even know the man, but quickly decided to accept. Apparently this was the custom here and she wanted to fit in. That dance was soon followed by another request by, judging by his heavy boots, a construction worker. Finally, she declined a dance so she could eat her dinner. After dinner she danced with both Al and Kevin. It felt good to just kick back and relax with people she liked. The country band carried a strong beat, though Corrie would have preferred half the volume.

Corrie and Earl, her ex, had never frequented taverns but managed to go to dances a few times a year, mostly at organizational functions. Although she loved to dance, those evenings with Earl had never seemed this carefree. He was always "on" for his business associates, always in control. This let-your-hair-down place seemed more relaxed, though a bit strange with the boldness of people asking perfect strangers to dance.

She wondered if J ever came here. What would that be like, dancing with him? It was difficult to imagine him in any other setting than his ranch. Another cowboy asked her to dance, a big fellow, about J's size. She tried to imagine it was J, then felt foolish. For Pete's sake, what difference did it make? She wasn't interested in romance. Anyway, there was Gretchen.

For some of the dances, strobe lights added more strangeness to the evening, making the dancers flicker in and out of view, giving the appearance of dancers jerking around like characters in an old movie.

Corrie loved the evening, and, frankly, enjoyed the attention from the men. She felt cherished and appreciated, even though, other than Kevin and Al, most of her dance partners were strangers. Nevertheless, she happily agreed when Joanne signaled she was tired and wanted to leave.

Kevin and Joanne drove Joanne's car home; Corrie rode with Al in the van back to the newspaper office to get their cars. She leaned her head against the seat. "This has been a eventful day. Thanks for including me, Al."

"Sure. I'm glad you could come. We'll be going back to the mountain now and then. You're welcome to join us."

"Thanks, that sounds great." Did it? Would she want to go back there again?

* * *

Corrie wandered to the big barn Sunday morning, still hoping to go riding. Bo ran ahead, making tracks on the frosted grass, turning occasionally to make sure she followed. Approaching the barn, she heard J's low voice coming from within. She hesitated, reached for Bo's collar, and then entered. J spoke in soothing tones as he brushed his big bay gelding, a quarter horse. His blue heeler lay curled up on a pile of hay, but rose when she saw Corrie and Bo.

J glanced up and gave her a friendly smile. "Ready for that ride?"

"Sure! I'd love to go." She released Bo, pleased when her big dog calmly greeted Julie.

J leaned over to pet Bo's soft ears. "All right, let's get you set up. We'll have you ride Nancy's mare. That horse doesn't get enough exercise so this will do her good."

J signaled Corrie to follow him to the corral behind the barn. On the way, he gathered halter and lead rope, scooped a handful of oats, and walked to a pinto mare, a sturdy white horse splashed with large irregular patches of brown. He offered her the oats, and then slipped on the halter.

"Oh," Corrie gasped, "she's beautiful. What's her name?"

"Fancy. She's a good horse, getting on in years now, but still has a lot of life." He led the horse into the barn and secured the halter to a rail. "Let's give her a quick brush down, get the dust off before we saddle her."

"Great. I'd like to do that."

He handed her the body brush he'd been using, showing her with a few strokes how to do it.

"Stand back a bit so you can put your whole body into it. Work front to rear, like this."

Corrie eagerly took over. J watched for a couple of minutes, and then took his horse, Nick, outside. He returned to the barn and showed her how to saddle and bridle the pinto. "Lay the blanket high, then pull it down, so the hair lays the right way." He saddled and bridled the horse with smooth deliberate movements. "When you cinch up the girth, tug it once or twice, then wait a few seconds before doing it again." He smiled a slow, easy smile. "They'll puff out their stomach, try to fool you into thinking it's tight. But if the saddle is loose, it can slide right under them and take you with it."

"Is this Nancy's saddle?"

"No, this is an extra. We'll adjust it for you. Okay, ready?" He handed her the reins.

She nodded and followed him out of the barn.

"Do you need help getting on?"

"No, I don't think so." She hoped not, anyway. While he stood by, she climbed on. "I hope it's like riding a bicycle and that I haven't forgotten."

Bo barked a single, alarmed warning as if to say, What are you doing on that big animal? "It's okay, Bo." She watched as J adjusted the stirrups. He swung into the saddle. Would it ever be that easy for her? "Should we take Bo?"

"No, let's not this time. We'll be around a lot of stock today. Let him get used to things gradually. We'll ride over to the cabin, leave him there."

"Bo, stay," Corrie commanded once they reached the cabin's front yard. She held her breath, hoping he would obey.

Ears plastered back, Bo sat, eyes clearly showing the betrayal he felt.

"You're doing well with him, Corrie. I'm impressed."

Corrie turned her horse and followed J. Julie ran ahead, apparently knowing where they were headed.

Corrie glanced behind. Bo still sat, dejected.

No one else was around, it seemed. "Where're Chad and Moe?" She zipped up her jacket against the cold breeze and fished out her wool gloves from her pocket..

"Moe's in the calving barn. One of us has to stick around while calving's going on. It'll be a week or so before we're finished with that."

"What about Chad?"

"He's putting out hay."

"Putting out hay?"

"Every morning we take feed out to the range cattle."

"Don't the cattle just graze on grass?"

"When they can, but right now there's not enough in most places because the ground is still frozen. It's starting to thaw but until the grass is growing strong, we have to take feed out to them."

He glanced up at the sky. His sharp eyes constantly took in his surroundings. "When Chad's through with that he's going over to the Wagner place. That's one of the ranches I've bought in the last few years. He's checking fences, getting ready to move the herd to summer pastures."

"What's the difference between a summer pasture and a winter pasture?"

"We bring 'em closer to headquarters during winter because we have to feed them every day. Then too, we can keep an eye on 'em. They're a lot farther away, in the high country, during summer months."

"So once you take them out to summer pasture you can just leave them?"

He smiled, making his eyes crinkle. "Not quite. We move 'em around so we can keep the range from being over-grazed. And we still need to check the herd over, make sure they're healthy." He glanced at her. "I can tell you're a writer. You ask a lot of questions."

"I know, I'm a regular question box. I hope you don't mind."

"No, I don't mind. I've just never had anyone ask me before."

"Really?"

He nodded. "Pretty much everyone I know grew up on a ranch." He chuckled. "And the others aren't interested."

They followed a small trail that led to what she learned was a winter pasture. "J, please tell me if you see something I should or shouldn't do. I want to do this right."

J nodded. "Will do. To begin with, don't let the horse graze along the way. She gets plenty to eat and that's a bad habit to get into. She needs to pay attention to you and not what's out there for her to eat."

Corrie pulled up on the reins and Fancy gave up her grazing efforts. The trail widened and J indicated to her to come abreast. He pointed to a coyote, standing still as stone, watching them.

"It looks hungry."

"They always look hungry, but this time of year he's getting plenty of food."

"Do they bother the stock?"

"I don't think so, but for years some ranchers have waged an open war on coyotes, setting traps or poisons. The coyote is great for cleaning up rodents and gophers. Those little critters cause us more problems than coyotes. If we have a dead calf or cow, we'll leave it for them to eat, but they seldom attack the stock. They're smart animals. Maybe they recognize me as a friend." He smiled gently.

It was obvious to Corrie that J loved this life. "Where are we going now?"

"To check on new calves."

"You mean there are more than what's going on in the calving barn?"

"Sure. Those are just first-time heifers, cows that have never calved. These range cows usually don't need any help from us. But I just want to check 'em out and make sure we don't have a cow in trouble."

As the two rode abreast, Corrie often felt J's eyes on her. She glanced over once and their eyes locked. Fancy stumbled on the rough ground, jerking her attention away, making her grab for the saddle horn.

"Easy now," J said. "Give her more rein. She knows what to do."

They rode to the top of a small incline and a dozen or so cow-calf pairs came into view. Seeing the riders approach, many of the cows mooed and stepped closer to their young.

J nodded toward a cow standing by a little form on the ground. They rode closer and J dismounted and approached the lifeless calf. He spoke gently to the cow. "Okay, now, let me see your baby."

"Is it dead?" Corrie felt tears forming.

"Yep. Well, that's too bad. I'll just drag it to this brush to get it out of the cow's sight." J's mouth formed a straight line as he bent to the sad task.

"What happened?"

"It's hard to say. Calves die, but not very often."

He climbed back on his horse. "We'll come back later and pick up that cow. We have a motherless calf at home. Maybe she'll take to it."

"Won't she know the difference?"

"We have our ways. We have some mother-up powder we give to both the cow and the calf. It confuses the cow enough that sometimes she's fooled into believing it's her calf."

J reined to a stop. "Okay, Corrie, what direction are we headed?"

Corrie blinked. "I have no idea." Why would he even ask?

"Let's figure it out. Do you know where the sun rises?"

Her cheeks burned. She hated this kind of thing. It made her feel so inadequate. He waited for her answer.

"In the east?"

"Are you asking me or telling me?"

"In the east." She stifled a sigh.

"Right. And where does it set?"

"In the west." Her stomach clenched.

"Okay, so now you can figure out which direction we're headed."

She stared at him.

He pointed to the sky.

"If that's east," she mumbled as she pointed, "that must be west, so that," she pointed in the direction they were headed, "is north!"

"Right."

"But there's no sun at night."

"No, but there are other signs then. If you keep track of your directions, pretty soon you'll just know. Out here you need to know this stuff, Corrie."

"Okay, I'll keep practicing."

They rode to another clump of cattle gathered around a galvanized water tank. J dismounted and checked the well plumbing. He mounted his horse again then trotted to a nearby fence and peered along the length of it. He leaned over and jiggled a fencepost.

"Is there something wrong with the fence?"

"It's starting to rot. We'll have to replace some of the posts this year. We're converting a lot of these wood posts to metal ones now." He took out a small notebook from his denim jacket pocket and made some notes with a stub of a pencil.

She hoped he didn't notice her staring at him, but she couldn't seem to get enough. She loved watching him work, seeing how expertly he handled his horse.

Corrie spotted several tiny calves, some of them probably only days old. At the sight of the first people they'd probably ever seen, many of the calves cried out to their mothers who answered with low guttural murmurs. J rode through a small bunch to an obviously miserable cow with head hanging, pus oozing from her vagina. Her malnourished calf stood beside her, bleating pitifully.

"What's wrong with her?"

"Looks like metritis, a bacterial infection they get sometimes after calving."

"Can you do something for her?"

He nodded. "We'll come back this afternoon with the stock trailer and pick up this cow and her calf, together with the one that lost her calf. We can treat the cow at headquarters and give this little one a supplementary diet if we need to."

He glanced at their surroundings. "Corrie, see that rock outcropping?"

"Yes. Why?"

"Remember it. Remember it's on our left."

Corrie sighed. He apparently was going to keep this up.

They rode through several more clumps of cattle, J scrutinizing each group and making notes.

Corrie loved the sound of squeaking leather, the jangle of tack, the soft thud of hooves. She felt surprisingly relaxed around J, watching his easy manner. He seemed okay with her tagging along, perhaps even glad for the company.

He reined up and turned to face her. "Time to head back. Which way to headquarters?

Corrie's eyes widened. "You're asking me?"

He nodded. He was. He was asking her. She glanced at the sky. The sun was straight up, no clue there. Sweat gathered on her brow, under her arms. She looked at him, trying to keep from showing how ignorant she felt.

He sat still in the saddle, giving her time to figure it out. A full two minutes passed. "Look around. Anything look familiar?"

She glanced around, spotting the outcropping of rock he'd pointed out earlier. "Those rocks over there, that outcropping."

"Where should it be when we ride by again?"

"It was on our left, so...to our right!"

He nodded approval. "Never give up looking for landmarks, Corrie. Make it a habit. You never know when it'll save your hide."

On the way back to the ranch, headquarters, as he called it, they were quiet. Even the silence felt good. This was wonderful, she hated to have it end.

As they neared the house another rider came into view.

J waved and the rider returned the gesture. "There's Gretchen. She spent the night at a girlfriend's."

Gretchen rode up to them, her face pinched. "Where have you guys been?"

"To check on the stock, Gretch. Did you have a good time at Pam's?"

"Yeah. How come?"

"How come you had a nice time?"

Corrie heard an edge to J's voice.

"No, Dad, how come you and.... Never mind." She wheeled her horse around and kicked it into a gallop, her slight frame stiff.

J watched her leave and shook his head. He opened his mouth to say something, but stopped himself, urged his horse on. "I'm going to check on Moe, get a bite to eat, then go back in the truck to get that stock. Want to come along?"

"No, thanks. I...ah...have some things I need to do."

He turned so he could look into her face. She tried to keep it perfectly blank, but squirmed inwardly. Obviously, Gretchen didn't like her. Fine. She was certainly not going to interfere between father and daughter.

"Suit yourself." His barely perceptible motion moved his horse forward. His back looked as stiff as Gretchen's.

Was he irritated at her? Well, it couldn't be helped.

The joy of the morning faded.

Chapter Nine

AS I SEE IT
Kevin Walsh
Clearwater News staff columnist

April 9, 1980. Earthquakes are becoming even more frequent and closer to Mount St. Helens. The mountain is changing in appearance. I talked on the phone to David Johnston, a geologist with the U.S. Geological Survey (USGS) team. He reports a small crater has appeared on the summit, 250 feet in diameter and 150 feet deep, surrounded by a dirty black ring of ash on the snow.

Representatives from USGS, Washington State Patrol, and Washington State Department of Emergency Services are cracking down on unauthorized visitors. Even though a Red Zone has been established, people are finding ways to get closer to the action, using the more than 8,000 miles of trails and logging roads. Silly people. What? They want to see action?

*O*n the morning after the ride with J, Corrie woke with muscles screaming. Her crotch burned, her backside felt like the skin had worn clear through, insides of her knees were raw where her jeans had rubbed against them. She groaned, feeling like an old lady. Although horse people would probably say you should just climb back on, she didn't know if she could even raise her leg that high. She walked as though straddling a barrel.

Corrie gave it a day or so and used that time to check out the local library and become more familiar with the town. She invited Nancy to lunch, pleased with their friendship. Although she would like to have discussed her strained relationship with Gretchen, Corrie hesitated, knowing that family was stronger than friendship. Nancy's loyalties would, should, go to family.

She also stopped by the newspaper office with a copy of her book, at the editor's suggestion, hoping it would be reviewed, Now that she lived here, there might be some local interest. She stopped at the bookstore and introduced herself, gave them a complimentary copy of her book and mentioned that she would be available to speak or do a reading if the occasion arose. The owner of the bookstore promised to buy copies. Corrie left her phone number and made a mental note to stop by again in a couple of weeks.

Corrie, although determined to learn about ranching, resolved to keep her distance from J. He was too polite to say anything, but she knew there was no room for her in his life. For sure, there was no room in Gretchen's. Corrie understood. J was the girl's life and she saw Corrie as a threat. No wonder J had been so reluctant to have her stay there. He didn't want trouble.

A few days later, after her body limbered up, she crossed the yard to the barn, hoping to find someone getting ready to ride. She'd kept track enough to guess that it was J's turn to deal with calving and either Moe or Chad would be riding out to check on the herd. She was catching on to the rhythm of the ranch.

Sure enough, she found Chad saddling his horse. "Hi, Chad."

Still shy, he only glanced up when she entered the barn. "Hi."

"Would you mind if I joined you today? There's so much I want to learn."

He brightened. "Sure. Want me to saddle Fancy for you?"

"No, I can do it myself." She hoped..

With a show of confidence, she lifted halter and lead rope off the tack rack, strode to the barrel of oats, dipped in for a handful of the course grain, and walked into the round corral to capture Fancy. Just as she neared, Fancy eyed Corrie and skittered to the side. Corrie, too, stepped aside with alarm. When she approached again. Fancy whirled completely around. Corrie jumped back to avoid a collision.

"Hey!" Chad yelled. "Settle down!"

"It looked so easy when J did this."

"Yeah, but she knows J, knows she can't get away with that crap. Hold your hand out, show her the oats."

Fancy looked down her nose, nostrils flaring at the treat, but stood her ground.

Corrie kept her voice soothing. "Come on, girl, let's be friends."

The horse pricked her ears firmly forward. She made a slight move, more of a sway, toward her.

Chad's voice was barely more than a whisper. "Just stand still, make her come to you."

The mare took a step and stretched out her neck to reach Corrie's hand.

"Bring your hand in a bit, make her get closer."

Corrie did as told. The horse stepped closer.

Finally, the horse stood close enough to Corrie to eat the oats from her open hand. The crunch of oats between the massive teeth gave Corrie a thrill of satisfaction.

"Okay, while she's chewing on that, slip on the halter."

Corrie whispered to the horse, "You twerp, you're just playing games with me." She rubbed the brown and white nose and soft whiskery chin. Fancy whickered, deep in her throat.

Chad led his horse out of the barn, mounted and rode to the corral fence. "Sure you don't want me to saddle her for you?"

"No, thanks, Chad, I can handle it."

"Okay. While you're doing that I'll ride over to the calving barn and check on Moe. If I'm not back by the time you're ready, ride on over there. Okay?"

"Sure. Okay."

"Be sure to cinch up the girth tight."

"I will."

She knew the job took longer than it would take anyone else, but at least she got it done, the grooming, the saddling and cinching. Everything seemed to take so much longer. At least more time than jumping into a car and starting it. Time passed differently on a ranch.

By the time she finished, Chad wasn't back, so she rode toward the calving barn and spotted Chad's horse, tied at a railing.

J emerged from the building. His eyes widened. "Hey."

"Hey, J. Thought I'd give it another try. Chad said I could tag along with him."

J nodded, silent.

Chad joined them and mounted. "Ready?"

"You bet."

J looked up at Chad. "After you check on 'em in the south pasture, go on over to Wagner's and push that bunch back there, too. I don't trust those fences."

"You want 'em all in the south pasture?"

"For now."

Chad turned to her. "You wanna bring your dog?"

"No," J answered for her, "wait until he can go with Julie. He'll learn from her."

Chad looked at Corrie and shrugged.

Corrie nodded. "That's a good idea. He could be a nuisance until he knows what to do. Or, what not to do." She noticed J hadn't offered to send Julie with them. Maybe he needed her.

Fancy made an attempt to graze along the way, but Corrie pulled up on the reins. Chad nodded approval. "That's right. Let 'er know who's boss."

Once they reached the small herd in the south pasture, which looked like any other pasture to Corrie, Chad did much as J had done as he checked the water supply, looked over the herd, counted the calves. Like his uncle, he kept a small pad in the breast pocket of his denim jacket and wrote occasional notes.

They rode on a gravel road, which ended at a big wooden gate. Chad dismounted and unlatched the gate, signaled her ahead, led his horse through, latched the gate and again mounted.

"Is this what J calls the 'Wagner place?'"

"Yeah. My uncle bought this place a few years ago. We tore down the house. It was a real dump. The barn's caving in, but the land is good, with plenty of water. He runs cattle over here."

"He mentioned he didn't trust the fences?"

"Yeah, they're getting pretty rotten. That's a summer job coming up for us."

They found a small bunch of cattle and Chad turned to her. "We'll move these over to that bigger bunch," he pointed with his thumb over his shoulder, "then move all of 'em back to the south pasture."

He rode in a wide circle, gently moving the cattle together.

A calf darted in front of them and ran into brush. It's mother bawled her alarm; the little fellow answered in a quavering bleat.

Chad went after the calf, crashing into the brush. "Haw, haw, get out of there!"

It allowed itself to be lead out, but then darted back, fear showing in huge eyes. The cow's mother, stepped forward, bawling a warning. To Chad? To her baby?

Chad smoothly reached for his lariat, swung it a couple of times, circling it above the running calf's head and dropped it neatly around the neck, dallying the rope around the saddle horn. The little fellow jerked to a stop, but Chad eased his horse ahead to soften the blow. He led the calf back to its mother, shook the stiff rope to loosen its grip and brought it back over the tiny head. It was all done casually and without a word, but Corrie was breathless with awe, even though she suspected a bit of that had been for show.

"When those little guys get scared, they get crazy. You never know what they might do."

"You're really good, Chad. It must take a long time to learn how to rope like that."

"Yeah, it does. My uncle and Moe taught me. One year, after spending the summer, it was time for me to go back to Seattle. I begged Uncle J to let me stay and go to school here, but he said my mom needed me." He shook his head. "I never knew if he meant that, or was just trying to get rid of me. I was kind of a pain in the...neck those days.

"I moped around 'cause I really didn't want to leave. I hate the city. To make me feel better, Moe made a wooden cow out of plywood for me to practice my roping back in Seattle. I stood that thing in the back yard and practiced for hours on end. My friends thought I was crazy."

"So when you came back you must have been pretty good."

"Oh, yeah, even J said so."

"So now you're out of school, huh? What are your plans?"

"To stay right here. This is what I want to do." Certainly no hesitation there.

"Have you thought about going to college? You could take agriculture courses at Central, in Ellensburg. That's where my daughter goes to school."

"J wants me to. He graduated from that college. He says I could still live here between quarters and summers, then come back full time. He's even offered to pay my way."

"That sounds good."

"Naw. I just want to do this."

At least he knew what he wanted to do. He seemed so at home, so in control. Chad was lean, not yet grown into his frame, but strong. He dressed like a typical cowboy.

"It's a good thing you're wearing chaps." She'd always just thought they were part of a cowboy's costume, sort of a decoration, but he'd demonstrated their usefulness. "When you went crashing into that brush, it could have scratched your legs."

"Yeah. This brush can be thorny."

"I don't remember J wearing them when I rode with him."

"I don't think he planned to move cattle that day, just check on 'em."

Chad didn't wear a Stetson like his uncle, put rather a billed cap. She wondered why, but hesitated to ask.

"What's your horse's name?"

"Ruby. My uncle gave her to me for my fourteenth birthday. I named her after that Kenny Rogers' song, 'Ruby, Don't Take Your Love to Town'. I still like that song."

"I do too."

He showed surprise. "You do?"

"Absolutely. I saw Kenny once when he was in Seattle. It was a terrific show. Dolly Parton was with him. What a great team."

"Who else have you seen?"

"Charlie Pride, George Jones, Conway Twitty and Loretta Lynn."

"Conway and Loretta together? That'd be great. That's the only advantage of living in Seattle. Nothing like that goes on here."

She laughed. "But here you've got the real thing!"

They rode abreast and Chad leaned forward in his saddle, holding reins high, to look into Corrie's face. She'd noticed J making that same movement. She smiled to herself. He was a nice kid.

"What kind of horse is Ruby?"

"Breed?"

"Right."

"Quarter horse, the best cow horse there is." His chest swelled with pride.

"Why's that?"

"Because of their speed. Ruby can go from a standstill to a full gallop in two seconds. There's an old saying, "A quarter horse can turn on a dime and toss you back nine cents change." He laughed and watched to see if she got the joke.

She chuckled, more at his enthusiasm than the story.

"At the rodeo, quarter horses are the most popular for the calf roping events. They can bring down a steer in three to four seconds."

"Wow, that's impressive. Are they always that color?"

"Normally they're what they call chestnut, like Ruby here, red mixed with gold, but J's is bay."

"Bay?"

"Brown with black mane and tail."

"So J's is a quarter horse?"

"Oh, yeah." Chad looked around at the gathered cattle. "Okay, you get on that other side and we'll take 'em over there." He was all business now.

On her side, a cow-calf pair darted away. Chad had his hands full on his side. Corrie hesitated, wondering how to go about getting these two back in line when Fancy took the lead and stood in front of them, blocking their way each time they attempted to go around.

"Just go along with your horse, Corrie, she knows what to do."

It was embarrassing having a horse know more than she did.

They joined the larger herd and Chad rode alongside. "I'll push 'em from behind. You watch that side, try to keep 'em together.

She nodded, hoping she could hold up her end.

So far, so good.

"Corrie!" Chad yelled from behind. "That calf got separated from his mom. See if you can get 'im back."

She broke away and maneuvered herself in front of the calf. Fancy darted back and forth, preventing the little one from getting away. Corrie had to pay attention, fearful that she'd be thrown off. Gradually, the calf's choice was limited to running in one direction, toward his mom. Corrie's stomach unclenched.

They worked their way back to the gate. Since Chad was behind the group, Corrie climbed down and unlatched the gate, leading her horse as she opened it.

Chad yelled above the din, "Okay, go ahead, take 'em on down. I'll close it."

They made their way back to the south pasture and left the bunch there, contentedly munching on hay someone had brought out while they were gone.

"Hey, Corrie, you did great. Thanks for the help."

Her heart raced. Wow. She'd done it, she'd actually helped.

* * *

J sighed, again. He felt foolish, being jealous of Chad. On the other hand, he was irritated with Corrie, not for anything she'd done, but just for being there. She'd unsettled things, interrupted the flow. He'd known that would happen.

He didn't need a woman in his life. Maybe some day, when Gretchen was raised and Chad took on more responsibility. But right now he didn't need this complication.

Waiting for the vet to return his call about that sick cow they'd found that morning, he stood at the window, absently looking at the plain yard. Who was he kidding? He'd love to spend more time with Corrie. He thought of the day they went riding. She was so alive and not afraid to show her interest.

The jangling phone jerked him from memories of Corrie's huge eyes when he'd asked her the way home. He chatted briefly with the vet who'd be out first thing in the morning. J hung up, his hand still resting on the receiver. He had wanted to show Corrie how they mother-up a cow to a calf that's not hers, but Corrie had made herself scarce for the rest of that day and even for a couple of days after that. He knew it was because of Gretchen's reaction when she saw them together.

He shook his head. Gretchen had somehow gotten it into her head that Corrie was a threat. The girl had made that pretty plain and Corrie got the message. He guessed that was why they warn about two women in the kitchen.

He didn't want to hurt Gretch, but she had to realize the world didn't revolve around her. He snorted. That was going to be news to her. They'd all made it pretty plain that it did. Gretchen didn't even know about the few times he'd dated. She'd just taken it for granted he was playing poker with the guys, and he'd let her believe that. Some of those women he wouldn't have wanted her to see; others he didn't really care one way or the other. But with Corrie...

Gretchen was fourteen. Did he really want to wait until she was eighteen before he got involved with another woman?

Chad stomped onto the porch, shaking loose dirt from his boots, and banged into the room. Gretchen was right. Chad didn't just walk into a room, he crashed in.

"Unc, you should have seen Corrie. She was a big help to me out there, moving those cows. She catches on real fast. Boy, she sure asks a lot of questions."

"Oh, yeah?" J tried to keep his voice calm. "What kind of questions?" About me?

"You know, stuff about horses, chaps, roping. She wants to know it all." He reached into the breadbox heedless of his filthy hands. "I like her."

J sighed.

"What's going on? Why're you here?"

"I live here."

Chad shook his head. "Right now. What are you doing?"

"I came in to call Doc Bradley about that cow. He's coming tomorrow morning."

Chad heaped peanut butter on the bread, slapped the two pieces together and wolfed down a huge mouthful.

J lifted his Stetson off the hat rack. This wasn't something that would just go away. He would have to talk to Gretch, make her see Corrie wasn't a threat.

His mouth formed a straight line. Good luck with that.

Chapter Ten

AS I SEE IT
Kevin Walsh
Clearwater News staff columnist

April 13, 1980. Two craters atop the summit of Mount St. Helens have now merged into one massive gash 1,700 feet across and 850 feet deep.

Prolonged earthquakes, one lasting nearly four hours, have jangled nerves from neighboring communities. Still, the general consensus among scientists is that there will be no major eruption of molten rock. "A small eruptive event" is what they foresee at this time with most of the effects limited to the mountain slopes.

Corrie woke troubled on Sunday morning. But why? What was wrong? Sadness enveloped her. Sunday had always been a family day, when she was a girl and after she had a family of her own. Now Sundays seemed hollow. Gwen was in college now, and it would never be the same with her, although Corrie hoped they would always be close. Would she ever have someone else again? A real companion?

No.

She didn't want, or need, a boyfriend, let alone a husband. It even sounded juvenile to say "boyfriend." Although she had been profoundly shaken by her divorce, she'd gotten over it. Gotten over the need to be a couple. She was free, free to pursue whatever she wanted. Right now what she wanted was to learn, and to write. That's it. It was nice to have friends, to be able to have fun. But no commitments. She would never, ever, go through that agony again. She didn't need anyone. She was fine alone.

She rolled over, adjusting the bedding around her, and stared through the tiny window. A watery sun tried to dawn. She'd wished it had been J instead of Chad the other day. No. Stop that. She sighed. Still, it would have been wonderful to spend another day with J. But Chad had been very kind and helpful. She was grateful to him for taking the time to teach her.

She wondered why Gretchen didn't like her.

She heard a soft sigh and turned over to stare directly into Bo's big, friendly face. Once their eyes connected, his tail swung wildly. I'm your friend, he seemed to say. When's breakfast? She reached out from under the warm covers and rubbed his muzzle and waxy whiskers.

Out loud she said, "I don't think it's me she dislikes, Bo, it's the idea of sharing her dad."

Bo's ears perked up and he tilted his head, trying to understand.

"For years, it's just been the two of them."

Bo rested his massive head on the mattress and watched her intently, probably hoping to get a clue about what she was talking about.

She sat up, swung her legs over the side of the bed and held his head in her hands. "J's a nice guy and I'd like to have him as a friend, but I don't want to cause trouble between him and his daughter."

Bo's tail swung low, slowly. Corrie stood up. The big dog jumped up.

"You hungry, boy? What a good dog. You're my best friend, Bo."

Speaking of friends, she should make a couple of phone calls today, connect with friends in Seattle. She needed to write to Gwen too, try to set a date for her daughter to visit.

She slipped on a robe and opened the door so Bo could take a quick potty run. He could be fast when a meal was waiting.

She poured food into his bowl and filled his water bucket.

At the wood-burning stove, she crumpled paper to build a fire. She'd finally gotten the hang of building an efficient fire. It was mostly patience that made a good blaze, starting with a little paper, topped with kindling and then small pieces of firewood. There was no hurrying it; the minute she did, the fire smothered and died. Each day she filled the small wood box near the stove to keep the wood dry and at room temperature. Soon the fire crackled to a glowing, leaping blaze. She stood in front of the stove, rotating like a rotisserie, warming her body in back, then in front. Then, comfortably warm, she ran water for her shower.

Later, she sat at her computer, keying notes and observations, while a pot of chicken stew simmered on the stove. She'd grown tired of fast meals and wanted something substantial for dinner and to freeze for future dinners. She jumped at Bo's sharp bark and a knock at her door. Opening the door, she found Nancy, grinning at her.

"I hope I'm not disturbing you."

"Of course not, Nancy. Come in. I don't think you've seen the place since I've moved to the ranch."

Nancy looked around with an experienced eye. "Corrie, it's darling. I wouldn't have believed you could fix it up so cute."

"Go ahead and look around. I love it here, Nancy, and I'm so grateful for your help."

"What an improvement. I can't believe the transformation. Has J seen it?"

"Briefly, when we moved your dresser out."

Nancy nodded thoughtfully, and then seemed to rouse herself. "Well, why I came over was to invite you over to J's. The whole family's there. My mother's been visiting this week and while she's here she wanted to see J, Gretchen and Chad.

Warning signs prickled, signs she had learned to pay attention to. "Thanks, Nancy, but it sounds like a family thing. To tell you the truth, I don't think–

"Not at all, Corrie! We'd love to have you, and I want you to meet the rest of the family."

It seemed there was no dissuading Nancy and Corrie didn't want to appear rude, so she allowed herself to be led to J's.

They entered through the back door and joined the others in the living room. J sprang to his feet. "Corrie!" He turned to his sister, "I wondered where you'd gone off to, Nan." A look passed between brother and sister and he nodded ever so slightly. The chatter had come to an abrupt halt and she was aware of being closely observed. More like dissected.

Nancy took charge of the introductions. "Corrie's a writer and is staying here to learn about ranching and ranch country." J came back with a mug of coffee and pulled a chair from the dining room table and offered it to her.

Corrie's eyes settled on Gretchen's cold stare. She smiled weakly. "Hi, Gretchen."

"Hi." Only a teen could have come up with such a totally indifferent greeting.

Corrie was aware of a movement from J. Gretchen glanced at him and her eyes widened. What?

Rick resumed what he had apparently been telling the others, something about a neighbor who caught his jacket in a piece of machinery. Corrie could see the family resemblance in J, Rick, and their mother. Chad commented on Rick's story: "He's lucky he didn't lose an arm."

She became aware that J's mother, Maude, was speaking to her. Corrie mentally caught up with the conversation.

"Are you published?"

The question was almost a dare. "Yes, I am. I've had a novel published, and several articles."

"Grandma, do you want to go out and see the new calves?"

Maud glanced at her granddaughter. "In a bit, dear." She studied Corrie. "How did you happen to come here, to this ranch?"

Nancy laughed. "Her friendly realtor."

"Yes, I was lucky enough to stop at Nancy's office and learn about J's cabin."

"How lucky can you get?" There was no mistaking Gretchen's sarcasm.

The whole room turned to the girl. Corrie instinctively realized Gretchen hadn't meant it to come out in such sarcastic tone, but it was clearly how she felt.

J, who had been standing in the doorway, jerked to attention. "Gretchen!"

"Well..." she hesitated.

Corrie, trying to fill the awkward gap, turned to Barbara. "Nancy tells me your son is graduating from high school this year."

Barbara blinked with the sudden change of conversation. "Yes, our youngest."

"Those kinds of milestones are important, aren't they?"

Barbara smiled. "Yes, as much to the parents as to the kids."

Tension filled the room.

Maude leaned forward. "Are you married?"

Out of the corner of her eye, Corrie saw J's hand go up and heard a sharp intake of breath. She smiled, what she hoped was a genuine smile and not just teeth showing. "I'm divorced."

Nancy glared at her mother.

Maude shifted in her chair. "Well, then, you're free to pursue your interests."

"Yes, I am."

"I can't imagine you'll want to stay in that dingy little cabin for long though. I saw it once, when Moe lived there and..."

"Mom," Nancy broke in, "you wouldn't believe how cute she's fixed it up."

"Well, why live there when there's this whole house?"

"Ma!" J's voice roared in disbelief.

"Grandma!" Gretchen's shrill voice expressed her alarm.

Maude, lips pressed together, nodded. She folded her arms across her ample chest.

Corrie stood and handed the coffee mug to J. "Thank you." She turned to the surprised, upturned faces in the living room, upturned except for Gretchen, who earnestly studied her hands. "It was so nice meeting all of you." She slipped out the back door. She couldn't leave fast enough, but forced herself to walk, not run.

As the door closed, she heard J's strained voice, "My God, I can't believe that just happened."

"Mother," Nancy's shocked voice, "I have never been so embarrassed."

Maude countered, "What? I..." Corrie couldn't hear any more.

Don't take it personally, she kept repeating to herself, as she speed-walked to her cabin. Don't take it personally.

But it was hard not to take it personally. Gretchen clearly didn't want her there. J's mother... well, what was she doing? At the very least Maude was suspicious of her. Poor Nancy was humiliated and J was angry, all on her account. Barbara and Rick seemed friendly enough, but... She stepped into the cabin and, for lack of something better to do, resumed work at the computer. Or tried to. She stared at the screen, random words swam out of control.

Another sharp bark from Bo and a knock at the door. With dread she opened it. Nancy, Barbara, Maude and Gretchen stood at her threshold. At a glance, Corrie had a hard time making sense of their mixed expressions. Looking past them, Corrie saw J, Rick and Chad as they stood facing away from the cabin, concentrating on some distant object.

"If you don't mind," Nancy said, her voice strained, "I like to show them how cute you've fixed up the cabin."

"Sure. Please, come in." Corrie couldn't bear to be around either Gretchen or her grandmother another minute. "Make yourself at home," she said as she joined the men in the yard. She left the cabin door open so it would seem less...final.

The men showed mild surprise when she joined them. "Rick, I understand you've had some rumbling from Mount St. Helens lately."

"Nothing much. As usual, I think the press is making a big deal out it. It doesn't help when they try to discourage people from going up there. It has the opposite effect."

She laughed. "I guess so. I went up last week with some newspaper people. It wasn't hard to get in. We just used a back road."

J spoke up. "They have those barricades for people like you."

She smiled. "I think they're just trying to protect their...themselves."

He cocked an eyebrow and smirked. "I think they're trying to protect yours."

Nancy's strident voice trailed out. "Mother, isn't this darling? Why would she go to all this work if she didn't plan to stay here?"

Gretchen said something that Corrie couldn't hear but to which Nancy responded, "Honey, it isn't like that."

The men looked down, studying their boots. Corrie filled the gap. "We met Harry Truman. What a character!" Her voice sounded hollow.

Rick took up the effort. "Yeah, he's an old coot. People either love him or hate him."

J chimed in, laughing. "Remember that time he took a shotgun after us?"

"Really?" Corrie asked, amazed. "Why?"

Rick laughed at the memory. "For fishing in his lake. We gave him our whole mess of fish. Better that than a backside of buckshot."

Chad looked at both his uncles. "I've never heard that story before."

The women joined them, Gretchen trailing behind. Nancy stood by her mother, arms crossed.

"Corrie," Maude began, "I hope I didn't offend you. I certainly didn't mean..."

"Oh, no, Maude, not at all." Corrie tried to look relaxed and care-free, but inside she was dying an inch at a time.

Nancy put her arm around her mother's shoulders.

"We're going into town for an early dinner," Maude continued, "and would like you to join us."

Gretchen's sharp intake of breath and wide-eyed horror left no doubt how she felt about her grandmother's offer.

Nancy's look of satisfaction disappeared, replaced with dismay.

"Sure," Rick chimed in, "we'd—"

"Thank you, but I have my dinner simmering on the stove."

"I saw that, but you could surely have that tomorrow." Maude said, her voice determined.

"No, thank you." Corrie kept the smile pasted on her face.

Maude's eyes widened, then narrowed.

Rick whirled around, but Corrie could tell he had a broad smile on his face.

J took his mother's arm as though to assist her back to his house. Corrie doubted if the woman had any choice but to follow where his iron grip took her.

"Well," Nancy stammered, "we'll see you...at bridge on Thursday?"

"Great." Corrie answered brightly. "I'll stop by for you. I don't know where Kim lives."

Nancy nodded, then shrugged, and shook her head in apology.

Corrie squeezed Nancy's arm in silent understanding. "See you Thursday."

J had said she could ride Nancy's horse any time she wanted. Well, she wanted to now. Returning to her cabin she paced the floor. Her mind babbled. She hated that J and Nancy were embarrassed because of her.

She wanted to wait until they left for town before going to the barn, but she simply couldn't stand it any longer. She stormed to the barn, anxious for escape.

Fancy allowed herself to be bribed with the oats and Corrie had just begun grooming the horse when J joined her in the barn.

"Corrie, I'm sorry about that."

"J, don't worry about it. It's fine." It wasn't fine, of course. Her voice sounded unsteady, her knees wobbled and she didn't know how much longer she could hold back tears.

"No, it isn't. My mother never seems to know when to keep her mouth shut. And Gretchen!" He shook his head and raised his hands in frustration.

"Well, your mom is just trying to understand." She couldn't think of an adequate comment to make about Gretchen, so she just shook her head.

"Corrie, if you're upset maybe you shouldn't ride."

"I'm not upset." Attempting to look casual, she reached up and gently pulled the mare's forelock from under the brow band. Was he forbidding her to ride? She really wouldn't be able to take that. She'd have a meltdown on the spot. "I just need to get away, get some fresh air." She finished grooming and flung the saddle blanket on, sliding it back like he'd shown her.

He reached for the saddle, plopped it on Fancy's back and cinched the girth in place. Their hands touched as he handed her the reigns. She started to pull back, but he caught her hand and gently held it. Time stood still as they gazed into each other's eyes. His warm hand felt so good, so comforting. He smiled. She tried to smile back, but knew it was a poor effort. Back there, with his family, she had just been given proof that this wouldn't work. There was just too much against any kind of a relationship other than casual friendship. She stepped back and he released her hand.

"Just ride 'er easy, okay?" His voice sounded like it came out of a barrel.

"Okay." Her voice came out thick.

"And don't get lost."

She smiled, but had the distinct feeling it was crooked. "I won't."

Corrie felt his eyes on her back as she rode out. The first gate latch could easily be handled on horseback. She let herself out and latched the gate behind her. She didn't dare look back, though she knew he still watched her. Finally, she couldn't stand it any longer and looked back over her shoulder. J stood, motionless, still watching. She faced forward again, tears gathering.

Once over a knoll she relaxed. She leaned forward and rubbed Fancy's muscular neck, speaking soothingly. "We'll just have a little outing, something nice for both of us." The horse's ears swiveled almost three-hundred-sixty degrees. Corrie urged her into a gentle lope. Riding Fancy was like sitting on a rocking chair. She was so privileged to ride this horse. She must remember to thank Nancy the next time she saw her.

She stopped, dismounted and walked along a stream, swollen with the winter thaw. She'd been warned about letting a hot horse drink water, but Fancy hadn't worked up a sweat, so she let her have a drink and scooped up the icy water for herself. She mounted again, feeling stronger and more in control of her emotions.

The sound of singing drifted toward her in the soft spring breeze. How incongruous. Birds twittering and human voices in song. She turned Fancy toward the music, following a winding dirt road and soon spotted a little white church with a tall, wooden steeple. She approached the back of the building and reined Fancy in. The congregation began a new song, one of Corrie's favorites, "Amazing Grace." She sat, spellbound with the magic of the scene. A sense of peace settled over her. Apparently, that was the closing song. She heard the murmur of conversations and the first people made their way out of the building.

She turned Fancy back the way they had come, not wishing to encounter anyone and break the spell. What luck to have stumbled upon that scene. She felt uplifted, realizing how much she missed going to church. For many years their family had been active members. After the divorce and her move to another neighborhood, she hadn't become established with a new church. She sighed. The memory made her long for those lost, serene days.

Her thoughts returned to her present situation. If she was going to stay here, she'd have to establish her independence to everyone, but especially to Gretchen. Corrie knew she must somehow convince Gretchen that she was no threat. She didn't know yet how she'd do that, but things would be miserable until she did. Nancy would have to take care of Maude, there was no way Corrie could take her on. She probably just wanted what was best for J and Gretchen, and was trying to understand. Seeing the cabin probably took care of that.

She thought back to when Gwen was fourteen. Those weren't their best years.

She wondered when Kevin and the others would go back to Mount St. Helens. A volcano seemed more pleasant to handle right now than Gretchen. At least it would be a good distraction.

Chapter Eleven

AS I SEE IT
Kevin Walsh
***Clearwater News** staff columnist*

April 15, 1980. The lure to Mount St. Helens is not only drawing sight-seers on the ground but in the air, too. The Federal Aviation Administration established a five-mile restricted zone around the mountain, but many pilots are disobeying the order. One of the pilots I talked to said, "It's like a dogfight up there." On a single day recently, 70 unauthorized planes were reported to be in the restricted airspace.

*A*s far as J was concerned, the dinner in town had been a disaster. His mother just couldn't let people run their own lives. She nagged Chad about college, she harped at J about needing a wife, to which Gretchen had said they didn't need anyone, they were doing just fine, thank you. It was a nightmare. Poor Nancy tried to calm everyone down. The whole dinner was so miserable he'd actually lost his appetite.

The family had taken separate cars so they could each go their own way after dinner. Rick was going through calving now, too, and he'd left their son in charge, but he'd been on his own too long and would need relief, so they and Maude were on their way back to Randle.

Silence hung heavy in J's truck as he, Chad, and Gretchen rode back from town. As they climbed out of his truck, J said, "Gretchen, go to your room. I'll be up in a few minutes."

She turned to her dad, started to say something, but one glance from him changed her mind. She ran into the house and up the stairs. He saw her bedroom light flick on.

"Chad, check on Moe, find out about that heifer."

"Okay. Unc, are you gonna talk to Gretch about...?"

"Chad, just go."

Chad turned on his heel, raising his arms in frustration.

J tried to calm himself as he climbed the stairs to Gretchen's room. He tapped at the door.

"Come in." Her hesitant voice sounded guilty. She stood by her bed, face blotchy, eyes huge.

J sighed. He sat on the chair at her desk and motioned for her to sit on her bed.

"What's gotten into you, Gretchen? This afternoon you were rude to Corrie and at dinner you were rude to your grandmother. I'm ashamed of your behavior."

Tears welled and she swallowed.

"What, Gretch?"

"I didn't mean to sound like that with Corrie. It just came out."

"It came out that way because that's how you were thinking. What worries you about Corrie?"

She shrugged.

His voice softened. "Don't give me that. Tell me what's bothering you. We need to sort this out."

"Dad, we don't need anyone else. We're doing fine, just us."

"We've talked about this before. I didn't ask Corrie to come here. It just happened. Nan showed you and your grandmother her cabin, how much work she's gone to, fixing it up. In my opinion, she's here for the reasons she says, that she wants to learn about ranch life so she can write about it. What makes you think she's some kind of threat?"

She shrugged.

"No. Tell me."

"I don't know. Nothing." she stammered.

He waited. "Tell me one thing she's done that makes you think that."

"I don't know. She's about your age, and she's pretty, I guess. I just thought...." She took a deep breath and swallowed.

"Gretchen, I haven't seen anything that makes me think she's remotely interested in me. As far as I'm concerned, she just wants to be friends, to all of us."

"But Grandma says—"

"Your grandmother has been talking about me finding a wife for years, Gretch. She worries about us. Mothers worry. She's made assumptions that just aren't true. But that doesn't mean you can talk to her in that sassy tone. Your grandmother deserves your respect."

Tears fell. "I'm sorry, Dad." She sniffed, plucked a tissue from her nightstand and dabbed her eyes. "I'll call Grandma tomorrow."

"That'll be good."

"How about Corrie. Do I have to apologize to her?"

"No. I'm afraid it would make it worse. Just be civil from now on, okay?" His voice turned stern. "Gretchen, I don't want to have to talk about this again."

She nodded and blew her nose. "Okay."

Their eyes met and held. J wondered if he'd really touched whatever it was bothering his daughter. In a way, she was becoming a stranger. Tears always seemed close to the surface. "Do you have homework tonight?"

"No, I'm done. I'm just going to bed and read for awhile."

With effort, he stood. He was beat–physically and emotionally. He bent and kissed her wet cheek. "Goodnight, honey."

"Goodnight, Dad."

He clumped down the stairs, made his way to the dark living room, and sat in his recliner. He leaned forward, elbows on knees, holding his head. His conscience prickled. What he'd said to his daughter wasn't entirely the truth, at least not at his end of the relationship. In his mind's eye he saw Corrie riding Fancy, looking dejected and miserable. Just like he felt right now. Gretchen was right. They didn't need anyone else. They'd been doing fine for years. But, let's face it, he wanted something else. He wanted Corrie.

Gretchen was just getting into those touchy miserable years. He could remember that turmoil, remembered it in himself and in Chad. But girls were different, even worse, with their tears and extreme highs and lows. He knew they were in for some rocky years and for him to have a relationship would only make things worse. Oh, boy. Would this ever sort itself out?

Chad banged into the kitchen and went straight to his room. He probably hadn't seen J sitting in the dark. J sat back and looked out the large window at the blackness and dark shadows, mentally bracing himself for the turmoil he knew would come.

* * *

Corrie woke the next morning, her heart pounding. She had dreamt of J. They were walking in a field, holding hands and laughing. Then they stopped and he'd embraced her. The dream faded. She closed her eyes, trying to recapture the dream, but it was gone, leaving her feeling empty.

But she knew a relationship with J was hopeless. There was just too much against it happening, considering how Gretchen felt. The poor girl had already lost her mother. Corrie was not going to be responsible for a strained relationship between J and his daughter. Corrie knew that she would be the eventual loser on that deal.

Besides, what had happened to her resolve to avoid getting into another relationship, inviting heartache and bitterness? Who needed that? She was miserable now, just thinking about it. That's what she needed to remember.

She would move on, build her new life without J, and not give Gretchen reason to worry about her. She dressed, ate a quick breakfast, packed up her laundry and headed into town. At the Laundromat she popped her clothes into a couple of washing machines, checked her watch and hurried over to the Clearwater News.

Kevin and Al burst through the door just as she arrived. "Corrie!" Kevin boomed, "we were just talking about you."

Al nodded to her. "We're heading over to Stella's for a cup of coffee." He motioned her to come along.

"Great. I just put my washing in so I have time." It felt so good to see them, to be welcomed and wanted.

Kevin ordered coffee and doughnuts for them. "How about another round at Mount St. Helens?"

"I've been thinking about that. Sure, I'm game."

Al lit a cigarette and reached for the ashtray. "What would you think about making it an overnighter? The best light is dawn or dusk and when we go for just a day we miss both."

"You mean camp?"

Kevin nodded. "We could camp. I can borrow my brother's stuff."

"Or we could stay in a motel," Corrie said.

Al took a drag on his cigarette. "Camping would be better, then we'd be right there."

Kevin shrugged. "Fine with me. Corrie?"

Her mind whirled. She remembered her resolve. "Will the others go too, Robert, Kim?"

"Naw," Al said. "Let's not make it a crowd. It gets too complicated."

"How about your wife, Kevin? Wouldn't Joanne like to go?"

Kevin chuckled. "Joanne and I aren't married, Corrie—but we've been together for a few years now. Camping isn't her style. That mountain isn't her style. She'll cheerfully pass."

Corrie considered. Since Al had never mentioned anyone in his life, she assumed he had no personal attachments. She felt comfortable enough with these two. "Okay. Sure. When?"

Kevin grinned. "How about this weekend? Let's do it while we're hot."

Corrie laughed. "Let's hope it's just us who're hot, not that mountain. What should we take?"

They worked out a simple menu, only needing food for three or four meals, which would be easy enough to handle.

Corrie glanced at her watch. "Okay, see you Saturday morning. I'll meet you at the office."

"I'll pick you up at your place. That way you won't have to leave your car in town overnight. I'm taking my own car. Robert isn't wild about us taking the company van up there again."

"Okay, see you Saturday morning, about eight?"

Walking back to the Laundromat Corrie had a few misgivings. Was this a wise thing to do? She hardly knew these guys, but her gut feeling told her that they were honorable. This was a professional venture, so Al could get good pictures and Kevin could get material for his column. She had shown an interest in going back and they were kind enough to include her. People did this nowadays. Don't be such a prude, she chided herself.

Her washing ground to a stop as she entered the Laundromat. She dumped the wet clothes into the dryers and again checked her watch. Good. I have time to go to the hardware, maybe even the grocery store.

Snow's Hardware, just across the street, was typically small-town with a variety of almost everything you could think of for a home. She found plastic containers of various sizes and stacked them on the counter. A middle-aged man, sitting in his office, looked around and then came out to wait on her himself.

"Sorry, I guess Margaret is out for coffee." He looked over his glasses at her and smiled. "I've seen you in here before, but we haven't met. I'm Leonard Snow."

Corrie extended her hand and smiled. "I'm Corrie Stephens. I'm fairly new here. You have a nice store with plenty of selection."

While they chatted Corrie noticed Leonard glancing at her left hand. Checking for a wedding ring?

His face colored, the flush going right up through his graying hair. "Excuse me, are you married?"

"No," she answered without hesitation, "I'm divorced." She looked at him, question in her eyes.

"I'm widowed. My wife died fifteen months ago."

He was still counting the months, like counting the age of a baby.

"I'm sorry. That must be so difficult for you."

He sighed. "In every way, I miss her. We'd been married thirty-two years, raised three kids. When the kids were almost grown, we bought this place and ran it together. We were a real partnership." He bagged Corrie's purchases and slipped the receipt in the bag, fighting for composure.

"I can only imagine how tough this must be."

"I...I...need to get out, do something. I'm tired of moping around feeling sorry for myself. My doctor tells me it's not healthy."

"No, it isn't."

"Would you care to go out sometime, maybe have dinner?"

For a split second she hesitated. Wait! What about her resolve to rebuild her life without J? This is a golden opportunity to make a friend. He didn't hold the tiniest bit of attraction to her, but all he was asking was for her to have dinner with him. "Sure, that sounds good."

He brightened. "How about Friday night?" His face colored and his eyebrows puckered. "I'm sorry if I sound forward. It's been a long time since I've asked anyone out." He shook his head.

She smiled. "Friday's fine." The situation did seem awkward, but she didn't want to add to Leonard's discomfort.

He showed surprised when she told him where she lived.

"J has a cabin out there? I didn't know that."

"He's never rented it before. His hired man lived there for years. I heard about it through his sister, Nancy."

"Sure, Nancy Abbot at the real estate office. I know J's place. Margaret can close the store. How about if I pick you up around six?"

She smiled. "Six is fine."

She'd used up her time at the hardware. She'd go to the grocery store after folding her laundry. Corrie smiled to herself. As it so often happens, once you've made up your mind to do something, doors open. She just hoped they were the right doors.

* * *

According to Corrie's calculations, Moe would be checking on the herd this morning while J tended to calving.

As she headed toward the barn, however, she saw the older flatbed full of hay, rocking away from her. Moe must have seen her through his side mirror. He waved from the driver's side. Corrie waved back, but then motioned them to stop and ran to catch up to the truck.

"You're going out to feed the cattle?"

"Yeah. Wanna come along?" Chad answered from the passenger seat.

"Sure, if I can be of some help."

Moe jerked his head, motioning her to climb in. Chad climbed out of the cab and onto the bales of hay stacked on the flatbed.

"Can't we all ride in front?"

"Naw. I'll end up here anyway. You can open gates."

The truck bounced along across pastures. Corrie's head actually hit the roof a couple of times. Occasionally they followed a road, but most of the roads were so rutted they were almost worse than the pasture. Corrie opened and closed gates as they distributed hay to various bunches of cattle. She was thankful for the leather gloves she'd recently bought as she handled the cold metal latches, or in some cases, wires looped around fence posts. Corrie watched Chad flake off several layers from the bales, spreading them out for the larger bunches of cattle.

Corrie loved the clean, wholesome aroma of hay. "I'm surprised it's so green."

Chad picked up another bale, cut the orange bale string and began flaking and methodically forking it over the side. "It's alfalfa."

"Do you grow it here?"

"No, we used to, but decided we'd just concentrate on raising cattle and buy the hay from growers. It takes expensive equipment and we had to hire extra people at harvest. J decided to leave that part of the business to someone else."

"You don't grow anything, then?"

Moe spit a long brown stream of tobacco, splattering it on a rock. "We seed pastures, for grazin'."

"Do you have to do that every year?"

"We alternate. Do each one every four years or so."

As the truck approached, the cattle pushed toward them. Some bellowed impatiently and crowded around the truck.

Corrie smiled. "They know why we're here."

Chad grabbed a bale and slid it off the back of the flatbed. "Yeah, we're a little late today 'cause we had trouble starting the truck. That's why they're irritated. They get used to a schedule."

"Is that why you're doing this together today, because you got a late start?"

"Yeah, it's quicker with two."

The countryside showed signs of spring, with grass shooting green sprouts, and trees and shrubs leafing. Corrie gazed toward the nearby rolling hills, now gray and partly obscured with morning clouds. At the edges of many of the pastures, scrub brush created borders, backed up with barbed wire fences. From a distance the pastures looked smooth; up close the ground was uneven. J's land gradually inclined toward the hills, taking a few dips now and then with patches of trees separating open sections of land.

As Chad distributed hay, Moe climbed out of the truck to check on watering systems.

"So you just do this until the grass grows enough for the cattle to graze?"

Moe nodded. "Yep. It won't be too much longer now."

"That will be nice, huh?"

Moe took out a pinch of tobacco and tucked it between his lower teeth and his gum. "Don't make much difference. There's allus somethin' gotta be done."

"You must like ranching though. You've been doing it a long time."

He shrugged. "All I ever done."

Cattle egrets, crow-sized white birds with long, graceful necks, combed the wide backs of the cattle. Corrie marveled at how nature provided and how much one living thing depended upon another.

Bumping along, back through gates, Corrie was glad she'd invited herself. She glanced at her watch. She still didn't instinctively know the time of day like the others seemed to. "What now?"

"I'm gonna saddle up and ride over to check on a bunch of cows over there," Moe pointed with his head.

"You can't reach them by truck?"

He shook his head. "They get in them draws where it's too rough for a truck."

She waited for an invitation but none came. Finally, as they neared the equipment shed, where he'd park the truck, she asked. "Do you mind if I come along, Moe?"

"Okay by me."

Corrie stepped into the corral, but Moe passed her with two halters. "I'll get 'em." She couldn't believe how quickly he gathered his horse, Roy, and Fancy. No bribe, no balk, no nonsense.

He handed over Fancy to her and they quickly groomed and saddled the horses. As they left the barn, and mounted, Moe looked back at her following him. "You should be doin' this with J, not an old fart like me."

She didn't know how to take his comment. She reined in. "Moe, would you just as soon not have me tag along?"

"No, I want you to come. What I'm sayin' is your charm," he stopped to give her a yellow-toothed smile, "is wasted on an old coot like me. J's the one who could use the company."

"Well," she said, "I don't know that he thinks so. Anyway, I just want to learn...."

"I don't care what he thinks, he's been alone too long."

She came abreast of him. The old man watched her, waiting for an answer, but she thought better of answering. Moe rode differently than J and Chad. He sat tall in the saddle and held his reins chest high. His motions were quicker, not the relaxed slouch she saw with the other two.

"You've been on this ranch a long time now, haven't you Moe?"

He spit. "Long time. Longer'n J by 'bout twelve years."

"Where were you before that?"

"Montana."

"Is Montana ranching very different than here?"

He glanced at her and nodded. "Harder. Them winters are bitch, er, killers."

"I hear it's rough here, too."

"Not like there. Go out to feed there and coffee freezes in yer cup. Ever' place you go, you're breakin' ice so's the cattle can git water. Spreads so big it takes all day jest to get to town. In winter, ya have to stay in town all night 'cause you don't wanna be travelin' at dark. Truck break down out there an' you'll be stiffer'n a board when they find ya."

She shook her head. "Sounds hard."

"It is, but life here can be hard, 'specially if you're doin' it alone, like J."

"You're alone, Moe."

"Thas different. I allus been alone. J had somebody and lost 'er, and he has the girl."

She nodded. "It must be tough for him, alone with a daughter all these years."

"Been too long."

"Maybe so. But it seems like he's handled it."

"He lived through it, if that's what you mean. Don't mean that's good."

She gave up skirting around it. "I don't think Gretchen particularly wants me around. Anyway, I just want to learn about—"

"Bull."

She stiffened. "What? Moe, I didn't come here to find a man. I came here to learn because I want to write about it." It occurred to her that Moe probably never would take her writing seriously.

He shook his head. "I mean 'bull' that Gretchen doesn't want you around. Kid that age don't know what she wants, what's good for 'er."

"Well, she thinks she does."

He snorted. "Before you know it, she'll be going off, doin' her own thing. J needs somebody."

"Well, that may be true. But Gretchen has made it pretty clear that they don't need me."

"It's high time Gretch thinks of somebody besides hersef. J and them have spoilt 'er."

Corrie shrugged and shook her head.

"You give up awful quick."

"Moe! I told you, I'm not here to find a husband, I'm here to learn."

"Bull."

She gave an exasperated sigh.

He glanced at her and chuckled. "Okay. Look out here now. Follow me. It's deep goin' here."

The horses hoofs made sucking sounds as they stepped through a wide span thick with mud.

"Where did this come from?"

"An underground spring. Dries up in the summer but it's like this all winter. 'Nother reason we don't bring the truck in 'ere."

It made Corrie nervous, seeing the horses struggling through the sticky mess.

"Don't let 'er stop," Moe called over his shoulder.

She urged Fancy on and when they finally reached hard ground, she sighed with relief.

"Is Roy a quarter horse?"

"Nope. Mustang."

"I thought mustangs were wild horses."

He nodded. "He was. Got 'im from Oregon. They brought 'im in at Hines. They got a gov'ment program. Bring 'em in from the wild."

"In a way, that's kind of sad."

"Better than starvin' to death. Them critters just keep breedin', more'n the land kin support."

"So how did you go about getting him?"

"Applied. Then I went down there and picked 'im up. Got a mare and her foal," he patted his horse's neck, "this guy. Them gov'ment people's fussy though. You gotta guarantee you kin take care of 'em."

"So you broke them in yourself?"

"Yep. Me 'n J."

"Where's the mare?"

"We had 'er for a long time but she got lame and we had to put 'er down."

"What color is Roy?" To Corrie he looked like a light brown, but no doubt there would be a 'horse color' to describe this particular shade.

"Sorrel."

"Is he a stallion?"

"Gelding. We don't keep stallions. They's knot-heads."

"So, when do you 'fix' them?"

"Castrate? Sometime before they's four years old. Then they're geldings."

"And you call a young female a filly until she's four years old, then she's a mare, right?"

"Yer catchin' on."

She took a deep, satisfying breath. Bit by bit, she was catching on.

Although she enjoyed this time with Moe, she fought back a deep aching. Was Moe right? Did J need somebody? Maybe J did, she despaired, but Gretchen apparently didn't.

* * *

Friday night at exactly six o'clock Leonard's car crunched on the gravel leading to Corrie's cabin. This wasn't an evening she'd particularly looked forward to. She felt like she was going through the motions of dating. But she was determined to act on her resolve to build a new life. With as much enthusiasm as she could muster, she invited him in.

He looked around with interest but made no comment. "Well, shall we go? I made reservations at the steak house for six-thirty."

As his big Buick glided toward the main driveway, they passed Gretchen and Chad, returning from the barn. The two stopped in their tracks as the big car passed them. Corrie waved and they half-heartedly waved back, their mouths open.

Corrie glanced in the side mirror and saw Gretchen's questioning look. Chad gestured to the car and said something to Gretchen and she shot something back.

"J's little girl is growing up."

"Yes, she is. Do you know Chad, J's nephew?"

"Sure, I've known him for years." Leonard glanced at her. "Corrie, I hope I didn't give you the wrong impression. I'm not looking for a wife. No one could replace Marsha. I just need to get out, to—"

"Sure, Leonard, I absolutely understand. I feel the same way. I don't ever intend to remarry, but I enjoy being with people and doing things."

"You don't intend to marry again?"

"No. Never."

His concerned look surprised her. "That doesn't seem right. A bright, pretty woman like you. To tell you the truth, when you told me where you were staying, I was surprised you and J...."

She laughed. "No, there's nothing there. I'm just here to learn about ranching and this lifestyle." Well, at least that was the original intent. Now she wasn't so sure. There was definitely 'something there' but it wasn't hers to have. Well, so what. She didn't need it anyway.

He nodded, but looked unconvinced.

Corrie took a bite of her steak and nodded at Leonard's attempt at conversation. Her shrimp scampi was excellent and créme brulée superb. But the evening was nothing compared to the thrill of having J point out a coyote, of watching him saddle a horse, of having him touch her hand, of being warmed by his smile. Even his attempts at teaching her which direction she was going was more thrilling than this dinner. Leonard was kind, and a perfect gentlemen. She hoped she didn't seem preoccupied. Her mind, when she wasn't thinking about J, skipped ahead to the next day, when they would take on that mountain again.

Chapter Twelve

AS I SEE IT
Kevin Walsh
Clearwater News staff columnist

April 18, 1980. According to geologist Dave Johnston, data shows increasing intensity at Mount St. Helens. "Records don't lie, it's building up," Johnston claims.

A large array of scientists are working together: seismologists, volcanologists, geologists and geochemists. Seismologists had wired sensors on the mountain even before the activity. Only hours after the first tremor, three additional seismic stations were installed. Within ten days, thirteen new stations were established. The scientists are taking turns manning posts set up in trailers at various sites.

*F*resh from his shower, J stepped into the kitchen. He'd expected to see dinner at least started. He and Gretchen had talked about grilling hamburgers and she had promised to put together the fixings. Strident voices from outside pierced the air. He looked out the window.

Gretchen and Chad were nose to nose, close to blows, it looked like. He opened the back door. "What's going on?"

Startled, they both looked up at him.

"Nothing," Chad answered, giving Gretchen a look of disgust. He roughly brushed passed her and climbed the back stairs.

"Gretch?"

The girl, stiff with anger, merely shrugged her shoulders and followed Chad into the house.

Still glaring at Gretchen, Chad plopped onto a kitchen chair.

Gretchen started to leave the kitchen, apparently heading for her room.

J frowned. "Gretchen, I thought you were going to start on our hamburgers."

She made an about-face. "I forgot. I'll do it now."

"Chad, you wanna start the barbecue?"

Chad hit his fist on the table and pushed himself up.

J put up his hands. "Wait, let's just hold it. What's going on?"

"Nothing," Gretchen and Chad answered, almost in unison.

"Don't give me that. What?"

Gretchen looked close to tears, so he turned to Chad. "Let's hear it."

"Did you see Mr. Snow's big Buick?"

"No. When? Where?"

"Here, Uncle J," Chad said with exaggerated patience. "Just a few minutes ago."

"What'd he want?"

"Corrie. He came to pick up Corrie." Chad said it slowly, as though explaining to a child.

"Okay." J didn't like the sound of that bit of news, but he'd think about it later. "So what? Did he run over your foot?"

Chad merely shook his head and rolled his eyes.

J turned to his daughter. "So, Gretchen, what's the problem?"

"Chad's blaming everything on me! He says I've chased her away."

Chad balled his fists. "You did! Your snotty comments, your attitude. Who'd wanna stick around here after getting treated like that!"

"Whoa. Let's just calm down." Chad's anger surprised J. He'd rarely seen him riled at all, let alone toward Gretchen. They'd always gotten along. She loved having him around. He'd been like a big brother to her and there was enough age difference that there was no real competition between them.

"Why is it all my fault?" Her shrill voice belied her feelings of guilt.

"Because you were the one that treated her like shi–"

"Okay. Okay, knock it off."

J turned to Gretchen, who was using the kitchen towel to dab her eyes and nose. "Dad, since we talked, I haven't even seen her. I was going to say something, but I haven't had a chance–"

"Well," Chad snorted, "that's a relief."

"Hey," J's stern voice cut in. "That's enough. Look, you guys, I think you're making a big deal out of nothing. "Corrie's free to come and go."

"I think it's going to be mostly 'go,' thanks to Miss Priss here."

"Chad, knock it off. Look, you guys, I don't want any more of this. What Corrie does is her business. What's been done," he looked at Gretchen, "can be patched up."

Gretchen's voice, thick with emotion, wasn't convinced. "Chad called me a bitch," she said, fresh tears welling.

J whirled on Chad.

"I called you a selfish bitch," Chad shot back.

"Chad!" This was getting out of hand.

"He says everything is my fault, that when I'm gone, to college or wherever, you'll be alone and it'll all be because of me." She hiccupped.

J looked at Chad and sighed.

Chad opened his mouth, but clamped it shut and shook his head.

J felt more shaken than he wanted to admit. "I don't want to talk about this anymore. What's done is done. Let's just take it from here."

Chad gave a lingering look of disgust at Gretchen.

"Chad," J's voice held warning signals, "I mean it." His voice softened, "Go start the barbeque." He turned to Gretchen. "Gretch, get out a clean towel."

Her sorrowful, beseeching eyes met J's sad smile. "Oh, Dad."

"Honey, it'll be all right." He stepped over to her and she leaned her head against his chest.

"I'm sorry. I've messed up everything."

"I don't think so, Gretch. Let's just show her we can be friends."

He gently peeled her off his chest and looked into her wet, flushed face. "Okay?"

She sniffed. "Okay."

All were silent as they went about organizing dinner. J steamed. Leonard Snow! How the hell had she linked up with him? He assumed they'd gone out to dinner. Then what? He always seemed one step behind.

* * *

After Leonard brought Corrie home, she remembered with a start that she'd forgotten to talk to Moe about taking care of her dog. By now Moe would have gone to bed, so she wrote him a note, asking him to take care of Bo until Sunday evening. She explained where the dog's food was and mentioned that she'd only be gone one night, but she didn't specifically mention her plans. She taped the note to his door, knowing she could rely on Moe.

A little after eight the next morning, Kevin and Al pulled up to the cabin in Kevin's brand new 1980 Subaru wagon. Corrie's sleeping bag, a small duffle bag and a box of groceries were on the porch.

"I don't have a cooler for the potato salad."

"Al brought one. We'll move the beer around to make room."

Kevin looked in disbelief. "Is this all you're bringing?" He pointed to her duffle bag.

"Yes, why? We're only going to be gone one night. All I need is one change of clothes."

Kevin laughed. "Corrie, Joanne would be lugging two full suitcases. Once there, she'd be looking for a place to plug in her hair dryer."

Corrie chuckled as she picked up her things and headed toward Kevin's station wagon. "Now we know why she always looks like the cover of a fashion magazine and I look like...I don't know what."

"Like you're ready for action," Al said, taking her things and stowing them in the back.

Corrie grinned at him. "Let's hope we don't get too much of that."

As they drove past the calving barn, Corrie spotted Moe and waved. It looked as though he'd been waiting for them. "Stop here a minute," Corrie said to Kevin.

She rolled down the window from the back seat. "Did you get my note about Bo?"

The old man gave her his barely perceptive nod and stepped forward.

"That okay?"

He nodded again. "'Course."

"Okay, thanks. See you Sunday night."

The old man narrowed his eyes at Kevin and dipped his head slightly so he could see Al in the front passenger seat. He spit a stream of tobacco juice, wiped his mouth with the back of his hand and stepped back.

As they pulled out, Al said, "I can't believe how J's aged."

"That wasn't..." Then Corrie realized he was joking and laughed. "You know Moe?"

Kevin swung onto the long driveway. "Everybody knows Moe, he's a permanent fixture."

Corrie looked around the car. "Nice car, Kevin. It looks brand new."

"He was waiting for you to say that," Al said.

Kevin laughed. "Al's jealous. I just picked it up this week. First new car I've ever owned."

Corrie sat back and relaxed. This'll be fun.

* * *

On his way to the calving barn, J noticed Corrie's car parked alongside the cabin. Bo lay in the yard. That's strange. The dog was usually with Corrie, either inside or outside. He whistled to Bo and the big dog trotted over, tail wagging. He stopped short of Julie and with reserve sniffed her. Julie made no move, then slowly wagged her tail. She at least tolerated him.

"Where's Corrie, boy? Huh?" He rubbed the dog's soft ears.

"She's gone 'til tomorrow night."

J's head jerked up to see Moe standing before him, hands on hips.

"How do you know?"

"I just talked to 'er. Saw 'em leave. I'm babysittin' the dog."

"Leave where?"

Moe shook his head. "Dunno. Looked like campin' stuff in back o' the car."

"With Leonard Snow?"

Moe spit. "Where'd ya come up with that? No, with them newspaper people. Kevin and some other guy."

"For the night? By God, I'll bet they're going to that damned mountain."

Moe nodded slowly. "You'd better do something, boss."

"I'll tell you one thing, I'm getting tired of people telling me what I should do."

Moe snorted. "You might try listenin'. Might learn somethin'."

J glared at the old man and started for the calving barn. "That heifer give us anything yet?"

"Nice bull."

* * *

As they neared the mountain, they didn't even attempt to take the main highway, but went directly to the back logging road from Randle they'd taken before. It was rough going at times with deep ruts and, in shaded areas, spongy from spring thaw, but Kevin's car handled it without too much difficulty. Al took a rough sketch out of his pocket. "According to this map, that Bear Meadow place should be north and east of here. Let's see what that's like."

They pulled into a small clearing bordered with lush salal and shiny Oregon grape, and a sweeping view of the mountain. Al climbed out of the car to look around. He returned to Kevin's side and leaned on the sill of the open window. "It looks just like what Darrell described." Al pointed to a circle of rocks and charcoal remains. " You can see where they, or somebody, built a fire."

"Who?" Corrie asked.

"Darrell Walters. A friend of mine, photo-journalist from Tacoma."

Kevin parked the Subaru alongside a huge snowberry bush. "He works for the Tacoma News Tribune, right?"

"Yep. Loves it there."

From the back of the station wagon, Kevin pulled out the tent and a nylon bag holding jangling metal stakes. "Let's set stuff up and then do some exploring."

Al helped Kevin figure out how to pitch the tent while Corrie found a place in the shade for the cooler. Kevin's brother had also sent a wooden box with a camp stove, a couple of pots and a frying pan, a few enamel-covered plates and assorted silverware. She made a cupboard of sorts out of the wooden box and put the stove on top and the cooking implements and dishes inside the box. That would work.

Corrie'd brought sandwiches and apples for lunch. Ready to go, she surveyed her sur-roundings, and took a deep breath of the chilly, fresh air and pungent smell of evergreens. The mountain itself was still covered with snow and beautiful from here. This northeast side didn't have the ugly black streaks they had seen from

Truman's place. Although dark clouds hovered over the top, mostly toward the north, Mount St. Helens still sparkled.

Kevin backed out of the tent. "Okay, we're set. Let's see what trouble we can get into."

Al noticed the cooler. "We'd better keep this in the car. I think the name "Bear Meadow" might actually mean there's bears around." He put the cooler in the back and turned to Corrie. "Why don't you sit in the front?"

"No, Al. I'm fine in the back. You'll have a better shot for pictures up there, anyway."

On their map, they found Ryan Lake and decided to stop there for lunch. A group of five had packed in with horses, set up camp, and were getting ready to eat their lunch. One of the fellows, a big guy who reminded Corrie of J, invited them to stay.

Corrie reached into the car. "I've brought our lunch."

"But we'll join you," Kevin said, and they found a log to sit on near the campfire. The campers, two couples and a brother of one of the women, had arrived the day before. According to them, Mount St. Helens was one of their favorite places to camp. "We come up here at least twice a year, more if we can," one of the fellows said. "Sometimes we pack in, sometimes just drive up. The fishing's good."

"Yeah," the other fellow said, "stick around and we'll have fish for dinner."

Al passed around beer from the cooler. "Thanks, but we're all set up at Bear Meadow."

One of the fellows, nodded. "That's a good spot."

After lunch Corrie wandered over to where their horses were staked out. Arnie, the brother of one of the women, the fellow who reminded her of J, joined her and smiled at her interest. "Like horses?"

"Yes, I do. I'm staying at a ranch near Clearwater, just starting to learn about all this stuff. You seem to know your way around horses."

"Yeah. Grew up with 'em. My wife, too. She couldn't come today because she's gonna have a baby in about six weeks. The doctor said 'no more riding.'"

"I guess that's reasonable." She watched as he strung a line between two trees, attaching the line to leather straps wrapped around each tree. "Are the leather straps to protect the trees?"

"Yep. Rope can kill a tree, especially with horses pulling against it. When I'm through here I'll tie the horses to this highline. That'll keep 'em from trampling tree roots and chewing on the bark. Horses can do a lot of damage."

Watching him tie the knots reminded her of J's capable hands and how he knew just which knot to use. A sense of longing surprised her. What was he doing now? Did he even know she was gone? Wouldn't it be fun to camp with J! Well, he wouldn't be on this mountain, that's for sure.

Kevin interrupted her reverie. "Ready to go?"

"Sure." She turned to the others. "Have a nice weekend."

They stopped by Harry Truman's place again. In the lodge, Corrie choked down a few swallows of Truman's eye-watering Schenley's and coke, then wandered outside. The others joined her.

Truman handed Corrie ancient binoculars. "Look up there," he pointed to the sheer mountainside beside the lake. "See the mountain goats?" His normal talking voice was a raspy shout.

She scanned the hill. "No, but I'd sure like to."

"They aren't originally from here, you know, they brought 'em in from Canada, 'bout eight years ago. There's about two hundred of 'em now. I see 'em all the time."

They chatted in front of the old lodge for a few more minutes and then climbed back into Kevin's station wagon.

Al turned to Corrie. "Got any more coffee in that thermos? Truman's drinks about finish me off."

He glanced again at the map. "I'm glad we're camped at Bear Meadow. It's far enough away, but we still have a good view of the mountain." He accepted the cup of coffee from Corrie and nodded his thanks.

"Yeah," Kevin agreed, "I wouldn't want to be in a straight line, like Truman is at Spirit Lake." He glanced at the map in Al's hand. "Where to next?"

Old mining shafts dotted the hills nearby. Kevin parked the car and they hiked up to one. He peered inside a musty, damp shaft. "I guess if the mountain blew, these shafts would protect us."

Al slapped the slippery wall with the palm of his hand. "I don't think I'd trust these old shafts to hold up under much rockin' and rollin'." His voice echoed as it bounced off walls.

Corrie peeked in. "You wouldn't want to go in real deep, but maybe stand in the entry. Actually, I guess I don't know whether to worry about something falling from the sky or oozing from the mountain, like lava."

Kevin chuckled. "It's tough not knowing what to worry about."

"Next time we see Dave Johnston, let's ask him," Al said. "I guess we should have some sort of plan in mind."

Kevin nodded. "Good idea."

At least they were thinking about safety, that was good. Corrie felt confident in their ability to take care of themselves. They weren't reckless. On the other hand, none of them were really knowledgeable about what they were dealing with here.

She found herself wanting to share a lovely scene, or a scary one, with J but then chided herself. She needed to stop thinking like that. He would think she was stupid to be here.

Al set up his tripod to take pictures of the old mine. Kevin found a stump and sat writing notes. Corrie wandered around the area, trying to concentrate on its beauty, but really thinking about J. Then Gretchen's pinched face came into mind and she stopped short. It would never work. Forget about it. The scene in the barn crept, uninvited, into her mind. What was J thinking when he reached for her hand? She closed her eyes and recalled his smile. He had such a genuine smile, but that one had been sad, too.

They returned to Bear Meadows and settled into their camp, gathering deadwood for their evening fire. Although the day had been comfortable enough wearing a jacket, the evening brought a chilly breeze.

Al set up his camera on a tripod and occasionally returned to it to view the mountain. "Wow, look at that." Kevin and Corrie moved to where Al hunched over his equipment, rapidly taking pictures of the mountain ringed in gold and crimson. As sunset progressed, the colors faded. Finally, a blanket of shadows surrounded them.

They gathered around the warmth of the campfire and while Al grilled steaks over the open flame, Corrie set out potato salad and sliced tomatoes.

Kevin watched the proceedings. "Cook mine to death, okay, Buddy?"

Al grunted. "No accounting for taste. Corrie, how you do want yours?"

"Medium."

"So, Corrie," Kevin asked, "anything going on between you and J out there?"

Corrie shot him a look. "No, why?"

He shrugged. "Just wondered. Seems like you guys have things in common. I thought–"

"I'm not interested in that kind of relationship, Kevin."

"You're divorced, right? Don't you want to get married again some day?"

"No."

"I can see you're anxious to talk about this," he chided.

"Not really, Kevin. I just want to live in the country. That's it."

Kevin studied her for what seemed like minutes. "J's a nice guy."

"I didn't realize you knew him."

"Yeah, we've known each other for a few years. As a matter of fact, we both dated the same girl a while back."

That perked her interest. "Really?"

"Yeah. I happened to win out, which didn't put me in very good favor with J. But she wasn't his type. Actually, she wasn't my type either. She's gone on to flashier things in the big city."

Corrie raised her eyebrows. So he had dated. She wouldn't ask any more. She didn't want Kevin to think she was interested. "Has he dated much, do you know?" She couldn't help it, it just popped out.

"Not that I know of. I suppose it's hard to get away, with the kid and all."

"Doesn't he have another kid out there, a boy?" Al asked, cutting into one of the steaks, testing for doneness.

Kevin shrugged.

Corrie spoke up. "That's his nephew. Chad. He lives there now, but he's been coming during the summers for years."

They both silently looked at her. "Well, I talk to them."

"Your steak's done." Al motioned to Corrie to get her plate. "Mine's done, too, so Kevin you can come over here and ruin your own."

They sat close to a dwindling fire for a while after dinner, but the cold forced them to crawl into their sleeping bags early. They gave her a few minutes alone in the tent to get into her sleeping bag. It seemed a little strange to Corrie, sleeping in the same tent with two men. They probably felt awkward, too. She was snuggled in her bag when they came in and she turned to face the tent wall while they prepared for bed. It wasn't long before the fresh air and the busy day caught up with them and she heard soft snores.

The last thing Corrie thought before drifting off was getting back to the ranch. She wondered what J's reaction would be to her camping with these two guys. Would he even know? Would he even care? For that matter, do I care what he thinks? Yes, I do. I don't want him to get the wrong idea.

Chapter Thirteen

AS I SEE IT
Kevin Walsh
Clearwater News staff columnist

April 21, 1980. Top caliber scientists are studying Mount St. Helens. Dave Johnston, often the spokesman for the USGS team, graduated from the University of Illinois with a degree in geology. His first geologic project involved studying volcanic rock in Michigan's Upper Peninsula. Later, he studied volcanic phenomena in Colorado and Alaska. He earned his Ph.D. from the University of Washington, and then returned to Alaska to study volcanic gases with USGS. "When Mount St. Helens started grumbling, I was one of the first ones here."

*A*l took charge of making coffee while Corrie scrambled eggs for breakfast. She placed a bakery muffin on each plate with the eggs, and they ate sitting on logs. Their campfire crackled and popped, its smoke rising straight up in the still, crisp morning air.

Al had already taken several rolls of film, which surprised Corrie. "It seems kind of foggy for good pictures."

"You don't need perfect weather for good pictures. Fog can be beautiful and give the place character."

Kevin helped himself to another scoop of eggs and offered more to Al. "I think this fog will burn off, though."

Corrie turned down more eggs. "You guys finish them. What's the schedule for today?"

"Let's see if we can find some of the USGS guys, maybe Dave Johnston," Kevin suggested.

Corrie nodded. "Good idea. I'd love to talk to him again. This time I have some questions to ask."

They cleaned up breakfast remains, tossing paper plates into the fire, and then broke camp.

After driving around awhile, they found a group of scientists gathered around a meter half buried in the ground, talked with them briefly, and asked about Dave Johnston. One of the fellows gave them directions to where he thought Dave was. Sure enough, they found him in a clearing by his truck, sitting on a folding metal chair, writing in a notebook.

He was friendly enough but chided them for being there. "This mountain could blow anytime, you know."

"Yeah," Kevin chuckled, "you'd better clear out."

"It's different for us." Dave's voice turned serious. "That's our job, conducting hazard assessments. To do that we have to accept the dangers of on-site monitoring."

Kevin took his notebook out of his jacket pocket. "We feel that's important in our profession, too. The people need to know what's going on and that's our job, to keep them informed. What's your assessment, doc?"

Dave scratched his head. "Actually, I'm recommending we close an even wider area to the public. Earlier this month a crater opened up and it's getting bigger all the time. It's going to erupt. We just don't know when."

"What's your background, Dave? Where have you worked?"

While Johnston gave Kevin a rundown on his professional background, Corrie warmed up to the young scientist. Although he seemed dedicated to his profession, he didn't appear "scholarly" and was open and friendly, with a ready smile. She liked him. "What's causing this activity, Dave?

The young scientist smiled. "It's pretty complicated, but in a nutshell the mountain has formed a body of magma, molten rock material, that's forcing its way to the surface. Once it reaches the top, the gasses within the magma will expand very quickly and cause an explosion."

Corrie felt a rush of excitement. "If it does blow, will there be flowing lava, like in Hawaii?"

"Not 'if,' when. Probably no lava like Hawaii. We're expecting a pyroclastic flow, which is hot mixtures of gas, pumice and ash. At this point it looks like it could be quite a blast, which is why we're recommending visitor restrictions."

Dave was in good shape and a marathon runner. He joked that he could dash in, take readings and get out before the mountain could catch up with him.

They left soon after, partly convinced by Dave that they should, but mostly because they still had a long drive ahead of them back to Clearwater.

At home, Bo greeted Corrie with a big grin and wagged his tail with joy so furiously he almost fell over. She unpacked, wrinkling her nose at her smelly campfire clothes. It's funny, she thought, the wood fire smells so good while it's burning, but clothes smell so rank afterwards.

When she finally finished putting things away, she sat contentedly in her chair, glad to be home. And even a little relieved. A motion outside caught her eye. It was J, slowly walking by, looking her way. She sat very still. He changed direction, like he intended to come to the cabin, but turned abruptly and continued toward the calving barn.

Well, that was interesting. She stood at the window, back a bit in case he looked her way, and watched. His head was bent as though he were deep in thought. Had he even known she was gone? Did he care?

* * *

The next morning she drove to town, loaded a couple of washing machines at the Laundromat and made her way to the bookstore.

A bell on the door jangled a greeting and Marie Clarke, the bookstore owner, looked up. "I was just going to call you. The middle school called in a panic and need a speaker for 'Young Writers Week.' It's an annual event and apparently the person in charge of lining up a speaker dropped the ball. Could you do it? It's really short notice. They need you on Friday."

"Sure. I've done that sort of thing before. Maybe do a little talk on writing, then do a reading?"

"Well...more like the keynote speaker."

"Oh." Yikes! Could she do that? "I think I can do that."

With obvious relief, Marie gave her a name and phone number to call. "I've ordered your books and they should be here by then. There's always a rush for the books after they've had a speaker."

Marie Clarke hesitated. "Corrie, these kids are going to go home and tell their parents about your talk. I'd like to schedule you to talk here, at the bookstore, too. Let's do it while the interest is high."

Feeling a bit overwhelmed, Corrie had to calm herself. "That's a nice offer, Marie. Sure, let's do it. Sort of the same kind of talk?"

"Probably not quite as formal. For sure do a reading. Adults love to be read to by an author."

Marie glanced at her calendar . "Okay, let's make it the first Friday in May, seven o'clock. That way I'll have time to put something in the paper and put a few posters around town. Do you have a picture I can use?"

While they discussed promotional details, Corrie's mind whirled on the various facets of writing she could talk about. Friday wasn't that far away. She'd worry about the bookstore event later.

As she drove down the long driveway leading to her cabin, she decided on the approach she would take for the talk. Research. She'd go into the extensive research she'd done to get material to write her book. Then, the challenge: how to make it sound interesting enough to read.

In her absorption with planning the talk, she didn't see J standing beside the driveway until he waved. She slowed the car and rolled down her window. "Hi, J."

He walked toward the car and she stopped. It looked as though he had something on his mind.

J had a dazzling smile–his teeth were so straight and white. He placed his hand at the open window. "Been to town?"

"Yes, I had washing to do and stopped at the bookstore."

"You're welcome to use our washer and dryer."

"No, thanks. I can take care of it in town." It would be nice though. Then Gretchen's dark look came to mind. "But I appreciate the offer."

"Suit yourself. Keep it in mind."

A long moment passed while they merely looked at one another. It wasn't an awkward moment–just a comfortable period of time spent studying each other's face.

J finally broke the spell. "I'm going to my brother's in Randle tomorrow. Wanna come along?"

Surprised, she laughed. "Randle? I just got back from there!"

He merely nodded. What was that expression? He knew something but wasn't going to talk about it? He waited for her answer.

"Sure, I'd love to go."

"I'd like to leave early, right after I get Gretchen off to school, about seven-thirty."

"I'll be ready."

For the rest of the day, concentrating on her talk was hopeless. Images of J kept popping into her head. She also wondered what prompted the invitation. Was everything okay? He seemed okay. She finally sat down at her computer and wrote an outline, so she could focus on what she needed to say.

Sleep didn't come easily either. What would she and J talk about tomorrow? Would it be embarrassing to see his brother's family again after that terrible debacle with their mother at J's last week? His wonderful smile floated before her, then his stern look. Gretchen's disapproval loomed. She noticed he mentioned he'd get her off to school first. She wondered if he would tell his daughter about this invitation. She tossed and turned, twisting her covers until she finally had to get up to straighten the bed. Disgusted with herself, she muttered to Bo, "If I don't get some sleep my eyes will be baggy in the morning. Seven-thirty! That's in just a few hours."

* * *

J pulled his truck up to the cabin, seven thirty-three. Uncharacteristically, he hadn't mentioned his plans to Gretchen. He just couldn't bring himself to do it, not knowing what her reaction would be and not wanting to send her off to school in turmoil. Chad, who was ecstatic with J's plans, promised to return to the house a few times during the day to check for any phone messages, in case something came up. It rarely did. Gretchen almost never called from school.

As Corrie climbed into the truck, she held up a thermos. "How about a cup of coffee? I brought a couple of traveling cups, too."

"Great. I'd love some. I just had a couple of swallows of yesterday's leftovers."

She settled in and they were on their way. "I'm surprised you can get away."

"Calving is winding down. Moe and Chad can take care of things today. My brother wants me to come over, take a look at a tractor he wants to replace." He chuckled. "I think he wants me to talk him into buying a new one."

"That kind of equipment must be expensive."

"It is. It's one of the reasons I quit haying. It's actually cheaper for me to buy what I need."

They rode along in comfortable silence. "Good coffee." J used his comment as an excuse to look at her. She always looked so together, so tidy. His heart swelled, just having her with him.

She nodded. "I can't imagine life without coffee."

He took a deep breath and dove in. "I saw Leonard Snow's car here the other day." Bit of a fib there, but he didn't want it to sound like he'd heard it second-hand, like they'd been talking about her.

"Yes, we went out to dinner."

"Oh? He's dating now?" Maybe it wasn't a date, maybe it was...

"Yes. I guess he figures it's time."

"He's a nice guy." But not your type.

"Yes, he is."

Well, she apparently didn't care to elaborate on that subject. "You say you were in Randle?"

"Well, we went through Randle on our way to Mount St. Helens."

"With Kevin and Al?"

"Yes. We camped so Al could get pictures during the best time of day, dusk and dawn."

He nodded. "They special friends of yours?" He tried to keep his voice even.

"Ah, I guess I'm not sure what you mean by special. They're friends, we have things in common...."

Damn it! Why did he feel so tongue-tied? What kind of drivel is this? Change the subject. "Corrie, I don't think that mountain is a good place to hang out right now."

She shrugged. "Right now is when something is happening. It's why we go."

He shook his head. "I still don't think it's a good idea." He glanced at her, expecting some sort of answer. She silently concentrated on the passing countryside.

"I wish you wouldn't go again." That got her attention. Wide eyes turned his way. He couldn't help smiling at her astonished expression. She remained speechless.

"Corrie, when you first came here, I'm afraid we got off to sort of a bad start."

Her eyes grew wider.

"Initially, I didn't think it would work, having you rent the cabin. I was wrong. I'm glad you're here."

"Really?" It was almost a whisper.

"Really."

It seemed like miles passed before she spoke again. "I don't think Gretchen is happy about me being here. I don't know what I've done, but somehow she seems to feel threatened."

"It isn't anything you've done, Corrie. Gretchen had some sorting out to do. I think she's thinking a little differently now."

"I don't know, J. I definitely get the impression...."

"I know, and I'm sorry about that. I'd appreciate it if you could give her another chance."

"Another chance?"

"You've been keeping yourself pretty scarce around us lately. We'd like to see more of you."

Could her eyes get any wider? He grinned at her. "Think you could manage that?"

"Sure." She dragged out the word, her voice reflecting disbelief.

As they drove through Randle, J pointed out the two schools he attended. "Now they have what they call a 'middle school,' but in those days, there weren't enough kids to fill three schools."

He drove past an apartment complex. "My mother lives right there, but we won't take the time to stop today." He didn't care to take the chance of creating another disaster like last time.

They left the small town and drove for almost an hour before reaching Rick and Barbara's ranch. Their driveway was even longer than J's. As they neared the house, Rick headed toward J's truck as Barbara bounded down the back porch steps.

Barbara hugged Corrie. "I'm so glad you could come with J today. I've just taken bread out of the oven. Let's have a snack before you guys do your thing."

The heavy scent of yeast bread permeated the house. Barbara placed a golden loaf on a small breadboard in the center of the kitchen table together with several jars of homemade jam and a crock of butter.

J's eye lit up. "Barb, you don't know what a treat this is." He held out a chair for Corrie. He loved how relaxed she seemed. She fit in so well, without pretense or the need to call attention to herself. She fit into those jeans well, too, he observed. Her green sweater made her hazel eyes look green. He felt his brother's eyes on him and he glanced Rick's way. Rick's slight nod and tiny, almost imperceptible smile showed his approval of Corrie.

Rick sliced the bread and placed a piece on Corrie's plate. He glanced at J. "Did you guys stop at Mom's?" His mouth quivered, suppressing a smile.

J snorted and shook his head.

Rick nodded. "Mom means well, but doesn't always think before she talks."

"Actually," Barbara said, "I think that's getting worse with age."

Corrie didn't add to the conversation, but became absorbed in the selection of jams for her bread.

They finished their snack and J turned to Corrie. "Do you want to come out with us and talk tractor or...."

"No," Barbara said, "stay here with me, Corrie. I'm dying for 'women talk.'"

Corrie smiled. "That sounds good to me, too."

Barbara showed Corrie through the old ranch house. "This is where Rick, J and their sisters lived. After we were married, Rick and I lived in that small house you might have seen as you drove up. After their dad died, Maude moved into town and we made this our home. By that time we had three kids and it seemed so good to be able to spread out. I love this old house.

Corrie learned that Barbara was a registered nurse and for years worked at the local hospital. "Now I do some home nursing, but I really prefer not to work. Rick calls me the 'resident medic.' Maude needs us more now, too. She can't drive anymore and Rick doesn't have that kind of time during the day, so I try to help her.

"Corrie, I hope you weren't offended by her comments the other day." She laughed. "Rick is right, she doesn't know when to keep her opinions to herself. But she just wants what's best for her kids. She's getting a little out of touch."

Corrie nodded. "I admit, I was a little taken aback, but it bothered me more that J and Nancy were upset on my account. No damage done, but I appreciate your concern."

They walked through the flower and vegetable gardens. "Things are looking a little scrubby now, but pretty soon we'll have lovely flowers and vegetables on the table."

"I notice that J has spaces for gardens, but nothing's been done for awhile. I understand his wife was quite a gardener."

"Yes, Tish was marvelous. She taught me a lot." Barbara smiled and looked as though she'd like to say more, but thought better of it. She merely touched Corrie's arm.

"While we're out here, let's go to the equipment shed and see what the fellas are up to. For two years I've been trying to convince Rick to replace that old tractor. I think he's close to it, now that he's asked J's opinion."

For a few minutes they listened to the men's tractor talk, then Barbara showed Corrie the big barn. Their calving area was in the back of the barn and didn't seem as efficient as J's newer building.

Typical in farm and ranch country, the main meal was served in the middle of the day. Corrie set the table. "J seems to have his main meal at the end of the day. From what I've seen, they just fix themselves sandwiches at lunch time."

"I guess that's because he does most of the cooking and doesn't have time during the day. Now that Gretchen is a little older, she'll be able to help more with that, but of course she's in school so their main meal will still be at the end of the day."

Corrie found she could just be herself around Rick and Barbara. They were fun and she felt as though she'd known them for years. It was interesting seeing the brothers together. They were much alike, though Rick seemed more jovial than J. Maybe he'd had an easier life.

The ride home seemed more relaxed than the trip over when J had said one astonishing thing after another. She hadn't been able to take it all in. First, he didn't think it was a good idea for her to go to Mount St. Helens. Like it was even any of his business. Then, he'd mentioned that he liked having her there. That, after she'd almost had to twist his arm to let her live in his cabin. On the heels of all that, he asked her to give Gretchen a second chance! It sounded like they'd been talking about her. She'd like to have been a fly on the wall for that conversation.

J broke into her thoughts. "I'm glad you could ride over with me today."

She smiled. "Thanks for asking me. I had a great time. It was fun to see Rick and Barbara's place. They're wonderful people."

He caught her eye. "I could tell they think the same about you."

"Oh," she said, flustered. "I..."

They were nearing Clearwater and she spotted the Roadside. It looked shabby in the daylight. She pointed to the marquee. "I see

Stampede is still there," she said, wanting to change the subject. "They're a really good band."

"You've been in there?" His voice was incredulous.

"Yes, one night with Kevin and a bunch from the newspaper. Why?"

He shook his head. "I dunno. It doesn't seem like your kind of place."

She laughed. "It really isn't. I've never been the tavern type. The Roadside is sort of rough and noisy, but it seemed okay since I went with a bunch of people. But the band is good, a little loud for my taste, but a great dance band."

"Sometime I'd like to take you there. I haven't danced in a long time, but I think I'd still remember how."

"I don't know...." She laughed, a nervous twitter.

"What? Know what?"

She immediately sobered. She really had to get this issue straightened out. J was a direct person and it wasn't going to work to skirt around this. "J, I'm really not looking for a relationship. I just want to—"

"Why is it that you can go out on a date with Leonard Snow and with Kevin and that crowd, and you can't go out with me?"

"It's different with them. Those were...other circumstances, not real dates."

"I doubt if that's how Leonard Snow looked at it. And I doubt Kevin..."

"Kevin lives with someone, Joanne. I know her from bridge. They're devoted to one another.

Kevin and I are both writers, that's all. Al isn't interested in me, he's just interested in photography. There's nothing there with those guys, or Leonard either, we're just friends.

"Okay, let's be friends."

Was he being sarcastic? No, he appeared to be serious.

"Okay. I'd like that, J, to be friends."

"Can you go dancing with a friend?" His smile showed his hesitancy.

She sighed. "Yes, I can dance with a friend." But no more than that. She wouldn't get involved again. But she couldn't get over the thrill of their conversation. He'd actually asked her to go dancing! Even though she wouldn't, couldn't, become involved again, it would be so good to have a friend like J. Why did her heart beat so wildly? He's just a friend. Calm down.

Chapter Fourteen

AS I SEE IT
Kevin Walsh
Clearwater News staff columnist

April 23, 1980. Geologists claim that Mount St. Helens is shifting by the hour. An instrument they call a Tiltmeter, which measures data, shows that the dome deflates and inflates measurable distances.

Meanwhile, keeping out anyone except official personnel is proving impossible for the authorities. Cowlitz and Skamania Sheriff Departments have established roadblocks on Spirit Lake Highway. In places, as a stronger control, the Department of Transportation has installed barricades with the State Patrol manning them.

Wednesday already. She'd better work on that talk. Friday was only two days away. When they'd returned from Randle the previous afternoon, Corrie had written her notes and planned to spend the day going over her talk. Before starting her work, she stepped outside with Bo for fresh air and spotted J walking toward the barn. She waved, then turned to go back inside.

"Corrie, wait up."

She turned, surprised. J always looked as though he sauntered but actually he covered the ground quite quickly. He stood only a few feet away, smiling his warm, friendly smile.

She smiled back, waiting.

"I'm just getting ready to ride out today, to check on the herd. Wanna come along? I thought we could take Bo today." He reached down and gently tugged Bo's ear. Bo leaned into him, soaking up the attention. Julie stood to one side, alternately looking at her master and at this intruder dog.

Corrie balanced the two possibilities: staying at home to work on the talk or riding with J, or rather, to check on the herd with J. "Sure, I'd love to." She could work on the talk tonight. It wasn't good to over-rehearse.

As they headed toward the barn, Bo scampered ahead, then slowed down when they entered.

"He catches on fast," J commented. "Let's just let Julie take over. She'll show him the ropes. Sort of a baptism by fire, but he'll learn. Okay?"

"Okay..." She couldn't keep the doubt from her voice.

He chuckled. "You worried about your baby? He'll be fine."

Corrie hurried to keep up with J as they saddled their horses, and managed the final cinch-up only a couple of minutes after he walked his big gelding to the hitching rail outside.

Bo's expectant eyes didn't leave Corrie's face. As she mounted, she called him. "Bo, come." He jumped with joy and fell in line. Don't blow it now, she thought.

As they neared a small bunch of cow/calf pairs, Bo started to rush toward them. Julie's growl came from deep within her throat. Bo stopped immediately, looking sheepish. Corrie relaxed. He'd get along.

A young heifer calf stood alone, bawling. They watched her for a while. She was apparently separated from her mother.

Corrie worried about the little one. "What do you suppose happened to her mother?"

"Hard to say. Cows and their calves usually stay together, but sometimes a calf will follow another cow and become separated from its own mother." J stepped down and scooped the calf in his arms. He draped the heifer in front of his saddle, mounted, then held the little critter across his lap. The calf contentedly observed her world from high up. She didn't struggle or act as if this were an unusual occurrence, yet it was probably the first time she had been handled by a human.

"What will you do if you can't find her mother?"

"We'll take her to headquarters and either match her up with another cow, or hand feed her."

The pastures verged on spring growth. The air hung heavy with rain from the night before. Rain threatened now with a darkening sky and chilly wind. Corrie buttoned the top button of her plaid wool jacket and jammed her western hat down tight over a stocking cap. Jeans didn't offer much in the way of warmth. J wore stovepipe chaps, which helped deflect weather, too. Leather chaps were expensive, but it might be worthwhile to buy a pair.

A black and white magpie darted to the ground, picked up a stick, and flew over to its large domed nest in a nearby bush. Gray barn swallows swooped for insects.

J pointed to a furry brown marmot hunched on a log, its beady little eyes regarding them with caution. The little rodent's jaws worked but otherwise he sat still as a fence post. When the horses drew very close, the marmot whistled, apparently warning the others, and scampered away.

"I love seeing all this, J. I can hardly wait to show Gwen, my daughter."

"She's coming soon?"

"Yes, on Saturday."

"Be sure to bring her over to the house so the family can meet her."

"Okay, I will."

A lone cow walked toward them bawling, leaving a small herd behind her. The calf J held perked up and started to scramble, its little hooves drumming against the saddle. J leaned over and freed it. The calf trotted to the cow and immediately attached herself to a teat. The mother cow stretched her neck back to her baby and emitted relieved guttural murmurs.

Later, they found another calf, this one thin and gaunt, apparently separated from its mother. Bo, forgetting himself, rushed over to the little fellow. Julie swooped down and nipped him on his rear flank and he immediately backed off with a bleak expression and plastered-back ears.

Bo had definitely been in the wrong, but Corrie almost felt sorry for him. "Boy, she doesn't take any crap, does she?"

"No, she doesn't. I've always been glad I'm the boss here. I'd hate to work for her."

J followed the same procedure as with the other calf, carrying the little bull across his saddle, but when it was time to return to headquarters, they still hadn't found the little one's mother.

"This little guy could be a bummer calf, a twin, and the mother couldn't handle both. Looks like Gretchen will have a job."

"Oh? Doing what?"

"She'll be responsible for feeding him. We're lucky; it looks like it's taken some nourishment from his mama. That's a good sign. He'll probably make it on the milk formula we give him. If they don't get a chance to get that first feeding from their mother, they don't always make it."

"Sort of like a human baby, huh?"

He nodded. "That's right. The mother's milk helps get the digestive system going. Otherwise, the calf can die of scours, especially if we can't get to it soon enough."

"I can sure see why you check on the cattle so often."

"It's especially important this time of year with all the new calves." J's eyes constantly scanned his surroundings.

"Is this very common, finding a stray calf?"

He nodded. "It's rare not to have at least one, sometimes more, each year."

They returned around lunchtime, unsaddled and prepared to turn the horses into the corral.

J glanced at her. "Want to stop by and have some sandwiches with us? We don't make a big deal out of lunch."

"No, thanks, I have some work I need to do." Enough is enough. She loved being with J. No, she loved being able to see the herd with J. To learn about ranch life, to....

"Suit yourself. Are you doing much writing? It doesn't seem like you've had much time."

She laughed. "No. I'm working at my profession, I guess, but not writing much in the way of new material. It goes in spurts."

That afternoon, she fine-tuned her talk, added a few details about the medical research she'd done so that her novel would be believable. That evening, she and Bo strolled to the calving barn. She hoped to see the little bull calf they'd found.

She heard Gretchen's voice. "Come on, now. Just try it. Oops. Stop that now. Okay, that's right...." The girl's voice turned from soothing to exasperation, then a forced calmness.

Stepping into the warm shed, Corrie found Gretch with the little bull, trying to hand-feed it. She held a bottle, not unlike a regular baby bottle, but much larger, maybe two quarts, with a huge dark red-brown nipple.

The girl glanced up. Hostility flickered across her sweaty face.

"Hi, Gretchen."

"Hi."

Gretchen had her hands full with this little guy. Although scrawny, he was a strong little devil and with every ounce of energy resisted the bottle she offered. She had straddled the calf's neck, holding him with her legs and was sticking her thumb into the corner of his mouth, trying to pry it open. The calf slobbered and snorted, trying to get away. The thighs of Gretchen's jeans were soaked from slobber and spilled milk.

"Can I help?" Corrie asked, not knowing how, but seeing Gretchen could use another two hands.

"No. Well, sure. As soon as I get the bottle in his mouth again, rub his throat. It'll make him swallow."

Together they wrestled with the calf, Corrie trying to restrain it while Gretchen forced the bottle into its reluctant mouth.

The calf's tongue wallowed the nipple, not knowing what to do with it. Gretchen persisted working it around his mouth until he finally grabbed the nipple and sucked. Corrie stroked its neck and for a few seconds, the little fellow sucked a few swallows, then again threw back its head.

"Here we go again," Gretchen muttered. "Okay, baby, calm down. Just let me help you," she crooned. The little guy sucked on the nipple again and Corrie again stroked his throat. This time, the procedure lasted a little longer. The third time was the longest and he seemed to catch on.

J stepped into the barn and came around to watch. Corrie glanced up to see his contented expression. She imagined it was pride in his daughter, but also that the two of them were working together. He nodded to her and said, "Good job, Gretch," and slipped back out.

"Wow, Gretchen, this is really a tough job!" Corrie said.

"He's catching on though. The next time or so that I do this, he'll know what to do. He's in pretty good shape, just thin. I think he had some time with his mother. This just feels different to him."

That was the most Gretchen had spoken to her. "What are you feeding him?"

"It's a powdered formula mixed with warm water."

"How often will you do this?"

"Three times a day. On school days I'll do it before I leave in the morning, then again in the evening. Someone else will have to do it at noon."

The calf threw his head back again and sputtered a loud bawl, drooling milk down Gretchen's sleeve. The girl persisted, again prying his mouth open and poking in the bottle. "Come on, Freddy, we're not giving up."

"Freddy?"

"I always name 'em."

"How long will you have to do this?" She couldn't believe that she was carrying on a normal conversation with Gretchen. A feeling of warmth coursed through her.

"We'll hand-feed for about six months, then he'll drink milk from a pail and eat some grain, too."

The little bull finished the bottle and Gretchen led him to a stall. "Thanks for the help." She gave Corrie a shy smile.

"Sure. I'm glad I came along in time to see this. That's really a huge responsibility you have, Gretchen. I'm impressed."

The girl shrugged. "I've done this for a long time. Somebody else used to start them for me, and I'd take over when the calf caught on, but now I can handle it all."

"You're a real part of the operation."

"I guess."

"I'll try to come back and watch again."

"Okay." Gretchen pressed her lips together, eyes wide. "I'd like that."

It seemed to Corrie that she floated back to her cabin. She felt as though a weight had been lifted from her heart.

* * *

Corrie was to be at the school no later than eight o'clock. Her talk would start the Young Writers' Week Conference. She had given thought to how she would dress, something appealing to young teens, but still professional.

Her stomach fluttered and she couldn't eat much breakfast, but she knew her material and from previous experience knew she would relax as soon as she stood in front of her audience.

Arriving at the school, she introduced herself to the principal who showed her the auditorium where she would speak. A bell rang and kids started to pour into the large room. She stood to one side and watched their funny mannerisms The boys ogled the girls, the girls giggled. There were a few loners, a few with strange hair. She spotted Gretchen who showed surprise at seeing her, stopping in the aisle before getting a shove from a kid behind her. Corrie smiled briefly, continuing to watch the noisy kids, vying for seats next to their friends.

The principal walked onto the stage and the din diminished quickly. He made a few announcements, then turned the conference over to the chairperson, an English teacher. When she introduced Corrie, her words were so flattering Corrie wondered if she were the one being introduced. She hadn't thought of herself as a "popular northwest writer" or how lucky they were "to have such prominence in their midst."

She took her place at center stage and launched into her talk, finding her audience attentive and absorbed. When she told about being mistaken for an in-coming patient when she went to the hospital to do research, her audience laughed. When she mentioned that the little girl about whom the story centered died, many eyes glistened with tears. She told them of the hours she'd spent at the University of Washington medical library studying this particular type of cancer.

After her talk the kids attended various writing workshops that covered creative writing, poetry, science fiction and research. Corrie had been asked to attend the entire day. They had set up a table for her with her books. At noon she autographed books for several parents who had stopped by to purchase copies. This was an annual event that the community welcomed.

After lunch, Corrie gave another informal talk in a classroom. She discussed the art of using strong verbs, delighting the teacher.

The conference ended at two-thirty. As Corrie gathered her materials, Gretchen appeared, girlfriend in tow. "Corrie, this is my friend Pam. She wants to be a writer."

"I'm happy to meet you, Pam." Corrie and Pam launched into writers' talk with Gretchen looking from one to the other, beaming.

Corrie realized that she'd never met a writer when she was a teen. That would have been a thrill. She tried to give the young writer suggestions, but most of all, hope.

As she left, Corrie smiled at Gretchen. "I'll see you later."

Gretchen grinned. "Okay."

Driving home from the school Corrie's spirits soared. She'd scored on several counts. She knew the talk went well, she could feel it in her audience. She'd become better known. And she'd made more headway with Gretchen.

* * *

Corrie peeked out her window for the umpteenth time. She was so anxious to see Gwen.

Finally, Gwen's black Chevrolet, a gift from her dad, rolled up in a cloud of dust.

Laughing and embracing, the two collided halfway between Gwen's car and the cabin. "Mom, your directions were perfect!"

"You don't have to sound surprised."

They laughed and Corrie led Gwen into the cabin.

"Mom, this is darling. When you described it over the phone I hadn't imagined it would be so cute."

"You would have gagged if you'd seen it before."

Corrie gave Gwen a few minutes to settle in. "I promised J we'd be over so you can meet them, then I'd like to take advantage of this beautiful day and go riding."

As they passed Gwen's dusty car, her daughter remarked, "You'd never know I washed my car yesterday."

"The trick on these dusty roads is to drive real slow." She told Gwen about her first encounter with J and skidding into a cow.

Gwen laughed. "And he still let you stay here?"

"Well, I had to do some fast talking."

Gretchen opened the door and, apparently expecting them, invited them inside. J joined them in the kitchen. Corrie suspected that he'd been working outside but saw Gwen's car arrive and returned to the house.

He invited them to sit at the kitchen table and poured coffee. A fresh pot, Corrie noticed.

Chad returned to the house, poured himself a cup and joined them. "Boy, you two sure look alike."

Corrie could see a crush in the making. But to Gwen, she knew, Chad would seem like only a boy. Two years at that age was a significant difference. She asked about a horse for Gwen.

J nodded. "Sure. Can you ride, Gwen?"

"Well..."

"I've talked to Moe and he'll bring in Sally, Tish's horse," J said. "She's getting on in years, but she's gentle and will give you a nice ride."

"I could go along," Chad offered.

J shot him a look. "You've got work to do."

Gretchen looked hopeful, as though she'd like to go along, but out of the corner of her eye Corrie saw J shake his head, ever-so-slightly.

In the barn, Corrie quickly saddled both horses.

"Wow, Mom, I've never seen you do that before."

"I'd never done it before I came here."

"J's a hunk."

"Gwen! He is nice. I'm lucky to have found this place."

Gwen rolled her eyes. "Mother. Nice? He barely took his eyes off you. I was afraid he'd spill his coffee."

Corrie shook her head, but smiled inwardly. It was strange hearing J described from a teen's viewpoint. "Okay, Gwen. Let's go. I'm dying to show you around."

Being careful to keep track of landmarks, Corrie proudly showed off the ranch, pointing out places of interest, as J had done for her.

"If it weren't the weekend, I'd take you into town and introduce you to my newspaper friends, too."

"You mentioned in your last letter that you'd gone camping at Mount St. Helens with them. Isn't that mountain about ready to explode?" Gwen had an edge to her voice. Corrie could hear herself through her daughter.

"We're careful, honey."

"Mom, I can't imagine why you'd go. What if it erupts while you're there?"

Corrie dismissed her daughter's concern with a wave of her hand. "We stay far away from where that would happen, Gwen."

The next day, Sunday, Corrie and Gwen lingered over lunch.

"I've got to go, Mom, but I want to talk about something."

Oh, oh. I'll bet she has a boyfriend.

Corrie smiled. "Yes?"

"Dad is mad that you didn't tell him you were moving."

Corrie bristled. "What concern is it of his? You knew, my brother knew, anyone I felt important knew."

Gwen sighed. "Well, he asked where and I couldn't refuse to tell him."

"That's fine, Gwen. I don't want you to feel you have to keep secrets."

Gwen brightened. "Mom, I'm so happy for you. This is great, and I think J's wonderful."

"Honey, I'm not here for any kind of relationship. I'm having a great time and I'm enjoying this lifestyle, but it's not going to lead into anything more."

Gwen's skeptical look made Corrie laugh.

"Mom, I don't think you should give up the idea of a relationship. Not every man would...do what Dad did."

Corrie shrugged. "I'm not willing to take that chance."

Gwen's sad eyes studied her mom's face. "I hope you change your mind."

After Gwen's car was out of sight, Corrie slowly returned to her empty cabin. The weekend had been so full of love and laughter with her daughter, her heart felt warmed. She washed the lunch dishes and lingered in the memories of the visit.

But she chided herself. She should have known better than to mention the trips to Mount St. Helens in her letters. She didn't want Gwen to worry about her.

It's amazing though how many people seemed so against her going to Mount St. Helens. She shrugged, knowing full well she'd go again when the opportunity presented itself. If anything happened, they'd be able to get away. They knew what they were doing.

Chapter Fifteen

AS I SEE IT
Kevin Walsh
Clearwater News staff columnist

May 1, 1980. Harry Truman, the crusty owner of Mount St. Helens Lodge, seems to be the exception to following Governor Dixie Lee Ray's order for all in the Red Zone to evacuate. He's steadfastly refusing to leave and apparently the government isn't going to force the issue as they have with other area residents. Media people love him and television and newspaper crews, sometimes flying in by helicopter, are frequently hosted by this old-timer. "Mount St. Helens has been my home for fifty-four years," Truman claims. "That mountain's part of Truman and Truman's part of that mountain."

Corrie pushed away her notes and book, weary of thinking about giving another talk. She really wanted to be outside, doing something physical. What was J doing? Her sensible side answered: What difference did it make? She wasn't supposed to be interested. She shook her head, disgusted with herself.

She slipped on a light jacket and stepped outside, holding the door open for Bo. It was amazing how quickly the nice, warm spring had blossomed. Although J's yard hadn't been cultivated for flowers in recent years, some shrubs remained from Tish's earlier garden care. Deep purple lilac buds would soon bring their sweet, tangy scent. She'd ask J if she could pick a bouquet for the cabin.

A soft light glowed from the calving barn. Gretchen was probably feeding Freddy. As she approached, Corrie heard two urgent voices from within. She grabbed Bo's collar to keep him from bolting into the calving barn.

"Pam, I told you. Dad won't let me date yet. I can't do anything more than be with a group of kids. He sure won't let me date an older guy like Ron."

"Gretch, just tell your dad you're going to my place for overnight. I'll tell my mom that I'm coming here."

"W-e-l-l, I dunno. My dad can always tell when something funny's going on."

"But you come to my place all the time. If you want to go out with Ron, now's your chance."

"I couldn't believe it when he asked me out. I really want to go, but..."

"Come on, Gretch, it'll be fun. We've never gone on a double-date."

Corrie guiltily clung to Bo, not wanting to intrude, but not willing to turn away. Bo finally grew impatient and barked a hello to the voices inside. Corrie immediately let go of his collar, her cover now blown.

She stepped inside and both girls looked up, eyes darting toward each other. "Hi." She glanced at Freddy, peacefully slurping his bottle. Gretchen sat on a bale of hay, holding it for him, while Pam stood nearby. The girl reached over to pet Bo's big head.

Corrie rubbed the calf's curly forehead. "I was hoping to watch you feed Freddy again. You've really tamed him down, Gretchen. It looks like he knows just what to do."

Both girls seemed to relax.

Gretchen wiped slobber off her forearm. "Yeah, he finally caught on."

Corrie turned to the other girl. "Have you done any writing lately, Pam?"

Pam nodded. "I'm working on a paper. It's really for school, but my teacher said if I polish it up, she'll send it to some Washington school contest."

"What's it about?"

"It's a story about when my dad was little."

"Family stories are always interesting. They make people remember their own childhood. Well, I'll be getting back." She smiled at them both, hoping nothing doubtful showed.

Approaching her cabin, her mind whirled with what she should do about the girls' clandestine plans. She sighed. That must be the oldest trick in the book, each girl telling their parents they would be at the other girl's house.

I'll do nothing, she decided. It's none of my business. After all, she didn't even know if they were going to go through with it.

Her phone rang and she quickened her step. Leonard's cheerful voice greeted her. "Hey, the word's out that a famous author is in our midst."

"Oh? How's that?"

"I just read in the paper that you were the keynote speaker at the school and now you're going to, ah, appear, at the bookstore."

Corrie laughed, "The press has a way of making things bigger than they are."

"May I have the pleasure of taking you to dinner before the big event?"

"Well, sure, that would be nice, Leonard."

They worked out the details for an early dinner to be at the bookstore by seven.

A knock at the door and Bo's sharp bark made her jump. Probably the girls. She opened the door and looked slightly down, as if expecting them. Her eyes traveled up and up. J.

He chuckled. "That was classic. You really gave me the once-over."

She chuckled, too. "I had just seen the girls and for some reason though it might be them."

"I think you've won some points there. Gretch went on and on about your visit at her school. And also when you gave her a hand feeding," he nodded and pursed his lips, "Freddy."

"That was fun at the school. And I was impressed watching Gretch feed that calf.

Can you come in?"

"No, thanks. I need to drive Pam home. I just came to ask if you wanted to play poker tomorrow night. Some friends have asked me over. I know you'd be welcomed, too."

"Thanks, J, but I have plans."

His face remained perfectly straight, but she could see disappointment flicker in his eyes. It crossed her mind to mention her speaking engagement. He must not have seen it in the paper, but then remembered her date with Leonard and decided to skip any explanation.

"Well, okay then." He turned stiffly away and descended the steps.

The next afternoon, Corrie found Gretchen in the calving barn feeding Freddy. She tried to sound casual.

"Hi. Looks like dinner time for Freddy."

"Yeah, I'm trying to hurry him up, but this is taking longer than usual. He sucks so hard now that he pulled the nipple right off and spilled the milk. I had to make up a new formula and start over." She shook her head.

"I can see you've got a death grip over the nipple now." The girls slim fingers straddled the nipple in a white-knuckled grip.

"I don't want it to happen again. My dad's waiting to drive me to Pam's."

"Hey, that sounds like fun."

"I'm eating dinner at Pam's and then we're going to game night at the school." She pressed her lips together.

"I understand your dad is going out tonight, too. That's why I came over." She handed a piece of paper to Gretch. "That's my phone number. I'll be out for awhile tonight, too, but if you ever need to reach me...."

"Okay, thanks." Both of Gretchen's hands were full of Freddy, so Corrie slipped the paper in the girl's shirt pocket." Gretchen glanced up and seemed to really notice her. "You're all dressed up."

Corrie laughed. "I guess slacks and a blouse is more dressed up than my usual jeans and flannel shirt."

Tires crunched on gravel and Corrie looked out as Leonard drove to her cabin. "Okay, Gretch, see you later."

She dashed into the cabin to get her purse and briefcase and joined Leonard in his big Buick. As they passed the calving barn, she saw Gretchen standing in the doorway, Freddy at her side, neck extended, sucking on his bottle.

During dinner she honestly tried to be interested in Leonard and his hardware store. He was a nice fellow and Corrie appreciated the attention he lavished on her, but, well, he wasn't exciting. She feigned enthusiasm about the meal, pretended interest in his grown children, but inside she yawned.

Getting to the bookstore was a relief, even though she faced another crowd, another session of being the center of attention. This program, much more relaxed than at the school, turned out to be actually fun. She talked about her book, covering much of the same material she had at the school, read part of one of her favorite chapters, and then opened the discussion for questions. People always seemed to want to know why writers write. How they go about it? Was it hard to get published? Corrie fought to not look at her watch and to graciously answer questions. She appreciated her rapt audience, mostly women but a few men, too.

Toward the end, Al walked into the store. She saw him flinch when the bell jangled. Corrie nodded and smiled to him as he clicked his camera shutter her way. He quietly stepped to the front of the room and took a picture of the audience. Later, as Leonard helped her gather her things, Al clicked his camera again. He slipped back out the door, wrapping his hand around the bell to silence it.

"How about going for a nightcap?" Leonard helped gather her things and carried her briefcase for her. He stood back to let her pass through the door.

"I'm sorry, Leonard, I need to hurry home."

"Oh?"

What could she possibly say to make this important enough to miss spending more time with Leonard. "Yes, I'm sorry, but...." There really was nothing to say. "I'm expecting an important phone call."

A tight little smile told her he was disappointed. He'd taken her to dinner, sat through what was probably a boring recitation and now wanted to have a relaxing evening.

"Thank you so much, Leonard, for the nice dinner and for coming to the program with me."

"My pleasure." Yes, he was ticked.

As they drove by the school Corrie noticed the full parking lot. Good. There really was something going on. Apparently, Gretchen was doing just what she said she would do. Corrie could change her mind and tell Leonard that she could go for that drink after all. No. Just the thought of it made her heart sink.

As Corrie climbed out of the car, she heard her phone ring. "There's my call. Thanks again, Leonard."

She ran up the steps and caught the phone on what was probably the fourth or fifth ring.

"Hello!" she said, fighting for breath and dropping her purse and briefcase onto her small desk. She glanced at the wall clock. Almost 9:00.

"Corrie?"

"Yes. Gretchen? What's wrong?" Something was wrong, she could tell from the girl's quivering voice.

"Can you come and get me?"

"Sure, where are you?"

"At the phone booth in front of the library."

Corrie knew the library would be closed at this hour. "Gretchen, isn't that right across the street from the Seven-Eleven? Can you go over to the store and wait inside? I think that would be safer." The idea of Gretchen waiting in a lit up phone booth in the dark was scary. Her heart pounded.

"Okay."

"Just stay there, inside. I'm leaving right now."

Her hands shook as she tried to slip the car key into the ignition. At the spur of the moment, she stopped at J's, leaving the motor running and the car door open. She didn't know if Chad would be playing poker or not, but she took a chance.

She burst into the kitchen and called out. "Is anyone home?" No answer.

She grabbed the tablet and pen by the phone and scribbled a note:

Chad: 7-11 town. Hurry Gretchen.
Corrie

She threw the tablet on the kitchen table and wondered briefly if it would make sense. Then she concentrated on just one thing, getting to the Seven-Eleven. She knew she was driving fast. If a cop stopped her, she'd tell him it was urgent and maybe even get an escort. Naturally, no cop in sight.

She screeched into the store's lot and parked in front of the store. Gretchen stood at the magazine rack, facing the door, a magazine in her hand. Relief flooded her blotchy face.

Corrie rushed to her. "Gretchen, what happened? Where's Pam?"

A woman customer lingered nearby. Corrie gently took Gretchen's arm and led her to the cooler.

With halting speech, Gretchen told her they'd met up with two older boys at the school and went out with them. They drove to the cemetery where a bunch of kids were having a party. She stopped, then in a strained voice continued. "They were drinking and some of 'em were already drunk. Ron and this other kid, started breaking grave markers, beating on them with sticks, knocking them over. I just wanted to get out of there, but I didn't know what to do."

She'd tried to talk Pam into leaving, but Pam's date, Paul, wasn't doing the damage and she wanted to stay with him. Besides, how could they leave? It was Ron's car they'd come in.

"I begged her to come, but she wouldn't, so I left without her. I hope she's all right," she finished in a small voice.

"You left? You walked from the cemetery?" Corrie knew where that was, about five miles away.

Gretchen nodded. "But after awhile I could hear somebody coming, so I hid. It was Ron's car. They drove right past me. I walked some more, but they came back and I hid again. By this time it was really dark. I could hear their voices. Ron was swearing and saying bad things about me." Tears welled and she wiped her eyes with her sleeve.

"Gretchen, do you think Pam's in danger? We need to do something about her."

The girl shrugged her shoulders. "I don't know. I hated to leave her, but..."

"No. Gretchen, you did the right thing. Let's get in my car and try to figure something out." Corrie put her arm around Gretchen's trembling shoulder.

A car squealed into the parking lot. Gretchen stopped and clutched Corrie's arm. "That's him. Ron." The parking spaces in the front were taken, so Ron double-parked his car at a strange angle off to one side.

Ron strode over to Gretchen, crowded in front of Corrie and grabbed the girl's arm. "Where the hell have you been? I been lookin' all over for you." Ron appeared to be about seventeen, maybe eighteen. He also appeared to be drunk. His breath smelled like cheap wine.

Corrie stepped between them. "Hey! Take your hands off her."

Ron's blurry eyes settled on her. "Butt out. It's none of your business."

"Oh, yes it is." She put her hand on Ron's arm, but he shrugged her off. A lady scurried by, apparently anxious to get into her car before something ugly happened.

"Lady, I tol' you. This is none of your damn business. Now back off." He didn't actually shove her, but rather turned his back to her, crowding between her and Gretchen in such a way that she had to back up.

The next scenes were such a blur that Corrie could hardly take them all in.

Before she could react, Chad stepped between Gretchen and Ron, pushing Ron aside. He took Gretchen's arm, his big hand circling her upper arm with a steel grip, and walked her outside and over to Corrie's car. Corrie barely recognized him. His stern face and stiff body was nothing like the ranch boy she knew. Chad opened the door. "Get in the car." His voice was firm, yet calm. As Gretchen started to climb into the car, she spotted her friend in Ron's car. "There's Pam and Paul in Ron's back seat! Can she come with us?"

"Okay," Chad said, pointing at the car. "Get in." He strode to Ron's car, jerked opened the rear door and said, "Pam, get into Corrie's car." Without a word, Pam left Paul's side, hurried across the small parking lot and climbed into the back seat of Corrie's Datsun, looking over her shoulder toward Ron's car.

Chad looked at Corrie. "Okay? Let's go."

"Oh, yes. Okay."

It would have all been over, except that Ron, in his stupid, drunken state, would not let it end.

"Hey, ass-hole, who do you think you are?"

Chad voice, still calm, said, "Corrie, get in your car. Go."

Corrie slipped in. "Lock your doors, girls."

She started her motor, but then sat transfixed. Ron swung at Chad but before he made contact, Chad grabbed Ron's arm and twisted it behind the boy's back, bending him over the Datsun's hood. Chad jerked Ron upright and marched him across the parking lot to his car, slammed him against it, and opened the rear door. After some discussion, Paul got out and took the driver's seat. Chad and Ron were obviously arguing about something and finally, with one arm firmly holding the furious boy, Chad reached into the kid's pocket, pulled out a set of keys and tossed them to the other boy. He pushed Ron into the back seat and signaled the driver to go. The boy drove off, bouncing off the curb as he left.

Chad stood by the road, watching them go. He shook his head with disgust as he walked to his truck, parked on the street. Corrie backed up her car and swung around to leave. She rolled down her window. "I'll leave Pam at her house, then we'll be right along. Good work, Chad. Thanks."

As Corrie pulled into the street, the car was quiet for about thirty seconds, when both girls burst forth at once.

"I couldn't believe Chad. That stupid Ron didn't have a chance!"

"Pam, why wouldn't you leave with me?"

"Paul wasn't doing anything wrong. He wasn't even drinking. I didn't want to leave him."

"But they were breaking up the cemetery. You can get into trouble, even being there."

"Pam, where do you live?" Corrie had no idea which direction to go.

"But we weren't doing anything wrong."

"Breaking up a cemetery? That's wrong. Drinking? That's wrong."

"But Paul and I weren't—"

"Pam, where do you live?"

Pam gave Corrie her address. "It's not far from Gretch's. Go just like you're going there." Then, "Wow, I couldn't believe how Chad turned that stupid Ron into a pretzel."

"Yeah. He's been bucking hay all winter. He's strong. I wish he'd punched that stupid Ron out. What a jerk."

"I'm glad he didn't," Corrie said. "I think he did just what he had to do. Any more would have been wrong. Ron was drunk and no match for Chad. I admire the way he handled the whole situation."

"Yeah, me too," Gretchen agreed.

They let Pam out. Corrie asked her if she wanted her to go in and talk to her mother.

"No, I'm going to tell her everything. She'd find out anyway."

As they drove away, Gretchen said, "She will, too. She tells her mom everything."

"How about you, will you tell your dad about this?"

"I don't know. He's going to be really mad."

"I imagine he'd be even madder if he hears about it from someone else, like Pam's mother."

Gretchen sighed. "This whole evening's been such a disaster." She looked at Corrie with somber eyes. "Thanks for coming to get me."

"Sure. I'm glad you called."

J's house was ablaze with light as they drove up. His truck was parked by the back door, not in its usual place by the barn.

Gretchen's eyes grew huge. "Oh, boy. He knows."

"See you later, Gretch. Just tell him the truth. It'll be okay." This was a family affair. She had no business being a part of it.

Chapter Sixteen

AS I SEE IT
Kevin Walsh
Clearwater News staff columnist

May 3, 1980. According to scientist Dave Johnston, USGS has established a new observation post about 5 miles north of the Mount St. Helens summit. Called "Coldwater II," the site houses time-lapse cameras and monitoring equipment. A travel trailer has been placed on site to provide shelter for scientists who are now located there around the clock.

Silence reigned at the breakfast table, accented by the sound of spoons clinking against cereal bowls. Gretchen's red-rimmed eyes darted toward Chad, then her father, as she choked down her oatmeal.

She'd better be upset, damned upset. J'd not only been furious about her sneaking around and dating, that older kid no less, but also that she'd lied to him about where she was going.

His words still hung in the air, and in his heart. "I guess this means I can no longer trust you, Gretchen." He ached with disappointment. Without trust, his work increased to an even higher level. Up to now, he could trust knowing she was where she said she'd be, that she was doing the right thing. Not now. Now he'd either have to watch her every minute, or have someone else do it. How else could he keep her safe?

She'd had nothing to say in her own defense. "I'm sorry, Dad," was all she could manage. Last night had been a nightmare. When Chad returned from the calving barn, he'd seen Corrie's note. Chad had called him before going into town and J left the card game immediately and headed into town himself. He'd met Chad who was on his way home and they'd stopped to talk. By then he knew that Gretchen was all right and that she'd be along with Corrie. He returned home to wait for her.

He was not only discouraged to think she'd lie to him, but that she'd pick such a loser as a boyfriend. They'd never had such a blow-up. It was all he could do to not turn her over his knee, but she was too old for that. Too young to date, too old to spank. What he'd dreaded was happening.

He sighed and pushed away his oatmeal. Gretchen glanced at him and tears filled her eyes. "Dad...."

"Just eat your breakfast," he snapped, leaving the table. Chad looked at one, then the other, steadily spooning the cereal into his mouth. Scraping the bowl, he pushed away from the table and reached for his billed cap. "You want me'n Moe to start gathering on the high north pasture?"

"Yeah. I'll be along in a bit."

Chad thumped down the back stairs. The clatter filled the tense kitchen.

Tears streaked down Gretchen's face. "Dad, I'm sorry. It won't happen again."

"How will I know that, Gretchen? How will I know that when you say you're going someplace, you're not lying to me again?"

He'd grounded her for two weeks though he'd like to have made it for two years. But it was almost harder to ground her, seeing that she followed through. If Tish were still here.... He gritted his teeth. She wasn't there and this was his problem. His alone.

"You've got your house work today, your homework and your piano practice."

She sniffed. "I know. I'll finish up and then come out and help sort—"

"No. You'll stay inside today.Her eyes flew open and her mouth dropped. "I was going to help sort today."

"No, you're not, Gretchen. I need to know exactly where you are, and that's going to be in this house." By the time she finished her work, he didn't know where he'd be. He'd have to stop whatever he was doing from time to time to check on her. My God, he didn't have time for this.

The phone rang. Gretchen froze, not making a run for the phone as she usually did.

J answered it. It was his sister. "Yeah, Nan, what's up?"

"Well, you're sounding cheerful. I take it you've seen the paper."

"No. What?"

"Maybe this isn't the time."

"What, Nan?"

"Did you know Corrie gave a talk at the bookstore last night?"

"No."

"I just noticed an article about it in the paper."

J waited for more, but she'd stopped talking. "And?"

"Nothing. I'm sorry if I've called at a bad time. I'll talk to you later."

Why was it that Nan could always tell when he was out of sorts? She hung up and, after a pause, he did likewise. He'd have to look at the paper when he had more time. Maybe tonight.

He hurried out. Chad had saddled his horse for him. He needed to thank him for all he did last night. He met Moe and Chad part way down from the upper winter pasture. He took over the bunch they were leading and sent them back to gather another bunch, to root the cows out of draws and that big rock formation they liked to hide behind.

He turned to see Corrie riding toward him. The cattle bunched up, walking along the narrow road between fences. There was no place for them to go, but forward. Corrie pulled off to one side as much as she could to let them pass and then reined her horse in beside J's.

J nodded. He really didn't feel like small talk. He was embarrassed and ashamed that she'd been exposed to his daughter's misbehavior. Family trouble was family business and he didn't appreciate others having to know about it. But he was indebted to her.

"Thanks for helping out last night, Corrie. I really appreciate your going after Gretchen." He glanced at her, but then looked straight ahead at the cattle's lumbering backs.

He could feel her studying his face. She was probably thinking that he wasn't much of a father, not even able to control a fourteen year-old.

"Girls that age feel a lot more sophisticated than they really are. I know that could have been a really dangerous situation, but for what it's worth, J, I think she did the right thing."

He reined his horse to a full stop. "The right thing? Going out with that jerk and lying to me about it? Going to a party where drinking is going on and smashing up graves?"

Corrie shook her head. "No, that was wrong, and I'm sure she's knows that. I'm also sure any attraction for that creep has totally vanished. I meant she did the right thing by leaving that bad situation. She tried to talk Pam into leaving, too, but Pam wasn't willing to go, so Gretchen struck out for herself. It took a lot of courage to follow her conscience."

"I wish that conscience had kicked in a little sooner."

"Still, she had the good sense to call for help."

"She broke the trust we had."

"It was a serious mistake, one that could have had terrible consequences. She knows that now."

"She'd better. It's going to be awhile before she has another chance." He shook his head. It was a relief to be able to talk to someone about this. "I've never had this kind of trouble before. Gretch has always been reliable. But now I'm stuck with this, with not being able to trust her, not knowing if she's where she says she is."

"I can speak from some experience, J. She'll learn more and be more responsible if you allow her to prove to you that she can be trustworthy."

"I've grounded her for two weeks."

"That's reasonable. But she'll still be going to school, helping out around here, right?"

"Sure. But I'll have to check up on her often, make sure she follows the rules. I need to get back to the house now to make sure she's there and doing her work."

"J, if you give her a little slack, she'll be able to prove to you that she can be trusted. If you keep too tight a rein on her, she'll have no way to show you."

J let that sink in. It made sense. "Okay, I'll keep that in mind. Thanks, Corrie."

A weight lifted from his heart. Kids do dumb things. It's a wonder they live through childhood. Some kids don't. Corrie was right. Gretch made a mistake and she recognized it. She'd tried to get away and even asked for help. He knew she was sorry. What more could he ask? They'd have a talk when he got back.

"Oh, and J, I was so impressed with Chad last night. He reminded me so much of you, how you would have handled that situation. He was in complete control. I don't know what we would have done without him. You've set a really good example for him."

Did the sun just come out? The day suddenly turned brighter.

Corrie, sensing that J needed to be alone, let him pass. "Maybe I can give Chad and Moe a hand at gathering."

He turned in the saddle, looking considerably more cheerful than when she first encountered him. "Okay. See you later."

Roundup for branding was starting. Corrie looked forward to it. She couldn't imagine it, but hoped in some small way she could help.

She found them by their noise, the strident bawls of the cattle and the sharp whistles of the men. She'd tried to whistle in the privacy of her cabin and even when she was alone outside, but she couldn't imitate that shrill whistle. Were cowboys born with that genetic trait?

Moe spotted her first and signaled with his arm, lariat in hand. "Go 'round by that draw and keep 'em from going back in there."

She raised her hand in acknowledgment and stationed herself by the draw. Fancy took over and effectively blocked any cattle with the notion of going back to where they had just been rousted. The horse stepped forward or stepped back, watching out of the corner of her eye. One particularly stubborn cow kept persisting, her calf complaining by her side. Finally, Fancy turned and directly faced the cow. After a stare-down, the cow bellowed and Fancy took one step toward it. Corrie wondered how safe she was, being so close to this test of wills, but the cow tossed her head and lumbered off, her calf scampering at her heels..

Apparently, Moe and Chad were satisfied that they'd gathered all of them from this pasture and pushed them toward home. Corrie fell in behind, knowing that newcomers rode drag, the least demanding, but also the dirtiest position. Dust, kicked up from the grinding hooves of about fifty cattle, settled on her face, head and shoulders, and on Fancy's once shiny coat.

At one point the cattle stalled with a commotion in the center of the herd. A tight knot of cows milled about, bawling with distress. Above the din, Moe, riding point, signaled Corrie to stop and then pointed to Chad.

With slow, deliberate moves, Chad forced his way into the center of the commotion, quietly soothing the cattle. "Hey, hey, what's going on? Come on, now, let me by." Cows parted, making way for him.

Once in the center, Corrie could see Chad through the dust. He had made his way to a little calf who had been separated from its mother. He gently accompanied the little one forward and reunited the two and the group moved on. He made his way back out and regained his flank position.

Moe signaled Corrie to move forward, but in the same motion made it clear to not crowd the stock. She'd noticed that cattle became nervous if you rode too close. They moved much better and much quieter if they were given space. There was sure a lot more to this cattle business than she'd thought. A lot of work went into putting steak on a platter.

* * *

J loaded his pickup with hay bales. While he had the truck out, he'd taken a run up to the end of the driveway to get the newspaper. He plucked the paper out of its box, picked up the mail, turned the truck around and headed back in time to meet the cattle just then in sight.

He opened the door and Julie bounded out, racing toward the approaching herd. J opened the paper, scanned the front page, then turned the page to see Corrie's dazzling smile. Standing next to her, Leonard Snow's beaming face looked at her with adoring eyes. The picture caption identified Corrie, a well-known northwest writer, and Leonard Snow, a local businessman and friend of the author. "Shit."

Julie's barking jolted J's musing. The cattle had picked up speed, smelling the hay in the back of the truck. J slowly swung the truck into a holding pen and the cattle followed him in while Chad and Moe, then Corrie in the rear, pushed the last of them into the confined area. Corrie swung the gate closed after the last one entered.

The three climbed off their horses. Moe glanced at J. "Boss, let's break for lunch. I'm starvin'."

J nodded and fell in step with Corrie. "Gretchen's putting together sandwiches. Join us."

"Sounds good." She couldn't read the expression on his face. He looked more relaxed than this morning, but something was on his mind.

"You didn't mention you were speaking at the bookstore last night."

That was it. "It was just an informal talk. How did you hear about it?"

He unrolled the paper in his hand, still turned to the page.

She glanced at the picture, then at him. What was that expression?

"I'd have liked to go to that."

He would? "You were playing poker."

"Not if I'd known about that. Why didn't you tell me?"

"Ah, well, I didn't know you'd be interested."

"I see Leonard knew about it."

"He read about it in the paper."

J nodded. "I guess I'll have to stay more current with the news."

After lunch J lingered at the house. "You guys go ahead. Let's bring 'em in from Wagner's and then we'll sort what we have today."

After they left, J signaled Gretchen to join him at the table.

"Gretchen, I want you to stay in the house the rest of today, but tomorrow I'd like you to help sort."

The girl brightened. "Okay, Dad. I want to help."

He looked into her anxious eyes and nodded. "Monday, after school, we need to stop by the sheriff's and tell him about Friday night."

Gretchen was stricken. "Dad! You mean tell him who was there...and everything?"

"Honey, he'll already know about the damage. You were there and unless you come clean, you could get blamed for the damage right along with the rest of them."

"But I left."

"Not before damage was done. Besides wrecking the graves, those kids probably left a mess. He may already know you were there. We've got to let him know the situation so we can clear your name."

Tears rolled down her pinched face. "That was the dumbest thing I ever did."

He reached over and put his big hand on her shoulder. "But you left after you recognized a bad situation, that's the important thing. We need to come clean and not have this thing hanging over your head. Talking to the sheriff is the right thing to do. I'll pick you up right after school on Monday and we'll take care of it. Okay?"

"What about Pam? Should she do that too?"

"That's her family's business. I have all I can do to take care of mine." He smiled gently. "I wouldn't talk about this around school, Gretch. The whole world doesn't need to know you're going to talk to the sheriff. Let's just keep it to ourselves."

"I need to tell Pam though."

"Well, tell her to keep quiet about it." He wondered if Pam could keep quiet about anything. She was a lot like her mother.

He hurried down the steps. He needed to talk to Corrie, yet he wasn't sure just how to go about it. Was she getting serious about Leonard? He didn't blame Leonard for falling for her, but damn it! I thought she said they were just friends. Those moon-eyes of his looked like more than that.

Chapter Seventeen

AS I SEE IT
Kevin Walsh
Clearwater News staff columnist

May 4, 1980. Concerned with the increasing instability of the growing bulge on Mount St. Helens, USGS scientists have issued an updated Hazards Warning. Based on this information, Governor Dixie Lee Ray and Forest Supervisor Robert Tokarczyk are closing additional areas near the volcano. New guidelines are shown by color-coded zones: the Red Zone's boundary ranges from three to seven miles out from the peak. Access to this zone is restricted to scientists, law enforcement, and other officials. The Blue Zone, roughly 10 miles from the peak, is restricted to loggers and property owners with special permits and may be used during daylight hours only.

J caught up with Corrie, Moe and Chad as they passed through the north gate, on their way to gather cattle from Wagner's. "Chad, can you stay home with Gretch this evening?"

"Yeah. Why?"

J glared at his nephew.

Chad shrugged. "Okay."

J turned to Corrie. "Can I talk to you?"

She reined in, curiosity compelling her to guide Fancy to face J. She looked at him expectantly.

Moe glanced at them both, then at Chad and winked. "Let's us just mosey on." It was said so deliberately, J narrowed his eyes at Moe and gave him a disgusted look, then glanced at Corrie. The old man nudged his horse and he and Chad trotted off, laughing.

Corrie laughed, too. "What was that all about?"

J shook his head. "Those guys are nuts."

"You wanted to talk to me?"

"Yes. Well....yes. Ah, Corrie?"

She leaned forward in her saddle.

"I need to pick up supplies for roundup. Would you like to ride into town with me?"

Her startled look flustered him even more.

He'd gone this far, might as well dive in even deeper. "I thought we'd go to the feed store, then grab a bite to eat. Maybe end up at the Roadside, give that band you like a whirl."

"Today?"

"You have other plans?" It came out rougher than he'd intended.

"Well, no, but I thought we were going to bring cattle over from..."

"Yeah, well, we'll do that too. He smiled, a shy boyish smile. "I wanted to ask before Leonard beat me to it."

She smiled back. "J, that picture in the paper looked...different than it really was."

"You weren't with him?"

"Well...yes, I was. We'd gone out to dinner before the program at the bookstore, but..."

He stiffened. "I don't want to interfere with something you have going on there."

"J, I've told you. I'm not looking for a relationship. Leonard and I are just friends, nothing more."

"That isn't how he looks in that picture."

"I can't help how he looks. All I know is how I feel."

"Okay. You feel like going into town with me? Having dinner? Going dancing?"

She grinned. "Sure. That sounds great."

"Okay!" He felt like he might float right off his saddle.

"It's only one o'clock. We've barely eaten lunch. When did you have in mind we'd leave?"

"We need to get to the feed store before it closes. Maybe leave here around five o'clock."

"Okay. So we have a few hours."

"Yeah. I just wanted to ask before you lined something else up. You're not the easiest person to make plans with." He smiled, looked her straight in the eye, then squared his shoulders. "Let's catch up with those guys."

As they gathered the cattle, J noticed how much Corrie had caught on, what a natural she was. His eyes rarely left her.

Chad sidled up to him. "So you want me to babysit Gretch? You guys going someplace?"

"Yeah. I don't want to leave Gretchen alone after last night. Get her to fix dinner for you, scramble some eggs or something, maybe you guys can watch TV." He explained his and Corrie's plans.

Chad whooped. "All right!"

* * *

The Roadside wasn't a dressy place, yet they were going out to dinner first. Corrie took out one thing after another from her closet, trying to decide how to dress. She finally settled on slacks and a dressy blouse. After seeing J, she was satisfied with her choice. Although he always looked good to her, he had never looked so handsome. His western cut pants and shirt with the bolo tie were perfect. Okay, stunning. He even wore a new Stetson.

As they settled into his truck she remarked how nice he looked. He smiled. "Thanks. So do you."

"I'll bet Gretchen and Chad razzed you about this, about your being all dressed up."

"Oh, yeah. They're not going to let something like this get by 'em."

"Does Gretchen seem okay with it?"

"More than okay. She really likes you, Corrie."

As they entered the feed store, Corrie was horrified to see Leonard at the counter, purchasing dog food. She hoped they wouldn't be seen, but of course knew how impossible that would be. J was hard to miss. Even without a hat he stood about six-four.

Leonard did a double take when he saw them. J nodded. "Leonard."

Corrie tried to appear casual. "Hi, Leonard."

Leonard seemed to gather himself as he graciously greeted them. "It looks like you two are going out on the town. Have a nice evening."

As Leonard left the store with a large bag of dog food propped on his shoulder, J touched Corrie's arm. "Okay?"

"Sure." And it was. She hadn't had so much attention in years. It was actually sort of nice.

J quickly gathered his supplies and paid for them. He turned to Corrie. "I could use a big, juicy steak. How about you?"

"That sounds really good." Going back to the Steakhouse would be a bit strange. She had been there just the night before with Leonard, but who was she to argue about eating steak two nights in a row at a nice restaurant?

What a difference between the two nights. With J she could relax, laugh and just enjoy being there. She felt an excitement, an exuberance, so unlike the previous evening.

Later, at the Roadside, she floated along in J's strong arms. "I thought you hadn't danced in a long time. You're a great dancer."

"I guess it's something you don't forget."

"Did you and Tish dance?"

"In our early years we danced a lot. Not much after Gretch was born. I don't remember the music being so loud."

"I know, it just bounces off the walls, doesn't it?"

For such a big man, he was light on his feet. Two-stepping or waltzing, he glided across the dance floor, the only movement from his waist down. She could have danced forever.

Between numbers, while they remained on the dance floor, she was aware of another man approaching them. She detected a slight shake of J's head and the man abruptly turned back. Relief surged through her. She wanted to stay with J.

From time to time she tried to remind herself that she wasn't interested in a permanent relationship, but she couldn't seem to concentrate on that thought. She finally just gave in and enjoyed being with him, having his arms around her.

* * *

Corrie stretched luxuriously as she woke the next morning. What a wonderful evening. She smiled, remembering J's kiss as they'd said good night. He hadn't made a big deal of it, just casually leaned over and gave her a warm, soft kiss. He'd lingered, maybe considered another, but seemed to check himself. His voice had been thick with emotion as he said, "Good night, Corrie."

She snuggled in bed a moment longer, then remembered roundup. She climbed out of bed and, out of habit, looked out her small window for any activity. She watched Moe and J carry branding supplies into the calving barn. J glanced over at Corrie's cabin. Instinctively, she shrank back.

After a quick breakfast, she hurried through a shower. Later, approaching the cattle pens, she found Gretchen and Chad on horseback sorting calves from their mothers. They systematically worked their way through the herd, Chad chasing the calves into one pen and Gretchen guiding their reluctant mothers into another. The noise level actually rivaled the Roadside's band.

"Gretch," Chad yelled. "Wake up. You let that calf get by you!"

"Don't yell at me!"

As Corrie approached, they all looked up from their work, making her wonder if they'd been talking about her. J and Moe tinkered with a chute gate. "Want me to saddle up?" Corrie asked J.

"No. We could use a hand right here if you're looking for a job. Where's your hat?"

"I won't need one. What can I do?"

"It's gonna get hot today. Get your hat and then I'll get you set up over here with the insecticide."

Corrie did have a western hat, but she'd bought it for good, not to get all gooped up. She knew J wouldn't be impressed with her reasoning. She rushed back to the cabin for the sparkling white straw hat.

By the time she returned, two pick-up trucks had arrived. A woman, waving to them, drove one of the pick-ups toward the house.

J noticed Corrie watching the woman. "During roundup, Shirley Ann cooks our noon meal for us. She's done that ever since Tish died."

"That's nice. Out here neighbors really help neighbors."

"Yeah. It'd be hard to make it otherwise." He glanced at her and smiled. "I'm afraid your hat won't look like that for long."

Three people sauntered up to them, looking with curiosity at Corrie. J introduced them, a married couple, Georgia and Robbie, and their hired hand, Raul. Shirley Ann returned. "I've put the food in the fridge. I can help out here now until about an hour before we eat."

J introduced Shirley Ann and her husband, Otis, then turned to Corrie. "If you don't mind, when the time comes, would you give Shirley Ann a hand?"

"Of course." She remembered their exchange when she first looked at the cabin and he'd asked if she could cook. They'd come such a long way since then.

Nothing could have prepared Corrie for her first roundup. Long, dusty hot days filled with shouting, bawling cows and calves, confusion, good-natured bantering, flaring tempers, splattered muck, and grinding hard work.

Corrie worked with different people, doing whatever job assigned her.

J gave orders easily: "Okay, listen up. Chad, you guys finished sorting?" At Chad's nod, he continued. "Okay, you, Robbie, and Georgia head those cattle from the south pasture over the top of the hill and down the other side. Shirley Ann and Otis will hold them in the flats until you come over with the last of 'em. Then bring 'em on in to that outside pen until we're through working the ones from yesterday. Raul, Gretch, Corrie, Moe 'n me will work the cows this morning."

Moe prodded a cow down the alley and into the squeeze chute. Julie nipped at the cow's fat stomach, coming away with a mouth full of winter hair. At the dog's nip, the cow plunged ahead with a loud bellow, sticking her head into the head gate, a V-shape device at the end of the chute. J slammed the chute gate shut behind the huge cow and her treatment began.

Corrie, wearing plastic gloves, dipped a ladle into a pail of strong-smelling delousing solution and drizzled it along the cow's spine. Raul replaced the cow's identification if it had broken off, or perhaps this was her first. He also put an insecticide ear tag on the other ear to keep flies away from the cow's face. To insert the tags, he punched holes in the cow's ears. To Corrie they looked like huge pierced ears. None of this seemed particularly painful to the cow, but the animal nevertheless resisted every move they made.

One cow entered the chute at a gallop but at the last second pulled her head back. Raul slammed the head gate shut, but without catching the cow's head. The cow, now trapped with a gate also shut behind her, bawled in panic and kicked her heels as high as the top railing. She slipped on her side and her eyes rolled in fear. Her terror was contagious and cows in the alley began stomping and backing up. J and Gretchen hollered, "HAW! HAW!" and quickly slid boards into the fence railings from one side of the alley to the other, creating a barrier to prevent the cattle from stampeding backwards. Corrie was so shocked at the commotion she stood transfixed, full ladle of disinfectant in hand.

"Corrie!" J bellowed. "Get back! Keep your eye on those hooves!"

"Right." Corrie ducked back from the cow's thrashing hooves. Raul dismantled part of the railing to free the terrified cow. Julie prodded her forward and this time Raul caught her head in the gate and her treatment began.

Shortly before noon Corrie handed the ladle over to Gretchen so that she could help Shirley Ann serve dinner. But first, she dashed back to the cabin to wash her hands and face and to get a clean tee-shirt, dismayed at the dirt and muck caked on her skin and clothes. At J's, she found an apron in a kitchen drawer to cover her dirty jeans. After the meal, she and Shirley Ann cleaned up the kitchen. Corrie liked the other woman and enjoyed sharing this chore with her.

Through in the kitchen, she reported to J for her assignment.

He smiled as she approached him. His cheek was already smeared with blood and grime. "I'd like you to work with me this afternoon."

Corrie stood by the calf chute with J and Moe while Gretchen worked the alley. A resisting, bucking calf made its fearful way down the alley and into the chute. The gate trapped its head and the sides of the chute compacted to hold the heifer fast while receiving treatment. Moe tipped the chute over on its side for easy access to the animal. The terrified calf bawled pitifully and its little hooves drummed against the sides of the chute.

Moe dehorned the calf using a tool shaped like a half-moon, and then splashed antiseptic on the horn cavities. In the meantime, J applied a hot, electric branding iron, stamping a graphic Circle J on its right hip, generating a stench of burnt hair and flesh. Corrie winced. This would take a little getting used to.

J showed Corrie how to administer vaccinations. She grimaced at first, but soon slipped the needle under the loose skin on the shoulder with confidence. As she worked, she kept a tally.

Moe righted the chute and released the V-gate. The heifer bolted out, bawling, in search of its mother.

"Bull!" Gretchen called out as a calf entered the chute, notifying her dad that a castration was next.

Corrie watched the swift, bloody process. "Do you castrate all the bulls? Why don't you use them for breeding?"

J tossed the testicles into a nearby bucket. "Yep. We do all of 'em. We build up the stock from bulls purchased elsewhere, so we don't have inbreeding problems. Let him go," he called to Moe.

"Is that the only reason, so they don't breed with cows? Why don't you just keep them separated?" Corrie prepared to inject the next calf, also a bull.

"No, we castrate them because steer meat is more tender than bull. Good, tender meat is the name of the game. It's why we're in business. But another advantage is that steers are more cooperative than bulls and less apt to fight." He glanced at Corrie with a twinkle in his eye. "What? You writing a book?"

She laughed. "Yeah, I'm soaking up all this, hanging on your every word."

By the time cattle were sorted, treated, and reunited, several hours passed. Corrie was dismayed with the amount of dung slung around by swishing tails and stomping hooves. Several times during the day she'd heard splats against her new hat. It would now be a working hat.

At the end of the first day she looked down at herself and considered burning her clothes. After a quick shower she changed into yet another shirt and clean jeans. Thank God for washing machines. She loaded J's washer with their dirty, sweaty, bloody, dung-plastered clothes. She was so tired she could scarcely move.

Shirley Ann had prepared enough food for them to have leftovers for supper. The others had returned to their homes, but Moe joined them at J's, already showered and wearing tomorrow's clean clothes.

"Corrie, sit down and eat," J said unceremoniously, gingerly lowering himself in his chair at the kitchen table. After dinner, the men planned the next day's work. While they talked, Corrie sat in a stupor.

Gretchen turned to her. "What did you think? Isn't roundup neat?"

"It is, but I didn't know a body could feel so tired and still be alive."

Corrie and Gretchen cleaned up the kitchen. She collected her clothes from the dryer, mumbled goodnight and stumbled to her little cabin.

Next day, it began again. The temperature hit 90, a record heat, they said. At least for early May it seemed hot since they were not yet acclimated.

By mid-afternoon the heat became oppressive. J peeled off his sweat-soaked long-sleeved shirt. Corrie glanced at him in his tee-shirt and her heart skipped a beat at the sight of his long arms, muscles rippling, brown hair tinged with gold darkening his forearms. Her stomach tensed. Confused and distracted, she turned to the instrument table.

"Corrie, have you done this one?" J waited for her to inoculate the calf before releasing it.

Corrie blinked. For heaven's sake. Pull yourself together."Ah, I'm not sure."

"I don't think you have. What's the matter? Are you getting tired?"

"No. I'm fine." She snapped her attention to the task at hand and vaccinated the bawling calf.

"Let her go." J yelled to Raul, who opened the gate while the calf scampered through.

"Gretch," J called, "bring Freddy out here."

Gretchen hesitated. J glanced up, giving her his don't-give-me-that look.

The girl shrugged and turned to get her special charge from the calving barn . "Poor Freddy," she muttered.

J nodded. "That's the problem with naming a calf and turning it into a pet."

"Couldn't she just keep him?"

"No, it doesn't work out. We'd have this two thousand pound maverick bull on our hands that wouldn't fit it. This isn't new to Gretch, it's just tough for her to give 'em up."

"She'll still feed him though, won't she?"

"For a few more weeks."

Corrie looked up, surprised. "This is Monday. Isn't it a school day?"

"Yeah. Gretch wanted to stay home and help with roundup. She can miss a day of school and we could use her help."

J and Gretchen stopped early to clean up and go into town and talk to the sheriff. Apparently, it went well enough. They came back looking relaxed and satisfied. They quickly changed their clothes and went back to work.

Corrie learned to pace herself and fell into a rhythm, so by the second night she wasn't as tired. She thrived with the demanding activity and by the end of the third day she had found her second wind.

"You're doing a good job, Corrie."

"Thanks, J. What an experience." She wished it would go on forever. She loved working with him.

"You do so much around here, I should put you on the payroll."

"Oh, no. My rent is almost free and I just work when I feel like it."

J shook his head in disagreement, but was distracted with Chad's struggle with a small bunch of cattle. He hurried over to give his nephew a hand.

Just as they were shutting down to call it a day, a dark blue New Yorker glided to a stop in front of Corrie's cabin. J noticed it first. "You've got company."

Corrie glanced at the unfamiliar car. As the driver climbed out, she whispered, "Oh, no."

"What? Who is it?"

Corrie's shoulders slumped. "Earl, my ex."

Chapter Eighteen

AS I SEE IT
Kevin Walsh
Clearwater News staff columnist

May 5, 1980. USGS Geologist Dave Johnston claims that precise laser surveys reveal that the bulge is not confined to the Forsythe Glacier, but also includes Goat Rocks dome. According to Johnston, it's very dramatic to see this much ground movement. "It is unusual in a volcano and demands explanation. It can't be anything but some type of dramatic change going on inside the mountain." He feels that even if the volcano quiets down, extreme danger persists until the north flank stabilizes. And, he adds, "The only way it can stabilize is to come down."

With dread, Corrie walked toward the cabin, toward memories she'd hoped to forget. Leaden legs carried her forward while her mind screamed with rebellion.

By the time she reached the porch, Earl was coming out the door.

"There you are!" His nostrils flared as she neared him. His brow rose with surprise at her appearance.

"Hello, Earl."

"What have you been wallowing in? You smell like shit."

"That's what I've been wallowing in. What do you want? Why are you here?"

He looked passed her. "What's going on over there?"

"We're in the middle of roundup."

"We?"

"We. I work here. I live here.

"Is that cowboy there the owner of the place?"

She followed his pointing finger. "No, he's a hired hand. The owner is the tall fellow walking toward the gate." Earl looked long and hard at J, sizing him up. He had always regretted not being taller.

"He have a family?"

"His wife died a few years ago. He has a daughter." She sighed and shook her head. Why was she even answering these questions? "What do you want, Earl? I need to get back to work." That wasn't precisely true, she was finished for the day, but it was the only thing she could think of at the moment to get rid of him. And she had looked forward to eating dinner at J's.

"Well, that's a hell of a way to greet me after I've driven all this way to see you."

How typical. He'd taken it upon himself to drive all the way from Seattle without calling to ask if it would be convenient, then was insulted when she didn't drop everything to greet him. Some things never change.

"Aren't you going to invite me in?"

"I see you've already invited yourself."

"You didn't answer when I knocked so I went in looking for you."

How had she ever stood this man?

"Well, can we talk?"

"Talk? About what?"

He smiled, involving his mouth only. His eyes showed impatient arrogance. "Let's just go in and have a chat."

She shrugged and brushed past him as he still stood in the doorway.

"Why don't you take a quick shower and we'll go into town for dinner?"

"No, thank you." She settled into her wooden rocker, the only thing she dared sit on with her filthy clothes. Removing her splattered hat, she placed it on the floor beside her.

"You don't want to take a shower?"

"I desperately want to take a shower. I don't want to go to dinner with you."

His smile faded. "What's the matter with you? You act colder than yesterday's coffee."

Shaking her head, she wondered how she could ever have loved him. And she had, for years. He sat opposite her on the couch, glanced around, taking in the small cabin, his mouth curling into a sneer. He wore a brand new western outfit. His striped shirt perfectly matched light blue jeans. She nearly choked when she noticed his western boots, his first pair ever, she imagined. He was trying to impress her!

"How come you're living here?"

"I want to live here."

"Seems like you could do better than this."

She made no comment. He looked so soft. She noticed his belly hung over his belt now. His hands were smooth as a pampered woman's. He obviously didn't put in the hard physical labor that the men here on the ranch did. Since he lived in an apartment, he didn't even do any yard work.

"You didn't even tell me you'd sold the house."

"I bought you out. It wasn't any of your business."

"I didn't know you'd moved here until Gwen told me."

Her hands, folded in front of her, broke into a little shrug, palms lifted upward. Oh, well.

He sat forward, earnestly studying her. "Corrie, let's stop this nonsense. Let's get back together."

She sat up so quickly the rocker shot back. "What?"

"We could start over, Corrie. Think how happy it would make Gwen."

"Leave Gwen out of this. While you were screwing around with Megan, you didn't give Gwen a thought. Or me, apparently. How is Megan, by the way?"

"I wouldn't know."

"Oh, you've split. What, another woman on the horizon?"

"It wasn't like that. Erica was just a friend." He clamped his mouth shut and frowned, obviously regretting his telltale statement.

She laughed. She knew it sounded hollow and she didn't care. "Megan was 'just a friend.' Just a friend that everyone knew about except me. Just a friend that broke up a marriage of eighteen years. Just–"

"Okay, okay. That was a mistake. One that I regret, but..."

"But what? There's nothing more to say, Earl. I could never trust you again. Actually, because of you, I'll never again put that kind of trust in anyone."

"What do you mean?"

She leaned forward and pointed her finger at him. "What do I mean? I mean you destroyed any inclination I'll ever have for a permanent relationship. I'll never put myself in that position again. Never." She hated that her voice shook, but she'd certainly gotten her point across.

Earl flinched. "My God, Corrie."

"Earl, just go."

He looked genuinely shaken. "Can you ever forgive me?"

"I forgive you. Now please leave." She'd said it with no expression, without a shred of sincerity.

The phone rang. Corrie walked to her desk and answered it, relieved with the distraction.

"Corrie? It's Kevin."

"Hi, Kevin."

Earl perked up, leaning his head over slightly to listen. She turned her back to him.

"How's it going?" Kevin continued. "You guys in the middle of roundup? I just ran into Nancy and she told me you guys were knee-deep."

"Knee-deep is right."

"Will you be through by this weekend? Al's talking about another trip to the mountain."

"Sure, this weekend would be fine."

"We'd like to leave on Friday, give us a little extra time. Is that a good time for you?"

"Sounds good." Although she didn't have a professional reason for going as they did, she appreciated their invitation out of friendship.

"You have company? You sound a little rushed."

"Yes."

"Oh. Sorry to bother you."

"No, no bother."

"Okay, then, Friday morning, around eight?"

"You bet. See you then. Let's talk later about what to take."

She hung up and glanced at her calendar.

"What was that all about? Who's Kevin? Go where this weekend?"

"Earl, that's none of your business. We don't have anything to talk about. Your marriage with Megan is over and it sounds like Erica has dumped you, too. None of this concerns me." She returned to her rocker.

"Look, Corrie, just give me a minute here...."

A movement outside caught Corrie's attention. Moe sauntered by. She suspected the old man was just making sure she was all right.

"Excuse me, I need to talk to this guy." She rose from her chair.

Earl looked up, startled. "What guy? Wait, Corrie...."

Corrie opened the door. "Moe, hold on. I have a message for you."

Moe stopped and watched her as she approached. He looked beyond her shoulder, apparently taking in Earl who had followed her to the door.

Corrie lowered her voice. "Moe, I need to get rid of this guy. He's my ex."

Moe stiffened. "I'll take care of 'em."

"No, Moe. It's nothing like that. I just want to get rid of him. Make up something. Just call me away."

Moe eyes sparkled with the idea of a conspiracy. "When?"

"Give me a couple of minutes."

She rushed back into the house.

Earl returned to the couch. Corrie had just settled into her rocker when the phone rang again.

Earl gave an exasperated sigh. "For Christ's sake...."

Kevin, again. "Corrie, I'm sorry to bother you again. I just checked with Joanne. This weekend isn't going to work It's her mom's birthday. How about the following weekend? Would that be okay with you?"

"The weekend of the sixteenth? Sure, no problem. See you then."

Corrie hung up and again returned to her rocker.

"So now you have plans for two weekends in a row? Who was that?"

"Earl, what difference does it possibly make to you? So...." she made an effort to rise.

"Corrie," Earl began again. "If I could just get in a word here...."

A hard knock at the door made Corrie jump. "Oops. Excuse me." She opened the door to Moe's somber face.

"Boss wants us to go over to Wagner's and fix that water system." The old man craned his neck to get a better look at Earl. He turned his head and spit a long brown stream, splattering Corrie's firewood.

"Right now?" Corrie noticed a stock trailer hitched to Moe's pickup. How had he gotten that all together so fast?

"Yep, Right now."

Corrie turned to Earl. "Sorry, I've gotta go."

"Now just a minute here!" Earl, now standing, obviously needed to take a stand. "Can't someone else do this? You're tired and I've come all this way—"

"Earl, we're through with this conversation. We're through, period." She walked over to him and said in a low voice, "Don't come back."

Earl's eyes grew wide and his lips parted. His eyes darted to Moe who steadily watched him and back to Corrie. His face turned red and he smiled a weak, fake smile. Just as he started to speak, Corrie abruptly turned away, unable to stand him another minute.

She picked up her hat and turned to Moe. "Okay, I'm ready."

As she climbed into Moe's truck, her hands shook. She wasn't used to being rude. Unexpected tears sprang to her eyes. Moe reached into his pocket and drew out a grimy handkerchief. Corrie accepted it with gratitude and dabbed her eyes. "Thanks, Moe."

"You bet."

They drove along in silence until Corrie could speak without her voice betraying her. "I think we can go back now. I'm sure he's gone."

The old man looked at her with surprise. "We gotta fix that water system at Wagner's."

"You mean there really is something wrong there? I thought you were..."

"'Course there's something wrong. Them cows don't care about your problems, they got a problem of their own. No water."

"But J didn't send you over to my place."

"No, I just put the cows and your problem together." Moe cackled and his eyes twinkled as he glanced her way. "I'd already had old Roy saddled; just had to do Fancy."

Corrie laughed. "That was quick thinking. Thanks for helping me get rid of him." She hoped Earl wouldn't come back. She was finally getting her life together and didn't need that anger and bitterness back in her life.

They arrived at Wagner's and bounced across the field until they reached a stand of trees. They led the horses out of the trailer. Moe gathered the tools he'd need from the back of the pickup and packed them into a saddlebag. They mounted and Moe led the way down a narrow path.

"Used to be a road here, but it's all growed over."

"This must be a cow trail. They always seem to walk in single file."

"Yep," Moe answered, letting a mouth full of chew fly.

A galvanized water tank in a clearing showed a water level of less than a third full.

"See that? The water level went down but the float's froze in place."

"It usually lowers with the water level? What does that do?"

"When the float gets down to a certain level, the valve makes the pump kick in and pumps water in the tank."

The cattle began milling around, curious about what was going on. These cattle had already been worked at roundup and brought to this pasture. "When J 'n Chad brought the herd over early this mornin', they'd noticed the water tank wasn't fillin'.

"This morning, before we started roundup?"

Moe nodded. "They were up and runnin' a couple hours before the rest of us got there. Had to get this bunch out of the way ta make room for the rest of 'em."

Moe began dismantling the valve and handed her the wrench. "Here, hang on to this so's I don't lose it."

She knew he wouldn't lose it, he was making her feel useful.

He scraped corrosion off the stem with his pocketknife. "We'd do this different, but this is 'ow old Wagner did it. Until we can change it, we have to put up with this 'ere system."

Corrie, fascinated, watched Moe demonstrate yet another skill. "You guys can fix anything."

"Ya got to, out here."

Moe reassembled the valve and they watched as the pump kicked in and fresh, clear water filled the tank. Cattle began crowding around and Corrie and Moe eased away.

"Okay, let's go home, see if that no good ex is hangin' around. I'll kick his ass if he is."

Corrie laughed. "You would, too."

"Damn right." He grinned at her, lighting up his entire face. His smile, along with his loyalty and support, warmed Corrie's spirit.

* * *

Because of Earl's visit, Corrie missed dinner at J's. She just didn't have the heart to face them. After showering, she opened a can of soup and as it heated, dropped a couple slices of bread into the toaster. Afterward, she sat at her computer, hoping to record impressions of roundup. During the previous days, she'd mentally noted sights and sounds, but now that she had the time, her mind danced around, not allowing her to gather her thoughts. The ugly scenes with Earl wouldn't leave her.

She finally gave up and sat on the porch steps with Bo. The dog sat on one step with his front feet on the next lower one. Bo hadn't been a part of roundup, he just didn't have the training. Corrie had tied him to the barn where he could watch, but where he would stay out of the way and not get hurt. He needed her attention now and she reached over and gently tugged on his velvet ear.

The dog responded to her touch by leaning into her.

The book Corrie had brought outside with her sat by her side, unopened.

She saw J approaching and fought the impulse to dash back to the house. She wasn't in the mood for company and above all else, didn't want him to see how upset she was.

J's eat-up-the ground walk always surprised her. He could cover ground faster than anyone she knew, yet still give the impression of strolling.

"Hi, J."

"Howdy. Mind if I join you?"

She picked up her book as she slid over, giving him room next to her, and scooting Bo over. She could feel J's body heat through his denim jacket, warming that side of her.

"How's it going?"

She sighed. "It was better before Earl came."

"He just come for a visit?"

"I think he came to see if there was a chance of getting back together. Apparently, he and his wife have separated and I guess his girlfriend dumped him too."

"He had a wife and a girlfriend?"

"Oh, yeah. That's Earl."

"That why you guys split up, him fooling around?"

"Yes, it is."

J shook his head. "I'll never understand that. He probably knows now what he threw away."

"I guess he has regrets. He should, anyway."

"Think he'll be back?"

"No, I think I managed to scare him off." She laughed without mirth. "With Moe's help."

"Well, then, that's good, right?"

"I guess. Every time I see him, I'm reminded that I'll never be able to trust anyone again, never lead a normal life." As she spoke, anger turned her voice harsh. "We were married eighteen years, but during the last five he was having affairs. Some of our friends knew, but I didn't see it until the very end. I'll never open myself up to that again. Never."

"Why? That part of your life is over and done with."

"It's over, but I'm not done with it. I'll never be."

"Not as long as you stay angry, you won't."

Her head jerked over to glare at him. "Well, wouldn't you be angry?"

He nodded. "I'm sure I would be. But I'm also sure you're not going to be able to find peace in your life until you can let go, move past this."

She shook her head. "He asked me if I could ever forgive him. I said I did, but neither one of us believed it. How can you forgive someone who wrecked your life?"

"You can't heal, Corrie, unless you do forgive him. I know that from experience. I was mad as hell when Tish died."

"But she didn't betray you. I can understand that you'd be terribly sad, but mad?"

"I was mad, at everything, everybody. At God, that he'd let that happen, at the doctors because they couldn't cure her , at myself for not finding a way to make her healthy. I felt like my life was over. If it hadn't been for Gretchen and having to go on for her...."

"So how did you do it?"

"I was driving myself and everyone around me crazy. I could see it in their eyes. I finally realized that I was going to have to live and I'd better shape up. I just let go of my anger. I guess God has his reasons and I had to accept that I'd probably never know why He had to take Tish."

"I don't think I'm that big."

"But look at him, at Earl. He's not happy, is he? He's done this to himself, wrecked his life. Don't let him wreck yours. He made his choices but he can't choose for you anymore."

"He already has."

"No, Corrie, he hasn't. You're the one that's doing that. You're not letting yourself be happy. How long have you been divorced?"

"Two years."

"Then it's about time for you to start living again."

"I have been living. I'm enjoying my life."

"But you've put restrictions on it."

"Okay. So you managed to forgive and move on. I don't see that you've married happily ever after."

"I've been waiting."

"Waiting?"

He nodded. "For the right person." He looked steadily at her.

She averted her eyes. "Are we through with roundup?"

He laughed at the abrupt change of topic. "Pretty much. A few loose ends. I appreciate all your help."

"I really enjoyed it." If it weren't for that stupid Earl, she could do it for the rest of her life.

He stood and she looked at him expectantly.

"Good night, Corrie. Would you think about what we've talked about?"

She opened her mouth, not sure of what would come out. He took her hand, turned it over and kissed her palm, a soft, tender kiss. He turned and walked with long strides to the calving barn.

"See you in the morning," she called.

Without turning, he raised his arm in acknowledgment.

Chapter Nineteen

AS I SEE IT
Kevin Walsh
Clearwater News staff columnist

May 8, 1980. Most USGS and UW scientists believe a major eruption at Mount St. Helens will be preceded by a change in the seismic activity or rate of bulging. However, if the patterns do not change, they might not be able to provide advance warning.

Professor Al Eggers of the University of Puget Sound warned reporters that tide-producing gravitational forces will be exceptionally strong on May 21. According to Eggers, this extreme force might trigger an eruption if the volcano were already set to erupt. USGS scientists do not totally discount Professor Eggers' ideas but many believe other factors such as magmatic pressure inside the mountain is more significant.

Corrie and Chad worked together on this drab, gray day, taking a small herd of about fifty head to a high summer pasture. It was hard to believe that it had been ninety degrees just a few days ago. The temperature had dropped thirty degrees.

They'd brought Bo. For the first time he'd be working on his own. Julie had gone with J and Moe to take a bigger bunch to higher pasture. Bo wasn't nearly as useful as Julie, but at least now he knew better than to scatter the cattle.

Nearing their destination, Chad suggested they stop at a protective rock out-cropping to get out of the wind and eat the lunch Corrie had packed. They quickly ate the sandwiches and apples and prepared to again mount up and get the cattle situated before the weather turned worse.

Chad scanned upward as angry clouds scudded across a threatening sky. "Looks like we're in for it. Why don't you head on back? I can get 'em settled in here."

"I won't melt, Chad. Let's just work together and get it done."

Glancing at Corrie, he nodded. They worked together, moving cow and calf pairs, taking care not to separate them. The stock, nervous after their roundup ordeal, resisted more change in their lives. One calf bawled pitifully. Despite their care, the little heifer became separated from her mother, darting first one way, then the other.

With a crash, the sky opened and a deluge of rain pelted them. Hunkered over their saddles, Corrie and Chad gathered the bunch they were working to coax them alongside the rock outcropping, away from the threat of lightning. Another loud crash of thunder caused Fancy to jump and skitter. Corrie grabbed the saddle horn to keep her balance.

Chad rode over to her and yelled to make himself heard. "Come on. We've got to get out of this." He whistled at Bo. "Here, boy."

They dismounted and stood by their horses under the outcropping, steadying their mounts as thunder roared and lightning snaked across the darkened sky. Rain splattered them, but the huge rocks offered protection from the worst of the storm. Gusts of wind screamed along the rock wall.

"Why don't we just head for home? We're through here, right?" Corrie shouted above the din of rain and whipping wind. She would have liked nothing better than the comfort of her cozy cabin.

He leaned toward her to be heard as a steady stream poured from the brim of his hat. "Because on horseback we'd be the tallest things around and a perfect target for lightning. We'll stay put until it lets up."

Corrie accepted his explanation. At half her age, Chad knew far more about the dangers of wild weather than she. In Seattle, she didn't remember a time she'd been frightened by thunder or lightning. Here, in this wide open country, it was a serious matter.

They waited almost a half hour, standing close, shivering and miserable. Any warmth the day had held vanished as the wind whipped at their wet clothing. The violence of the storm eased, leaving only a steady, wind-driven rain.

"Corrie, I'm going to look for that heifer, try to get her back with her mama. I saw her bolt over there, just down that draw with the first bunch.

There's no sense in both of us doing it. The draw's slippery with mud. As soon as I get her, I'm heading back. I think the worst of the storm is over. Ride on over that ridge and look for strays. If you find any, push 'em back over here. Then go on home." He mounted his horse, turned, and trotted away. Mud splattered his horse's belly.

She rode over the ridge to look for strays, but it was hard to see with the driving rain stinging her eyes. Rain penetrated the seams of her yellow rain slicker, soaking her shirt. Her clammy jeans stuck to her legs; her boots and hat were heavy with rainwater. Her icy hands, even with leather gloves, felt stiff and weak.

"I'm drowning in my saddle," she grumbled aloud, shivering.

Finding no strays, she returned the way they'd traveled earlier that morning. She neared a creek and sharply reined in, astounded. The stream, already full, spilled over its banks. It was now a small raging river, debris bobbing in the swift water. The place where they normally crossed formed a bend in the river and now water flowed more swiftly at that spot. Studying the situation, she decided downstream would be a better, safer crossing.

At Corrie's urging, the mare picked her way a distance downriver. Corrie sat for a few minutes trying to decide what to do. She didn't know of another way to get home, other than crossing this river. It wouldn't be too deep for the horse. Horses can swim. Bo was a strong swimmer, labs even have webbed feet. He'd be okay. And she could swim, although she was pretty loaded down with wet clothes. The longer she delayed, the worse it would get.

She coaxed Fancy to the edge of the swift, muddy river. The horse stamped and snorted, uneasy about entering the water. Corrie eased forward in the saddle, kicking the horse's belly. "Come on, girl." She felt Fancy's tension as she walked stiff-legged into the rushing waters. Water and debris washed past their legs with surprising force. The horse neighed and laid her ears back in fear. The rushing water sounded like a waterfall. The horse didn't have to swim; the water wasn't so deep that she couldn't reach the bottom.

Just past the middle of the river, Fancy lunged and sank. She struggled, tossed her head and sharply whinnied. Sick with fear, Corrie tried to urge the mare on, praying she could free her legs. The horse was mired.

Bo had plunged into the river with Corrie and crossed to the other side. Now he stood at the opposite bank, looking worried and confused with his mistress still in the river. He barked sharply, standing with his front feet in the water.

"Bo, stay," Corrie shouted. The dog obediently sat on the muddy bank, watching intently, trembling.

What should she do? She slid out of the saddle and into the cold water, hanging on to the stirrup to keep from being washed downstream. The force of the water made her gasp for breath.

Reaching for the reins, she worked her way to Fancy's head, searching for solid footing in the muddy rush of water, which now reached her chest. The mare's rolling eyes showed her panic. She screamed a heart-wrenching whinny.

Finding rocky bottom for leverage, Corrie pulled the reins. Fancy's neck stretched out, but her legs, deep in the soft bottom, could not obey. Corrie hated to leave, but didn't know what else to do.

She had to get help. Oh, my God! How could this happen?

The water continued to rise. She had to reach Chad. Should she turn around and go back? No, she didn't think so. She'd head for home. It wasn't that far and maybe J would be back by then. Chad must have crossed downriver, where they usually crossed. She'd better go for the bank on the closer side.

Reluctantly she let the reins drop with an agony so great she moaned.

Heart pounding, Corrie waded against raging water toward the closest bank. A tree branch swished by, catching on her legs. She kicked free and fought on, inching her way to the water's edge. At last, she reached the riverbank and flopped on her back for a moment to rest. Bo stood above her and licked her face.

She struggled to a sitting position and called to Fancy. She wasn't straining any more, but appeared terrified. The horse looked at Corrie out of the corner of her eye, exposing the white.

Corrie scrambled up the slippery, muddy bank, grasping at weeds and exposed roots. Bo dug his way ahead of her, splattering mud at her head. By now she was weak with cold. Hurry, she must hurry. Mud sucked at her boots. She stumbled on. Bo trotted along beside her, fur matted, ears plastered against his head.

Thank God she knew the way home. Now she could see why J had made her pay attention. That would be all she'd need right now, to get lost.

Her anxiety mounted with every shivering step. What would she do if anything happened to that horse? What would she tell Nancy? Just last night, at bridge, she'd told Nancy how much she enjoyed riding Fancy. And now look what's happened to the poor horse! What if the water rose even more?

As she rounded a bend, she saw J coming toward her at a fast trot. He skidded to a halt and stepped off his horse in one fluid motion. He grabbed her shoulders.

"Corrie, are you okay? What happened?"

Her teeth chattered so hard she could barely speak. "J! Fancy's stuck. In the water. I can't get her out."

Rain bounced off their hats, the ground, and surrounding brush.

J climbed back on Nick, slipped a foot out of the stirrup and held out his hand for Corrie. She swung on behind and J goaded the horse into a gallop, Corrie pointing the way.

When they reached the river, Corrie gasped. Fancy's head was barely above the rising water. At the water's edge, J secured one end of his rope to his saddle horn and dismounted. Fighting the current, he half waded, half swam to the frenzied mare and tied the other end of the rope to the left cinch. Then he lifted Corrie's rope from her saddle and made his way to Fancy's other side and secured that rope to the right cinch.

As Corrie watched with pounding heart, tears flowed in streams down her face. "Be careful, be careful," she whispered over and over again. "This is all my fault. What have I done? J, be careful!"

Struggling back with Corrie's rope and again mounting Nick, J wrapped the second rope twice around his saddle horn and held it tight with one hand. The two ropes now formed a V from the mired horse to his. J pulled the reins, backing and applying steady, constant pressure to the bogged-down horse. "Back, back."

Corrie's breath caught as she saw jerking movements. But then nothing, no movement. Nick strained, his huge muscles stood out with the tremendous effort. "Back, back." J's voice was calm, yet insistent.

The suction broke and Fancy staggered, pulled one leg free, then another, then stepped out of the mire. Finally, the trembling horse reached the bank. Corrie threw herself against the horse's wet neck, tears of relief mingling with the rain.

J stood behind her, resting his hand on her shoulder.

The rain let up, suddenly.

Chad galloped up. "What's going on?"

As Corrie collected herself, J explained to Chad what had happened.

Corrie looked at them both, her face pinched with anxiety. "I worried about crossing, but didn't know what to do. I tried to cross where it wasn't as swift."

J nodded, understanding.

Corrie looked at him, her eyes searching for relief. "What should I have done? Why did Chad make it and I didn't?"

"I think what happened, Corrie, is that where you crossed, the ground was soft and loose. It might have been better to cross at the place we usually do where the ground is packed and rocky. But you didn't know." He laid his hand on her arm. "Don't feel bad about it; anyone can get a horse bogged in mud. You did the right thing by getting help. We could never have gotten her out without another horse."

Chad looked stricken. "Corrie, I'm sorry. I shouldn't have left you."

"It wasn't your fault. I should have retraced our steps, like you did." She looked at J as he examined Fancy's legs. "Is she all right?" Her heart still raced.

J walked the mare around the small clearing. The horse favored one leg, but didn't seem seriously injured.

"She's okay. I don't think you should ride her for a few days. We'll keep an eye on her." J mounted Nick, still with Fancy's reins in hand.

"You're leading Fancy?" Chad asked. "Okay, here, Corrie." Chad slipped his foot out of the stirrup and offered his hand to her.

J started to say something, but with a soft "tsk," shook his head and turned his horse to lead the way, Fancy in tow.

Tears threatened again as Corrie prepared to mount Chad's horse. Chad leaned over and, in his most instructional voice, chided her, "Corrie, real cowboys don't cry."

Astonished, Corrie's eyes and mouth flew open. She began to laugh, a silent gasping laugh.

She laughed so hard she didn't have the strength to mount. Afraid she'd wet her pants, she staggered over and sat on a soggy log, still laughing, shaking, gasping for breath. Tears streamed down her cheeks.

J trotted back. "My God, now what?"

Corrie laughed all the harder, giddy from relief and fatigue.

Chad dismounted and walked over to her, scrutinizing her as he might an ailing calf.

She shook. She couldn't stop laughing. She hiccupped.

"I dunno, Unc. I think she's gone weird on us."

Corrie smeared her tears with her gloved hands and gasped, "He said...he said....'real cowboys don't cry.'"

J chuckled, shaking his head. "Get her up in that saddle, Chad, before she freezes in those wet clothes."

J again turned toward home. He wondered if his life would ever be normal again. He really didn't care, as long as he was with her.

* * *

Saturday evening Corrie cooked a special dinner at J's house in honor of Nancy and Roger's thirtieth wedding anniversary. When Corrie had suggested the dinner to J, he radiated pleasure. Before Corrie arrived with an armload of groceries, J, Chad and Gretchen had made a big effort to straighten up the house. During roundup it had been neglected, but this was a special event and they wanted the house to look nice.

Corrie enjoyed bustling around J's spacious kitchen. While J barbecued steaks on the patio, she baked potatoes, tossed a large salad, and basted baked squash with melted butter and brown sugar. She'd baked a strawberry-rhubarb pie earlier and it sat cooling on the counter, its tangy aroma drifting throughout the kitchen.

Tired of jeans, she's donned a casual floral cotton dress with a full skirt, and slipped into sandals rather than boots or tennis shoes. It made her feel festive and she'd enjoyed the double take J and the others gave her. Chad even whistled. Moe, of course, had been invited and Corrie noticed him sidling up to J with some comment after he'd observed her.

J seemed to have a special glow about him, serene and content. She was happy for him. It just felt right, being in his kitchen, in his house, if only for the day.

Gretchen wandered into the kitchen. After seeing Corrie in a dress, she returned to her bedroom and changed from jeans and a tee shirt into a nice blouse and slacks. "What can I do?"

"You could set the table."

"I think I'll use our good dishes."

"That's a great idea. It's good to use nice things, especially for special occasions."

In the dining room, Gretchen opened the china cabinet and gingerly picked up a dinner plate. Corrie, passing by the doorway, noticed and joined her.

"They're beautiful dishes, Gretchen."

The girl nodded. "They were a wedding gift to my mom and dad, from her parents."

"That makes them really special, doesn't it?"

Gretchen nodded again.

"Do you feel a little hesitant about using them?"

"I guess." Her voice was almost a whisper.

"Maybe you should ask your dad what he thinks about it."

Gretchen carefully placed the dish back into the china cabinet. "Okay, I will."

Returning to the kitchen and standing at the sink, she watched Gretchen approach her dad as he stood on the patio by the barbecue. He dipped his head to hear what she said. He smiled gently and nodded his approval. He put his arm around her slim shoulders and gave her a warm hug and kissed her cheek. She looked up at him, adoration shining in her eyes.

The tender scene made Corrie smile. What a special relationship those two had.

Corrie busied herself as Gretchen returned to the house, her step brisk.

"We're gonna use 'em."

"Good. What a lovely recognition for Nancy and Roger's anniversary."

The party proved a wonderful success. The weather had again turned sunny and in the early evening the group sat on the patio visiting, enjoying the warmth of the lingering spring day. Later they filed inside, played poker and chatted long into the evening.

The guests eventually straggled home, first Moe with his usual, "I gotta get my beauty sleep."

Nancy yawned and Roger nodded, "Me, too." Gretchen said her goodnights and retired to her room.

"Come on, I'll walk you home," J offered to Corrie.

Since Corrie and Kevin had made their plans to return to Mount St. Helens, Corrie had intended to mention it to J. But somehow she kept putting it off. Not ordinarily a procrastinator, she was also aware this would be unwelcome news for J. It weighed heavily on her mind now, as they walked to her cabin, but she didn't want to ruin his evening.

There was nothing wrong with her going to that mountain. He knew, as well as she, there was nothing besides ordinary friendship between Kevin and Al and her. He just didn't approve of people going up there when the authorities were saying to stay away. She couldn't get very excited about those rules. The government didn't want to be liable, that's all.

So, why couldn't she get her nerve up to tell him? Oh, well, she had a whole week before they planned to go.

They reached her little home. "Good night, J."

He tenderly turned her around to face him, his big hands on her shoulders.

She looked up, surprised.

"Thanks for making this such a nice evening, Corrie." His deep voice turned husky.

"Sure..." The rest of her words were silenced by a gentle kiss. She felt his body's urgency and her own body, deep within, responded. But too soon reality set in and she was saddened.

Corrie slowly pulled away. "Oh, J." She lowered her head and rested her forehead on his chest.

"Corrie, just let it happen. Trust me." He ran his fingers through her hair and gently massaged her neck.

She shook her head. "I can't."

He kissed the top of her head. "It's your life, Corrie. Don't let something that happened before ruin your happiness now."

Worries flooded her mind. Even though she didn't want to concern him about their trip to the mountain, she felt guilty keeping it from him. She feared that her resolve to not get involved was weakening. For her to give in to him now, would be a commitment that she wasn't ready to make. She worried that he was getting impatient, yet....

"I can't, J. I'm sorry."

He sighed. "Good night."

"Good night, J."

Chapter Twenty

AS I SEE IT
Kevin Walsh
Clearwater News staff columnist

May 14, 1980. Explosions at Mount St. Helens have resumed after an almost two-week break, sending steam and ash plumes 13,000 feet into the atmosphere. The bulge is pushing outwards at the rate of four to five feet a day.

When most of us think of a volcanic eruption we think of hot lava flows, as in Hawaii. According to USGS, that is not always the case. Geologist Dave Johnston says the mountain itself will blow apart, not just spew lava.

In the meantime, earthquake activity is impressive. Since March 20, 2,550 earthquakes larger than magnitude 3.0 have been reported, including 291 larger than 4.0. There's a lot of shaking going on which isn't doing much toward steadying the nerves of local residents.

Corrie spotted Kevin at the grocery store. She laughed when she saw his selection of boxed ready-made pizzas, potato chips, and clam dip. No wonder he was out of shape. "I see you're on a health kick."

"Yeah, whenever I can get away with it, I eat this junk. Joanne keeps trying to get me to eat salads." He grinned, evidently not the least bit upset with others' ideas of what he should eat.

Corrie laughed. "I was going to call you about what to bring for our camping trip." They quickly put together an easy menu for the three days.

He made room for a six-pack of beer in his grocery cart. "I'm glad you're willing to leave on Friday."

"I think it's a good idea. That gives us a whole uninterrupted day on Saturday."

Kevin nodded. "The days are longer now and we'll still have daylight when we get there to set up camp. Al will have both Saturday and Sunday mornings to take pictures, in case the weather isn't great both days.

"And then some property owners are howling about getting up to their property on Spirit Lake to gather their belongings and it looks like Governor Ray will give them permission Saturday morning. I'd like to talk to a few of them. Should make a good story."

"Sounds interesting. Still can't talk Joanne into coming? I wish she would."

"Are you kidding? She's not even happy about me going."

"Well, then, Kevin...."

He shook his head. "She's just getting antsy about that mountain blowing up. Remember, she's a devout coward, and proud of it. Anyway, she doesn't like to camp. 'It's so messy'."

"I'm sorry she won't come. I like Joanne. She's a lot of fun."

Kevin nodded. "She is. But she's just not a camper. I'm really not either, except when it allows me to be places I can write about. Same with Al. He's dying to be the one to take the most famous picture of the mountain when it blows."

* * *

On Thursday, Corrie met a friend in Yakima, about a two-hour's drive from the ranch. Susan had been a close friend for many years, since their college days, and was in Yakima visiting her parents.

As old friends do, they caught up on each other's news. Corrie glossed over J's role in her life, but Susan picked up on it.

"This J, is he married?"

"He's a widower, but anyway, you know I'm not interested in anything more than friendship."

"Corrie, that's silly."

Corrie waved her hand in dismissal. "Guess who came calling." They thoroughly discussed Earl's visit.

"What a creep. But, Corrie, all men aren't like that."

"I'm content to just do what I'm doing without the worry of complications."

Driving home from Yakima, Corrie basked in her close friendship with Susan. She really must stay in touch with these friends who had meant so much to her over the years. With guarded reserve, she replayed the conversation concerning her feelings about remarriage. She skidded away from that topic and began mental preparations for the next day's camping trip to Mount St. Helens.

Darn! She'd forgotten to make arrangements for Bo again. She briefly considered taking the dog with them, but decided against it. Kevin's car wasn't big enough for three people, their equipment and a big dog, to say nothing about the dirt and hair in Kevin's new car. She'd leave a note on Moe's door again. He wouldn't mind feeding Bo. She'd be gone two nights, so he'd have to feed the dog four times. She'd have to remember to do something for Moe to repay him. Maybe after the camping trip she'd bake him a pie. Moe had such a sweet tooth.

By the time she drove down the long driveway, it was ten o'clock and velvety darkness shrouded the ranch. The place was a classic example of 'early to bed, early to rise.'

She knew she'd be rushed in the morning, getting the last minute things ready for the camping trip, so she wrote a note that night and taped it on Moe's door. She could ask J, or Gretchen or Chad for that matter, but she didn't want to have a confrontation with J and deal with his disapproval.

Maybe she'd luck out and be gone before he even found out about it. What she did was her business anyway.

* * *

The next morning, Corrie bustled around her small kitchen, gathering the last-minute items for the camping trip. It was a little past seven-thirty and Kevin and Al would be along soon. The phone rang as she checked off items from her list.

She answered, feeling certain it would be Kevin saying they were running a little late. Leonard's voice surprised her.

"I hope I'm not calling too early. I know you ranchers get started before the rest of us even have our first cup of coffee."

"No, it's fine, Leonard."

"Ah, Corrie, I tried to call you last night, but couldn't reach you."

"I met a friend in Yakima for dinner."

"Yes. Well." She heard him take a deep breath, "My daughter called yesterday, the one who lives in Tacoma, and she and her family are coming for a couple of days. I'm hoping you can join us tonight for dinner."

Oh-oh. She had already decided not to accept any more invitations from Leonard. He appeared to be getting too serious, despite what he'd said earlier about just needing to get out. But she didn't have time, or the inclination, to explain all this now. "Thanks, Leonard, but I'm leaving in just a few minutes for a camping trip."

"That sounds like fun, but I'm sorry you can't join us. Where are you going?"

"To Mount St. Helens." She glanced at her list.

"Mount St. Helens! Corrie, do you think that's wise?"

She laughed. "You wouldn't believe how many people go up there now. The restrictions are a joke."

"But why would you want to do that? From what I hear, it's really quite dangerous."

"I go with newspaper friends. They're always looking for a story. This is a hot one."

"Maybe hotter than you think."

"Well, anyway, Leonard, thanks for the invitation. Have a nice time with your daughter." She didn't want to be rude, but she really had things to do.

* * *

J called Gretchen for the second time. Getting her going this morning was tougher than usual.
"Gretch, get a move on."

Gretchen sighed. "I'm so glad it's Friday. This has been the longest week." She brightened. "This is my last day of restriction, isn't it?"

"Yep." His look told her this freedom was not free.

"I know, Dad."

"Have you made plans for this weekend?"

"Not yet. Would it be okay if I make plans with Pam?"

"If I know where you'll be."

"You'll know."

He nodded. "You're going to miss the bus if you don't leave right now."

The phone rang. "Gretch, you don't have time to talk on the phone this morning."

"How do you know it's for me? Nobody calls me this early."

J answered on the second ring.

"Ah, J, it's Leonard Snow."

"Yeah, Leonard." J's eyebrows lifted in question.

"I...ah...hesitate to call...about this...."

"Just a minute, Leonard, I'm getting my daughter off to school." He put down the phone, handed Gretchen her lunch that she'd packed the night before, gave her a quick kiss and gently shoved her out the door. Chad was warming up the truck to take her to the school bus stop. He picked up the phone, wondering what was on Leonard's mind.

"Okay, I'm back."

"J, I'm concerned about Corrie."

J stiffened. "Concerned about what?"

"About this camping trip she's going on. I know it's none of my business, but—

"What camping trip?"

"Oh. I guess you haven't heard."

"No. What camping trip?"

"She's apparently going camping with newspaper friends to Mount St. Helens."

"The hell she is."

Leonard's voice brightened. "You'll talk to her? I couldn't seem to make any headway, but I really think it's dangerous up there now. She's leaving in just a few min...."

"Leonard, I've gotta go. Thanks for the call."

He knew there was no time to spare. He had to talk to her before Kevin got there. He rushed out the door, not even taking the time to put on his hat.

Moe hurried toward him, looking like he had something on his mind.

"Moe, I'll catch you later."

"No, boss. We gotta talk now." The old man held up a piece of paper, the note from Corrie asking him to take care of Bo.

J snatched it out of the old man's hand without slowing his pace and glanced at the note. "I'm gonna put a stop to this right now." He jammed the paper back into Moe's hand.

Moe stopped. He couldn't keep up with J anyway. "Good."

* * *

Corrie put her backpack on the porch, along with her sleeping bag. She was ready except to finish packing the groceries. She'd better check her list, make sure she had everything. J was barreling toward her. His determined walk told her everything she needed to know. She'd just stepped back into the cabin when he burst inside, not even waiting for an invitation. The door banged against the wall, then hung open.

She turned, startled at his dark, flushed face.

"Good morning, J." How could he have known? Moe, maybe.

"What's this about you going camping at Mount St. Helens?"

"Yes, I'm leaving as soon as Kevin and Al get here."

"The hell you are."

"I beg your pardon? Since when do you tell–."

"Why didn't you tell me about this?" he demanded.

"What's to tell?"

"Answer me."

"Why didn't I tell you? I can't imagine. We're having such fun discussing it now." Her eyes tried to avoid his glowering face.

"Corrie, this isn't a good idea. Do you know about that bulge forming on the side of the mountain?"

"Of course."

"I can't believe you would take a chance like this. You're asking for trouble going up there." Incredulity strained his voice.

"J, for Pete's sake. We don't plan to climb up to the volcano itself."

"Corrie, please reconsider." Now alarm tinged his voice.

"J, I hope you're not upset about my going with Kevin and Al. I've told you before, we're just friends. I'd like Joanne to go too, but she just doesn't like to camp. They want to take pictures and Kevin hopes to get a story from the Spirit Lake property owners."

"That tells me why they're going. Why are you?"

"Because I want to. Because I'm a writer, or am supposed to be. It's good for me to see different situations and experiences." Cornered and hemmed in, she couldn't seem to explain her position. "J, what is it to you anyway? I don't owe you an explanation." She opened the refrigerator and removed a dozen eggs and a pound of bacon and placed them in the grocery box. When Kevin came they'd sort out what needed to go into the cooler.

"What is it to me?" he exploded. "What do you mean, what is it to me?"

He took two quick strides and turned her away from the refrigerator. "Corrie! Will you stop that and talk to me?"

Her temper flared as she jerked her arm away from him. "J, this isn't any of your business. I don't even understand why you care." She turned back to her task of packing the groceries.

"Isn't any of my business?" he thundered. "You know how I feel about you! Corrie, I love you. Look at me!"

What? What did he say? Did he just say that to make her change her mind? She turned to look at her list, now blurry with her confusion.

He roughly turned her around again. Reluctantly, she looked up at him, his face was a picture of frustration and anger.

"J, I'm sorry you're upset. But I have never tried to encourage you. You know my position."

Her knees felt weak; she lowered herself to a chair at the kitchen table.

"No, I don't know your position."

"How many times do we have to discuss this? You know about Earl, about how he—"

"No, ma'am," J shot back. He slammed his hand on the table. A yellow daffodil petal from a bouquet Nancy had given her fell softly to the table. It caught Corrie's eye, but J continued to glare at her. "Earl may be ten kinds of bastard, but you can't hang this on him."

Corrie stiffened. Her eyes narrowed as she glared at him. "What do you mean?"

"Not letting yourself get involved with me is your decision. You've made up your mind you don't want to take a chance on being happy. You're content to spend the rest of your life blaming Earl for your unhappiness."

His harshness took her breath away. She blinked, trying to clear her mind.

"I have to protect myself," she quavered. "I can never go through that again."

He leaned over the table toward her, only inches away from her face, resting his weight on his knuckles. "Bullshit."

She looked up at his furious face, his throbbing temples. She bit her upper lip and nervously glanced away.

Kevin's white Subaru pulled up to the cabin.

J straightened, eyeing her.

"I've got to go." She stood and again turned to pack milk and jelly into the grocery box.

Kevin came to the open door.

"Hi, Kevin." She forced herself to sound casual. "I'm ready to go. My pack and sleeping bag's on the porch, and groceries are in this box. We'll have to sort them out, put some things in the cooler."

Kevin stepped in and took the box from her. He nodded to J. "Hi, J."

J returned the greeting with a curt nod.

Kevin returned to the car and began sorting the groceries. He glanced up and noticed Corrie on the porch, holding her sleeping bag and pack. He opened the back door for her and climbed behind the wheel to wait in the car with Al.

Corrie started down the steps.

J spoke quietly. "Corrie, you're being foolish."

Corrie stopped, dropped her head, then slowly turned to face him, her gaze steady.

"I'm going. See you Sunday night."

"I don't know about that."

Her startled eyes swept up to his angry face. Was that a threat? She refused to ask what he meant, and continued on. She had almost reached the car when he called her name.

"Corrie?"

She tossed her pack and sleeping bag into the back seat. He called again.

"Corrie!"

Reluctantly, she raised her eyes toward him, clearly irritated.

"Do you remember where my brother lives?"

The question surprised her. "Yes, in Randle."

"Do you remember where in Randle?"

"South of town."

He nodded.

Corrie punched her sleeping bag aside and slid into the back seat beside it. She slammed the door.

J briskly walked to the car. He leaned over and placed his big hands on the open window frame on Kevin's side. "Kevin, is this necessary?"

"Necessary? I don't know what you mean by `necessary' but it's what we're going to do."

"Do you know about that bulge?"

"Sure we know about it. That's why we're going. J, this is what I do. I'm a reporter. I go where the action is. I can't write about things unless I can see them happening. You couldn't pay me enough money to do the stuff you do, ride broncs and wrestle cows. I don't like broken bones. I get paid to write."

"Okay, but do you have to risk other people's lives too?"

"Now wait a minute. I haven't twisted anyone's arm here." He turned to Corrie in the back seat. "Corrie, do you still want to go?"

"Yes," she answered through clenched teeth.

J mustered great restraint. "Kevin, I have a brother in Randle. If you need to, call on him. Corrie knows where he lives."

"Okay, thanks."

"Do you have any idea where you're going to set up camp?" His voice showed his doubt that these guys were that well organized.

"Yeah, we've camped there before. A place called Bear, something."

"Do you have a map?"

"Sure." Al pulled the crude logger's road map out of the glove box and handed it to Kevin.

"My God," J muttered when he saw it. "Okay, where?"

Kevin studied the map. "Al, where was that place?"

Al leaned over Kevin's shoulder. "Right in there someplace." He pointed a yellowed cigarette-stained finger to the area.

"Bear Meadow," J nodded.

"Do you know Bear Meadow?" Kevin asked.

"I grew up near Randle. Mount St. Helens was my back yard. I've hunted and fished around there for years."

Kevin looked impressed. "You're welcome to join us, J."

J shook his head. "No, I don't think it's a good idea, for anyone." His steely blue-gray eyes glowered at each in turn, settling on Kevin. "You're playing with fire, Kevin."

"Let's hope so," Kevin laughed as he started the car.

J stepped back. As they drove off they heard "Stupid-assed fools," from the still opened window.

When they were out of J's sight, Corrie's eyes met Kevin's in the rear view mirror. Kevin had never seen her any way but cheerful, but now she knew her face was red and blotchy.

"Corrie, is everything all right? Do you still want to go?"

"Yes, I do, Kevin." She wiped her eyes with the back of her fingers. "It's my fault J's a little upset. I didn't tell him beforehand we were going." It was an outrageous understatement, but she hadn't yet figured it out herself.

"Okay. You're a grown woman, you ought to know what you want to do. Let's go give that mountain what-for."

Chapter Twenty-One

AS I SEE IT
Kevin Walsh
Clearwater News staff columnist

May 16, 1980. No explosions have been reported on Mount St. Helens in recent days, although steam has been emanating from the summit area. USGS Geologist Dave Johnston tells me the shape of the volcano has changed considerably during the past 10 days. The north and northwest rims of the crater have huge cracks filled with snow and ash. The area appears to be moving downward as a mass, toward the crater. The bulge now appears quite broken and distorted.

Before dawn this morning the Department of Energy personnel made an aerial infrared survey of the mountain. The results of the data will be available on Monday.

The sunny day, the view, and the companionship were lost on Corrie. Her anger at J consumed her. She managed to answer with civility when directly spoken to, but inside she seethed. Who did he think he was, dictating to her like that? For months, she had made it perfectly plain that she only wanted to be friends.

He said he loved her.

Despite her anger, her mind nibbled on how she would, or rather could, fit into J's family. Gretchen finally seemed to accept her; Chad was fine. No, wait. Nothing had changed, she simply could not become involved again.

She realized Kevin had called her name more than once.

"Sorry. I let my mind wander and it never came back."

Kevin chuckled at her joke. "I asked if you wanted to set up camp before we explored around."

"Sure. Let's. We can claim our spot and then we'll know we have something to come back to. I didn't have a chance to make sandwiches, but we have the fixings."

She didn't have a chance because that stupid J barged in at the wrong time. Well, she had to forget him and pay attention to the here and now. She would not allow herself to be a wet blanket. It wasn't these guys' fault that J was being such a jerk.

As before, they drove directly to the unsecured backcountry logging roads. A Jeep turned onto the road just before they did and they waved to one another.

"It's funny," Al said, "it's as though we're all in this together, like old friends."

They made their way to Bear Meadow. The roads were still rutted in places. It had been a long time since these roads had had any maintenance, but Kevin managed to navigate without too much trouble.

They were relieved when they again had Bear Meadow to themselves. The woodsy essence of a nearby campfire told them that someone was nearby, but the forest was so dense they couldn't see another camp or even their fire. From this ridge top, ten miles from the peak of the mountain, it was a straight shot to the newly formed crater. The mountain loomed over them, dark and sinister, blackened with ash. Was it just her dark mood, or was it more threatening this time?

Kevin and Al pitched the tent while Corrie arranged the cooking gear. They had the routine down pat. "I'll go ahead and put sandwiches together and we can eat before we take off, okay?"

"Sounds good," Kevin grunted as he tried to straighten the center pole.

Corrie built deli sandwiches and set them out with potato chips and apples, a soft drink for her and beer for the fellows, thankful that her companions were easy to please. As Kevin had said at an earlier time, camping was simply a means for the story and for Al's pictures.

Try to tell J that, she grumbled to herself. His angry face, especially the scene at the kitchen table when he'd been only inches away, forced all other thoughts from her mind. She shook her head, trying to clear away the gloom.

They quickly consumed lunch and cleaned up the mess, mindful that there could be bears in the area.

"Let's go up to Ryan Lake and see if Arnie and those guys are there," Al suggested as they piled back into the Subaru.

Much to Corrie's surprise, the same five people were there and had packed in as before. They laughed at the coincidence and shook hands. These people hadn't been back here since they'd first met on that April weekend either. Corrie sought out Arnie, the fellow she had talked to the last time, who reminded her of J. Again, he was tending the stock, five handsome horses and a pack-mule. "How's your wife? Isn't she about due to have that baby?"

"Yeah, in a couple of weeks. Her sister is giving her a baby shower at our house. I didn't think I could take a house full of women so I came with these guys." He looked a little wistful, as though he wished he were at home with his wife.

Corrie admired the ease with which Kevin talked with people. She understood why he was such a good reporter. He gained people's confidence with his easy, relaxed manner. Al quietly went about taking pictures of the people, the scenery, and the horses.

Later, they made their way back to their Bear Meadow camp, eager to get away from the ash which, other than a fine dusting, had not yet accumulated in quantities there.

Al began collecting small, dried branches. "We're having steaks tonight?"

Kevin reached in the trunk of the car. "Yeah, they're in the cooler."

Corrie rummaged around in the grocery box. "I've brought potatoes to bake in the coals and I'll slice tomatoes."

Al started the fire and cracked open a beer for himself, offering Kevin and Corrie the same.

Corrie sat down near the fire, soothed by the mindless flames, sipping her beer.

Al gently elbowed her. "How ya doing?"

"Okay, I guess. I don't like arguments. I've never even seen J that mad before, let alone at me." She hugged her knees.

"He looked pissed all right."

Corrie nodded, her lips compressed. "When they're working, he yells a bit, but it's just a momentary thing. But today...." She shook her head, wanting to forget the memory. "Well, I won't let it spoil our time this weekend." She picked up a stick and toyed with it at the fire's edge.

Kevin dropped a load of firewood and joined them. "Corrie, if you need to talk, do it."

"No, that's all right." The kitchen scene flashed through her mind. "I've told him all along I can never get involved again. And now look." She poked the fire savagely with the stick, scattering coals.

Kevin patiently rearranged the coals. "I think J showed a lot of guts in letting you know how he feels."

Al nodded.

Corrie wasn't comforted. "Yeah, well, he can just keep his feelings to himself."

The coals glowed and Corrie, using tongs, turned the foil-wrapped potatoes. Finally, it was time to cook the meat, and they busied themselves with the meal. Determined not to spoil the others' trip, she refrained from mentioning the issue again that evening.

Which, unfortunately, didn't end her misery. It was late by the time they finished dinner and cleaned up. A velvet darkness settled around them, capped with a twinkling starlit sky. They sat by the fire for a while, then doused the hot coals and crawled into their sleeping bags.

Sleep eluded Corrie for a long time. When she closed her eyes, she saw J's face, sometimes angry, sometimes smiling. She relived the dinner they'd given for Nancy and Roger the previous weekend. J had shown such contentment and pleasure. Her skin warmed with the memory of his gentle kiss. But then she recalled his anger this morning when he'd leaned across the table, glaring.

She tenaciously held on to her right to be at Mount St. Helens. Even if they had an understanding of some kind, there was nothing wrong in her being there.

But were they talking about rights, or concern? Whatever. She was there. She tossed and turned, afraid she would disturb the others. Apparently she didn't bother Al. He snored in the darkness.

Corrie awoke next morning to the sound of Al tinkering with his Nikon and 500mm lens, mounted on a tripod. The lens, about eight inches across, dwarfed the camera. An Olympus hung from a strap around his neck. The inevitable cigarette drooped from his lips.

She crawled out of her sleeping bag and carefully made her way out of the tent so as not to wake Kevin.

Al proudly stood aside. "Have a look."

Corrie bent over the viewfinder. "Wow! What a great picture that will make. I see what you mean about the lighting at dawn. Everything looks so crisp. Why is that?"

"When the sun is at a low angle, like early morning and evening, the atmosphere filters out the blues, enhances the reds and makes the colors appear more brilliant. That's why the green trees are so bright now and evening sunsets appear red."

She stepped back to let him begin taking pictures, knowing he would use many rolls of film. He told her sometimes out of twenty-four pictures, only one might be worthy of consideration for publication.

Corrie put on a pot of coffee and searched through their breakfast things. They'd have scrambled eggs with croissants.

Al looked up from his camera. "Want me to build a fire?"

"No, I'll use the camp stove. Don't you think we'll be going to Spirit Lake soon after breakfast?"

"Probably."

Kevin joined them, stretching hugely and patting his ample stomach. He'd slipped on walking shorts and a Hawaiian shirt. "Coffee smells good."

After breakfast the three piled into Kevin's car and went off in search of adventure. As before,

Corrie was taken with the area's beauty. Fully green now in many places, the forest burst with life, though in shaded areas crusty snow banks persisted and in the higher elevations snow still covered the ground. Ash covered some exposed areas, taking away from the lush beauty.

By this time, they had certain haunts they liked to check out, plus they wanted to go to Harry Truman's place and interview Spirit Lake residents. Driving the back roads, they tracked down the caravan consisting of thirty-five Spirit Lake property owners and a few reporters.

Although relieved they could finally retrieve belongings, the property owners were angry they had been denied access to their own homes. As Kevin interviewed a few of them, they repeatedly expressed their profound disappointment in the condition of the mountain. Many of them had owned their property for years, for generations even, and now these cherished vacation homes were threatened.

When they reached Spirit Lake Corrie and her friends were sobered by the condition of the properties. Porch roofs sagged with the heavy ash fall resulting from constant small eruptions from the north side of the mountain. It smothered grass and small shrubbery, tree branches drooped from the weight of the heavy stuff. There seemed to be an eerie silence about the place. People hurriedly loaded their belongings, and left.

Corrie brushed her Levi's, then wiped her gritty hands together. "What is this ash? Why does it keep falling?"

Kevin picked up a handful and let it sift through his fingers. "Dave Johnston told me it's particles of lava. Mount St. Helens is a relatively new mountain and is formed by layers of cinders and lava that built up, erupted, and fell back down around the cone. They call it a stratovolcano, which means layers. These small eruptions keep sending ash out of that new crater. It's surprisingly heavy. Dave says it weighs thirteen and a half pounds per gallon."

Al carefully put his camera back in its case, blowing away the ash. "I don't care if I come to Spirit Lake again. This place is a downer."

"Even the poor trees look depressed," Corrie observed, "weighted down with this stuff."

Kevin nodded. "Yeah, I agree. Dispiriting." He grinned, but the others groaned at the pun.

They drove over to Harry Truman's Spirit Lake Lodge but didn't find Truman. Corrie observed the bleak surroundings. "That's okay. I couldn't stomach another one of his bourbon and cokes."

Kevin observed her, humor in his eyes. "You don't have to drink it."

"I wouldn't want to be rude." She grinned.

Although the day and the company were pleasant, Corrie's frame of mind churned, uneasy and troubled, unable to dismiss the episode with J. At times she buried her concerns, yet they were never far from the surface.

Later, after a grilled hamburger dinner, they sat close to the fire as the evening chill settled around them. After getting little sleep the night before, Corrie's spirits sagged, her heart heavy.

Kevin saw the far-away look in her eyes. "How's it going?"

"Okay, but I can't seem to get anything resolved in my head."

Surprisingly, Al offered a suggestion. "Sometimes, when I can't decide something, I play-act, pretend I've already done it, and see how it feels."

Corrie nodded. "I might try that."

She poured herself another cup of coffee. "I don't understand why J was so angry."

Kevin held up his hand, turning down the offer of more coffee. "I think he feels there's a certain amount of risk here. He wants you to be safe."

"I guess. But this mountain is crawling with people. I can't get too excited about the danger of it."

Al shook his head. "Apparently the State thinks it's unsafe or they wouldn't be restricting visitors. Remember, we're not supposed to be here, either."

Kevin thought a minute. "I can imagine J isn't wild about you going off with us."

"Kevin, he knows there's nothing to this except friendship. We've discussed that. Besides, I told you, he and I aren't actually involved."

Al stretched and yawned. "Night-night."

Kevin continued to sit with Corrie a while longer. After a few minutes of silence, she shared her thoughts with Kevin.

"J thinks I'm using Earl, my ex, as an excuse not to get involved again."

"Seems to me the real issue is what you think about J. But it's your life, Corrie. I don't want to influence you one way or another."

With that, Kevin stood, put his coffee cup by their gear and bent over to climb into the tent. She heard him zip up his sleeping bag.

Left to herself, Corrie hung her head, deep in thought. She had to figure this out. Her life had become such a jigsaw puzzle. With missing pieces.

She'd do what Al suggested. Okay. She dismissed J from her life. That would probably mean she'd have to move. There would be no way she could still live at the ranch.

Corrie sat for a long while, engulfed in despair. She didn't think she could stand not seeing him, at least. Even though she'd resisted it, he'd become a part of her life. They could never go back to how it was a few weeks ago, only casual friends. They'd gone too far for that. Wrapping her arms across her chest, she shivered, then remembered the warmth of J's embrace. Face it, she couldn't bear not to be near him.

But maybe now she didn't have a choice. He was so angry. What did he mean, `I don't know about that,' when she said she'd see him Sunday night? Did he mean he didn't know if she'd be back, or that he wouldn't welcome her back?

Her mind flashed on something she had seen a couple of years before in her Seattle neighborhood. Someone's belongings in boxes and plastic bags were stacked on a porch. It had seemed so stark to Corrie, so cold. They'd had a fight, she assumed, and someone got kicked out. The items had remained for two days, and then disappeared. Corrie imagined the hurt and anger involved.

I wonder if J is that mad. Will I go home and find my things packed and waiting for me? Oh, my God. What have I done?

She hadn't been fair, not to herself and especially not to J, even though she'd tried to be honest. He'd welcomed her into his life, well, eventually anyway. He'd even shared with her how he felt. But she'd wanted it both ways. Trying to protect herself, she had withheld her love, but still allowed him to hope. No, that wasn't true. She'd told him over and over how she felt, how she could never again become involved. Then she had no business spending time with him, knowing what he needed.

He loves me.

The thought filled her heart with joy, and she smiled. But her internal battle raged. She rehashed again why she couldn't allow herself to fall in love. The old anger rushed in, bitterness and resentment gripped her soul. Anger.

Lord, help me to get rid of this anger. I'm sick of it. It's killing me. Maybe if I.. no. But maybe. She ran her fingers through her hair, then held her head in her hands, forcing herself to look at the anger.

The image of Earl's face during their last visit surfaced and his need to be forgiven.

She'd told Earl she forgave him, but they both knew she didn't mean it. Does forgiving mean taking Earl back? She couldn't, knowing she could never trust him again. Since taking him back was out of the question, did that mean she didn't forgive him? In a way, it would be simpler if he were still with Megan, then that wouldn't be an issue.

She would forgive him, but not go back to him. There was no love there, she could no longer be with Earl. But she could forgive him by going on with her life, allowing herself happiness. She had thought she could be happy being alone, but now that she'd met J, she could no longer settle for that.

What about getting hurt again? Could she take that chance? Corrie scrambled to her feet, feeling too antsy to sit. She circled the fire pit, feeling trapped in her own body, then sat again. It was too dark to wander around.

She tried to imagine J being unfaithful to her. She felt certain it would never happen. It was unreasonable for her to give up happiness with J because of something that happened between Earl and her.

She sighed.

J was right. She had been blaming Earl for her decision to remain alone. She honestly thought she'd made the right decision, but it wasn't. Not if being alone was what she no longer wanted to do.

J was so eager and ready for marriage. He'd told her that he'd been waiting for the right person, and she knew he meant her. He'd been alone for a long time. He was gentle and kind, yet a real man. He was everything she loved in a man.

She thought of Gretchen and how their relationship had blossomed. She doubted if Gretch would be an obstacle, or an excuse.

What in the world had been her problem? Her fear had blinded her to what she could have.

For a moment she felt better, joyous even, but then her spirits plunged again.

Maybe now J wouldn't want her. He'd probably given up on her. He had every reason to think she was an angry, bitter woman. Coming up here didn't help. He thought she was foolish.

Her stomach knotted. She thought again of her things bundled up on the porch and shuddered.

She imagined herself in his strong arms, tucked in under his chin. The image was so real she sensed he was there, with her. She loved his outdoorsy smell, the blend of horses, fresh hay, him.

She wanted to be with J. Life without him would be horrible. She loved him. There, she'd admitted it.

Comfort warmed her breast. Tears sprang to her eyes. She experienced a peace she hadn't felt in years.

What she wanted right then was to get off that damn mountain and go home. She couldn't wait to go home.

She sighed.

She hoped Kevin and Al wouldn't want to stay late Sunday. She would encourage breaking camp right after lunch, maybe even after breakfast. Al could get his morning pictures, they could do a little more sight-seeing and go home. She thought they'd all had enough of this dingy mountain.

A remaining piece of glowing wood collapsed, making a soft puffing sound and reducing the fire to coal fragments and ash. Corrie scooted closer and hugged her knees against her chest, trying to keep warm. Blackness and soft night noises settled in around her.

Her mind soared with her thoughts of newly found freedom. She could be happy, happy with J. Fear rose again. Was it too late? She needed to go home and talk to J. She had to tell him how she felt. She ached with her need to be with him, to go home.

Chapter Twenty-Two

*A*fter Corrie left, J stormed into the barn and paced the length of it, pounding on a door jamb with his fist, then swearing with the pain of it. "Son of a bitch! What the hell is the matter with her?"

Eventually, as he groomed Nick, he calmed himself. He hung the curry brush back on its peg then slumped onto a bale of hay, regretting their last words had been spoken in anger.

Later Friday evening, he stopped by her cabin. He found Bo lingering on the porch and let him in. Although he felt a little guilty entering, he had such a strong need to be near her things, he did it anyway. He noticed the fallen yellow daffodil petal on the kitchen table. It looked like he felt, dejected and forsaken. He settled in her rocking chair, turned off the light, and sat in the dark, blinking back tears. The dog sat by his side, also sad and lonely, his big head on J's knee.

He berated himself. Way to go, J. The first time you tell her you love her is when you're yelling at her, telling her not to do something she wants to do. Great timing, fella. He shook his head in disgust.

Bo plunked down at his feet and sighed deeply. J reached down to pet the dog. "I know, big guy. I screwed up."

He sat, elbows on his knees, hands holding his head. He'd had no right to talk to her like that, to show her that kind of anger. It was just that he'd been so scared she would go. And she did. He could have been more gentle about it, told her he was worried, rather than act like he was bossing her around.

He slowly stood. Gretch was probably waiting for him to say goodnight. Opening the door, he let the dog out. Bo circled his big pillow on the porch and with a dejected sigh, collapsed on his bed.

J woke early Saturday morning with a huge knot in his stomach. He couldn't shake a feeling of doom. He tossed and turned, twisting the sheets. It was past time he got up anyway. He climbed out of bed and absently looked out his bedroom window toward her cabin. In the half-light it stood empty and forlorn. He watched as Moe walked toward the cabin, entered and came back out with a bowl of food for the dog. The old man again walked inside, carrying the dog's water bucket and in a moment was out again with a full pail.

His mind raced. Get busy, there was work to do. Get those kids up and ready for the day. Find out what Gretch's plans are, have Chad clean up that calving barn. It had been a mess since roundup.

The morning dragged on with J forcing himself to do mundane chores. He sat at the kitchen table, trying to concentrate on writing checks, a stack of bills before him. Gretchen practiced her piano lesson. Usually her music pleased him but this morning he found it irritating. How many times was she going to play that passage, anyway?

Chad pounded up the back steps and slammed into the kitchen. "What's this about you letting Corrie go to Mount St. Helens?"

The piano abruptly silenced and Gretchen rushed into the kitchen. "What? What did you say?"

J glared at Chad. "What do you mean, I 'let her.' I don't have any control over Corrie."

"Moe said you tried to stop her but couldn't."

Gretchen stood in the kitchen doorway, her eyes huge with concern. "Dad! That mountain isn't safe. My geography teacher said it was gonna blow up any day! Why would she want to do that? Why would you let her?"

J put down his pen and looked at his agitated nephew and distraught daughter. "What makes you two think Corrie needs my permission?"

Gretchen looked at him in disbelief. "But she would listen to you."

"But she didn't."

Chad sank into a kitchen chair. "I can't believe you just let her go."

"Just how do you think I could have stopped her?" The knot in his stomach wouldn't let up. A feeling of urgency consumed him. Looking at their worried faces, he knew what he had to do.

"Okay. I'll go get her, bring her back."

Chad sprang to attention and slapped the kitchen table. "All right! Can I go with you?"

"Me, too?"

"No, I need you guys to stay right here. I have enough to worry about without having two more people on that mountain." He looked at Gretchen.

"Gretch, you'll have to cancel your plans for tonight."

"Dad, you said—"

"I know, honey, but I need to know you guys are here, safe. I need to have a clear mind and I can't if I don't know just where you are."

He could see her slump with disappointment. She'd looked forward to going out after the long two-week restriction. But then she straightened up and looked directly into his eyes.

"It's okay, Dad. I'll call Pam. Just bring Corrie back."

Chad's eyes brightened and he nodded. "We'll take care of everything, Unc. Just go."

"I'll be at Rick's tonight. By the time I get there, it'll probably be too late to go to the mountain. If you need anything, call there."

J phoned his brother.

"Rick. J. Are your mules there?"

"Sure are. You wanna talk to 'em?"

J wasn't in a jovial mood.

"You going packin'?"

"Maybe. I'll need a string of four, don't let anyone take 'em." Rick maintained two strings of mules and rented them out to packers. "I'll be there in a few hours."

J threw clothes and equipment into saddlebags, tossed them into his truck, hung his 30-30 on the gun rack, and left.

On the trip to Randle his mind whirled. Had he gone crazy? No, those kids were worried too. He couldn't imagine how he would pull it off, talking Corrie into leaving, but somehow, he'd have to find a way. What if she refused? The way they'd parted, he could hardly blame her. At least the tension in his stomach eased a bit. Doing something helped.

He thought of her smile, her warm eyes that had such depth, her sweet gentle ways. She fit in so naturally. He loved her eagerness to learn about ranching. He'd never known anyone who tried harder than Corrie. She had so much energy, so much life.

But my God, she could be stubborn.

He wondered if he'd ruined whatever chances they had.

She had so much courage in other areas of her life, but her hurt was so deep she no longer trusted even herself when it came to love.

He'd been out of line, talking to her like that. Somehow he'd find a way to help her get over her fear of love. If it took a lifetime, he'd find a way.

Fear gnawed at his gut, fear for her safety. At least he was doing something. By that night, he'd be closer to her.

By the time he arrived at Rick's, he'd almost convinced himself there was still time to go to the mountain.

Rick shook his head. "Bro, I think it would be a mistake. By the time you get up there it'll be dark and it would be too tough to find 'em. Why don't you get a good night's rest and go out in the morning?"

J sighed, then nodded. "You're probably right. Even if I did find her, we'd be traveling in the dark to get back."

"Come on in the house. Barbara has chicken fryin'."

* * *

Corrie woke Sunday morning longing to be with J. Kevin and Al were already up, tinkering around camp. She eagerly crawled out of her sleeping bag, rolled it up and slipped on her jeans and a clean red, long-sleeved cotton shirt. Glad they were going home today, she could hardly wait. At the first opportunity, she'd suggest they break camp right after lunch. Earlier would be better, but she knew the men wanted to make the most of the trip.

The sun shone this flawless morning, bright and warm. As Corrie emerged from the tent, Al signaled her to take a look through the viewfinder of his Nikon, mounted on its tripod, focused on Mount St. Helens.

She looked through the viewfinder. "It's an amazing view, isn't it?"

Kevin handed her a steaming cup of coffee.

Corrie almost whispered. "It's so quiet."

Kevin nodded.

They ate a simple breakfast of cold cereal and bananas.

Al gulped his breakfast and hurried back to his camera. He suddenly shouted. "Oh, my God. Look!" He began to take pictures furiously.

Shocked, Corrie and Kevin stared at the mountain.

As if in slow motion, the entire north side of Mount St. Helens collapsed into itself. A roiling, frothy, brown mass slid downward.

While Al frantically shot the scene, Corrie and Kevin watched in horrified fascination at the crumbling mountain. At one point Al stopped and looked away. "That motion makes me seasick."

A giant mushroom cloud began to form, exponentially increasing, a pulsating evil mass, billowing out to encompass all that surrounded it.

Corrie cocked her head. "It isn't making any sound. How can that be?"

Kevin and Corrie noticed it at the same instant: The menacing, huge black cloud rolled, boiled, churned toward them.

Corrie's stomach clenched at the thought of being swallowed by that monstrous cloud. It wasn't like a vaporous storm cloud, it appeared heavy and solidly dark, a killer cloud.

Kevin sprang to action. "Let's get out of here. Come on!"

Al was intent on taking as many pictures as he possibly could. "Okay, okay, just a minute. I want to finish this roll."

Darkness from the cloud threatened to engulf them. Corrie made a dive into the tent for her daypack that she'd stuffed into her large one. She had packed a few emergency items for their day excursions, container of water, a few candy bars and first aid supplies.

As she reached into the tent, the first rocks pelted her back. Startled, she cried out in shock and jerked her head back out only to be struck on her cheek with a jagged piece of pumice about the size of a baseball. She yelped. It wasn't a deep cut but it drew blood.

Rocks and debris rained from the dark mass with alarming force. Al hunched over his camera and continued taking pictures, but visibility rapidly diminished. The mountain became shroud-ed with the ugly ash cloud, turning everything it covered into a black hell.

Kevin yelled at them. "Come on! We've got to get out of here!" With the last shred of light, he pulled the tent stakes out of the ground and wadded the whole works together, stuffing it into the back of his car.

Al shielded his camera with his body as he frantically broke down the tripod and placed the Nikon in his camera bag. He threw the tripod into the back of the car and climbed in after it, clutching the camera bag to his chest.

Kevin started the Sabaru as Corrie jumped into the front seat. Rocks and debris pelted the car.

Kevin turned to peer out the rear window so that he could turn the car around. "Oh, my God. Oh, my God! Al, I can't see anything. Check to see if I'm clear."

Al jumped out of the car, glanced back, and dove back in, ducking pelting rocks. "You've got about five feet."

Kevin managed to turn the car around and pointed it back down the logging road, their only route to safety. Terror filled Corrie's heart. Would they make it in time? How bad was it down this road?

* * *

At Rick's ranch near Randle, J, Rick, Barbara, and their youngest son Tim, finished a blueberry waffle breakfast. Waffles were one of Barbara's specialties, but this morning J hardly tasted them; his anxiety and dread almost consumed him. He shared his fears. "I just have a hunch, that's all. There's nothing saying it's going to blow today but I can't shake this feeling."

After breakfast J hurried out to check his truck and get ready to leave. He'd decided not to bother with the mules, just take the truck and go. The morning sparkled bright and beautiful, unlike his dark spirits.

He became aware of Rick's mules and horses in the corral. Two of the mules made such a racket, it sounded like something terrible was after them. The horses ran in circles, skittish, whinnying. Rick's bay mare trotted by. J blinked and took a second look. Ash dusted the horse's rump. As J watched, an accumulation of ash built up on the horse's shiny back.

He looked around him. Ash fell, like a soft rain.

He glanced up at the crisp blue sky. His eyes darted to the south. A huge dark menacing cloud, growing by the second, churned toward him.

"No. No!" he roared.

From inside the house Rick heard his brother and ran outside. "Good Lord, it's happening."

J ran to his truck and turned it around to hitch up Rick's stock trailer. There was no doubt about it now, he'd need those mules. Rick gathered the string of mules and loaded them into the trailer while J tossed in sacks of grain, saddles, water jugs, and pack equipment. He wasn't sure what he needed, he threw in everything he could think of.

Barbara ran out with a canvas bag of food and drink, things she had hastily thrown together.

She stretched up to kiss her brother-in-law's cheek. "Be careful."

J nodded and squeezed her arm.

He opened the truck door and turned to face Rick. "Thanks, brother." They embraced.

"You bring that girl back here." Rick's voice strained with emotion.

J climbed into his truck. "You bet."

Night fell from the daytime sky. It appeared as if it were a moonless midnight, rather than 8:55 a.m. As J sped down the streets of Randle, automatic streetlights blinked on.

Chapter Twenty-Three

*B*ear Meadow plunged into total darkness. Thunder clapped and orange lightning blazed through the sky, though there was no rain. The pelting of falling rocks against the car roof subsided, replaced by the thudding of steaming ice-and-mud-balls. That, too, abated and now all that could be seen was a heavy ash fall. The sulfur content stung their eyes and noses, even in the car.

The car window felt hot to the touch. Corrie felt as though she were suffocating. Hot stuffy air, heavy with ash, made breathing difficult. She pulled her shirt up to cover her nose.

They leaned forward, squinting, trying to see through the falling ash. Corrie, though she felt she were being roasted alive, shuddered. "I never dreamed it would be this bad."

Al leaned forward so far his head was between Corrie and Kevin in the front seat. "I can't believe how stupid we were to come here. What were we thinking?"

Kevin didn't seem to hear the conversation. It took all his concentration just to drive. To see the road at all, he had to lean out the window, using as his guide barely exposed blades of grass along the left side of the narrow road. The other side of the road dropped off. Corrie couldn't see the drop-off, but knew was there. Her skin prickled as though raw nerves had been exposed. They crept along. While on the way up, they'd heard the crunch of tires on dirt and rock, now they heard the whine of the car in low gear as they made their way downward and felt the rough jolt of tires bumping over unseen, rutty terrain. Outside, the ash muffled thunderclaps and all but obliterated the jagged lightning as it streaked across the sky.

* * *

J took the logging road he suspected they had chosen. Thankful he knew these back roads, he crawled along at a maddening pace, stopping frequently to clean out the truck's air filter. He regretted not bringing spare filters. He knew Rick had them, but he hadn't thought about the toll this ash would take on a vehicle. It was slow going, but he made progress. He fought panic for Corrie and the others.

Where were they? Did they stay at Bear Meadow like they planned? He hoped so. He could probably reach Bear Meadow, but if they weren't there....

* * *

Kevin brought his head back into the car. Ash, forming mud, caked on his face and in his eyes. "I can't see." The wet ash smelled like damp cement.

The cooler sat perched on top of gear in the back seat. Al rummaged around and found a towel and swished it in the melted ice water at the bottom of the cooler. Kevin washed his face and then wrapped the towel around his nose and mouth. Al offered Kevin his reading glasses for eye protection. They continued their slow journey. The three hardly spoke, each with their private, terrified thoughts.

The car coughed and stalled. Corrie inwardly screamed. "I can't believe this!" she said aloud.

"Al, what's wrong?" Kevin cried. Al knew more about cars than Kevin.

"I think the ash is clogging the air filter."

"Can we fix it?"

"Probably. Pop the hood."

The three leaned over the engine. Kevin held the flashlight while Al removed the filter. He shook it out, banging it against his leg to dislodge the thick layer of ash, Al replaced the filter and they returned to the car, covered with ash. The engine started. Corrie breathed a sigh of relief.

They repeatedly had to stop to clean the air filter. The headlights now proved useless; ash covered the lenses as soon as they were cleared. The windshield wipers had long since ground to a halt.

* * *

J's tracking skills were of no help. Ash obliterated everything.

He strained to see through the windshield. Again, he stopped to clean the truck's air filter.

Before climbing back into the truck, he brushed off a thick accumulation of ash from the windshield. The stock trailer swayed as the mules shifted their weight. The forest looked unreal, lifeless, like he'd been caught in a time warp. His mind churned, trying to outguess unforeseen incidents.

Corrie, hang on, hang on. She was tough, sometimes he'd been surprised with how tough she was. Be tough now, Corrie.

* * *

Kevin's car skidded on the ash and swerved to the right, toward the drop off. Thrown forward, Corrie's forehead bumped against the dash. Her panic blocked any pain she might have felt. She hadn't worn her seatbelt, fearing she might be trapped should some nameless thing happen. Al was nearly thrown into the front seat. A small tree stopped the car from going farther down the steep drop off. In seconds, the car sank to its axle in pumice.

Al gingerly climbed out of the car and helped Corrie out. Attempting to climb the embankment to the road, she slipped in the ash, falling to her hands and knees. A cloud of ash engulfed her. She choked and coughed. Al helped her to stand and brushed her off.

Kevin joined them. "Looks like we'll be walking down this mountain."

Corrie turned toward the disabled car. "I'll get my daypack."

Al took her arm. "I'll get it." He got her pack and his camera bag. He slipped both over his shoulder and reached in the back for something to use as face coverings. He climbed back to the road and handed Corrie her pack.

Kevin removed the wet towel he had been using as a mask and both men tied tee-shirts across their noses and mouths. Corrie had a large handkerchief in her pack, which she used. The air was hot with falling ash and wearing face coverings seemed to make it even more difficult to breathe, but they knew it wasn't good for their lungs to inhale the ash. Corrie struggled into her pack.

Al slipped his jacket off. "Wait a minute. I want to wrap my camera. Here Corrie, hold my coat over us." They made a tent against the thick, falling ash as Al wrapped a shirt around the camera and film, and then securely zipped the bag.

Kevin crawled back down to the car and reached into the car's glove box for his flashlight.

He joined Corrie and Al on the dark road. "Okay, let's stay as close as we can."

Corrie's heart ached for Kevin. That car had been his pride and joy. She glanced back at the once-shiny white Subaru now covered with filth. Dents showed where it had been pelted with falling rocks. The front bumper rested against the small tree. If the tree gave way, the car would surely roll down into the ravine.

But worse than the loss of the car, was the loss of protection it offered. Now they were exposed to the elements.

Danger lurked everywhere. Would she ever see J again? She wished they'd listened to him.

Chapter Twenty-Four

*J*ust beyond Wakepitch Creek, J stopped again to clean the truck's air filter. He'd lost track of how many times he had done it. And again, he checked the mules. They appeared to be fine and, as usual, staunchly patient. He wiped ash from his watch. Three hours since he'd left his brother's place, a distance normally traveled in about a half hour. He climbed back into the truck and inched forward. Moments later he found a car blocking the road.

He reached for his flashlight and walked over to the empty car, a red 1978 Chevy sedan. He called out, but no one answered.

Strange, he hadn't seen anyone on the road. He could probably push the car out of the way, but driving was as slow as it would be with the mules. Time to leave the truck and trailer. From now on, he'd be hoofing it.

A short distance back he'd noticed a turnout. The truck engine whined in reverse as J slowly backed it and the trailer to the turnout. Even this simple task proved difficult in the murky darkness.

He unloaded the mules, tying each one to a tree until they were all out. He put handfuls of oats in nosebags and secured a bag around each mule's ears.

They'd better eat and drink now. No telling how long it would be before he could feed them again. He saddled three mules and packed grain, water, a chainsaw and gas can into canvas panniers and secured the packs onto the fourth animal. When he found Corrie and the others he'd distribute the load between the mules and ride the unsaddled one himself.

He ran a small breakaway line from each saddle and pack saddle, along the mules' rumps. If one mule slipped down a ravine or drop off, the small rope would easily break. For well-trained stock, as these were, he needed only this small line to lead them.

He watered the mules and took a few swallows himself. Sitting in the truck, he forced himself to eat the roast beef sandwich Barbara had packed for him, and then put the rest of the food into a saddlebag. He slipped his rifle into the scabbard and checked the saddlebag for extra ammunition. After tying his old Army-style canteen onto the saddle, he stood a moment. Had he forgotten anything? His flashlight. He fetched his three-cell flashlight from the truck and placed it within easy reach in the saddlebag.

Ash fell steadily. Would it never let up? It seemed to be even denser than before. Everything turned gray in the stark landscape. Scrounging around his truck, he found rags and draped them over the mules' noses, securing them to the bridles.

After mounting the largest mule, he tied his neckerchief over his own nose and mouth, clamped his hat securely, and set out.

About a half mile down the road, a heavy limb blocked his way. It must have fallen after that car passed. He unloaded the chainsaw from the pack animal and cut out a section large enough to pass through. They plodded past the opening into a strange, gray world.

* * *

Exhausted, fear sapping their strength, Corrie, Kevin and Al slogged along. Corrie struggled for breath. She heard Al's wheezing. Kevin, overweight and out of shape, huffed and puffed too. Ranch work had toughened Corrie and, of the three of them, she was in the best physical condition, but still found it hard to walk, like wading through deep sand. The heat of the ash penetrated their shoes.

Walking on the logging road was even tougher than it had been to drive on it earlier. The road's unevenness made it impossible to walk in steady strides. They constantly slipped into grooves, turning their ankles or stumbling over ruts. Occasionally one or another tripped and fell. It was slow, miserable going.

Tremors rumbled under their feet. Jagged lightning lit up the steel gray sky, and the countryside vibrated with frequent thunderclaps. Trees snapped and cracked, weighted down by the heavy ash. Eerie darkness, as though it were the edge of night, cut visibility to a few feet. They needed to conserve their flashlight; besides, it didn't do much good. The light bounced back, like car headlights in a dense fog. Nerves wore raw as their nightmare dragged on.

Much of their tension stemmed from the unknown. Would the mountain blow again? This time, the destruction could be even closer. What happened to the other people? They had seen no one, but had come upon several abandoned cars. Were they the only survivors?

Where birds had cheerfully warbled just yesterday, now only silence reigned in this drab bizarre place, punctuated by the occasional snap of branches and thunder claps. They heard no animal sounds at all, no rustling in the brush, no scolding from squirrels for territory invaded. The world was devoid of life, empty, forsaken, and profoundly dead. Where were the little critters like the frogs, squirrels, gophers? Where were the deer, the bear? Panic choked Corrie as she contemplated her own fate.

They said a few words to each other occasionally, but found the effort too strenuous to keep up. At one point Kevin said, his voice hoarse, "I've never really prayed before, but I'm giving it all I've got now."

Corrie stepped over a branch. "Me too. I've prayed a lot in my life, but I've never had to pray for my life. Kevin, let's rest for a couple of minutes."

They stopped but found no respite. They didn't want to sit in the hot ash and, anxious to get away, they pressed on, Kevin in the lead, Corrie in the middle, followed by Al.

Corrie thought of her daughter. If something happened, it would be so unfair to Gwen. My dear Gwen, I'm sorry. I'm so sorry. With a sinking heart she thought of Gretchen and what a terrible example she had set for that young, impressionable girl.

Her crotch itched and burned from the coarse ash. With every step, the chafing ash scoured her skin raw. Ash collected under her arms and her shoulders ached from trying to hold them away from her body.

In front of her, Kevin, lumbering along on the rough terrain, looked like the uniformly gray tin man from the Wizard of Oz. He wore shorts, and although he didn't complain, the ash must be sticking to the hair on his legs. At the very least, he must be feeling the heat even more than she.

Corrie heard a loud crack, then something suddenly shoved at her shoulder from behind. She staggered forward, stumbled, and fell face down. Her handkerchief slipped off and ash, tasting like chalk, filled her mouth. She fought to regain her breath, coughing and gagging. Her shoulder throbbed.

Kevin spun around and lurched back to her. He knelt and patted her back while she fought for breath. He looked around.

"Al!"

No answer.

He helped Corrie to her feet. "Are you all right?"

She gasped for breath. "I think so. Where's Al?"

They retraced their steps and stumbled into tree branches, raising clouds of swirling ash. Weighted down, a large limb from a Douglas fir had broken and fallen across the road, stirring up ash as it fell.

"Al!" Still no answer.

They stepped over the small branches, working their way to the larger limb. Corrie stepped on something soft. She bent over to look. Al's hand.

"Oh, my God. No. Al, no! Kevin, it's Al!" They tore at the small branches, but they couldn't move the large, main branch that had struck him. Kevin fumbled for his flashlight.

Al was dead. From the odd angle of his head, Corrie knew his neck was broken. He lay on his side, facing the sky, eyes closed and mouth open. Blood trickled from his mouth and ears. His face covering had slipped to his throat.

Feeling suddenly light-headed, Corrie feared she might faint. She knelt and reached for Al's hand while tears cut muddy tracks in the ash on her face. She stared at the body in disbelief.

"Something pushed me forward, Kevin. I don't know if Al did it or a limb. Kevin, I'm so sorry. I know what a good friend he was."

Kevin merely nodded, awkwardly patting Al's shoulder. His eyes filled with tears. With a shaking hand, he absently brushed away a small branch that scraped against Al's closed eyes. He gently pulled the camera bag off his friend's body, untangling it from small branches, and put it over his own shoulder. It had been Al's most prized possession.

Corrie didn't know if they had it in them to go on. Would this ash never stop falling? What would become of them? They could die on this mountain, too.

She reached over to brush Al's still face. She couldn't stop the ash from falling into his open mouth. It began to collect again, forming lumps around his eyes. Again she reached out to brush it away, but Kevin caught her wrist.

"Leave it."

"Should we try to get him out?"

"We can't lift this heavy branch, Corrie. We've got to keep going. I've no idea how much farther it is, but we have to get off this mountain."

"We can't just leave him."

"We have to. We can't carry him."

"But he'll be buried in ash!" To leave him horrified her.

"I know," he said, his voice cracking.

They knelt very close, both holding on to Al. Kevin squeezed his eyes closed. His furrowed forehead twitched. Corrie cried, painful, wracking sobs.

Kevin stood and pulled her to her feet. "Come on. Put your scarf on." He pulled his tee-shirt over his nose.

He carefully unfastened the tee-shirt Al had been using as a face covering, gently slipping it from around his neck. He tore a strip from it and, reaching as high as he could, tied the strip to a small branch, as a marker. He stood still, his head bowed. Corrie stepped beside him and took his arm.

Her voice was barely a whisper. "Lord, please take care of Al. Take him home with you."

She turned to Kevin. "Do you know the Lord's Prayer?"

Kevin nodded.

"Let's say it together, then. 'Our Father, who art in Heaven...'" They recited the prayer, their voices cracking.

They picked their way through the branches and resumed their laborious trek, heartsick and scared.

Corrie's mind whirled. Was this the end of the world? At Christ's crucifixion it turned dark too. Breathing came with greater difficulty. Had they been forsaken? Were they being punished for taking this kind of chance with their lives?

Limbs continued to snap off trees; at times a whole tree fell. An umbrella of branches covered the road; they never knew when it might happen again. Once, a tree fell only a few feet in front of them, making Corrie wonder what would have happened if they had been a few seconds farther down the road. They climbed over the fallen tree and proceeded on.The strong sulfuric sting and smell of the ash had lessened, but the density had not. If anything, ash seemed to fall heavier.

"Kevin?"

"What."

"If I don't make it," she gasped for breath, "will you tell J something for me?"

"Corrie, I don't want to hear that kind of talk." Corrie knew it was hard for Kevin to talk, too. His words were drawn out, his voice strained.

"Please."

Kevin sighed. A cloud of ash blew off of his scarf. "Tell him what?"

"I want you to tell him I love him and, well, just that."

Kevin stopped. In spite of their difficulties, through the dim light she saw his red-rimmed eyes soften, and even through his scarf Corrie knew he smiled; crinkles formed in the corners of his eyes.

"You got it sorted out, huh?"

She nodded. "Not too late, I hope."

He put his arm around her shoulders and gave her a squeeze. "All right, I'll tell him. Will you tell Joanne the same, that I love her? She knows it, but I want her to hear it again."

"Yes, I will."

Chapter Twenty-Five

J stopped again to clear a large pine branch from the logging road. At least it was small enough that he didn't have to use the chainsaw this time. As he struggled with the ash-laden debris, his chest hurt with the effort of breathing. He pulled the limb to one side and sat on it for a minute to catch his breath.

He was getting tired, and that wasn't good. He needed to conserve his strength. Returning to the mules, he took a long drink of water, and chewed on a piece of beef jerky.

He prayed for guidance in finding them, and for their safety. He mounted, gave a gentle tug to the lead mule, and continued.

The road climbed sharply here. J turned in his saddle to make sure the pack mule's load was secure.

A short distance off the road he heard twigs snap and branches thrash. The mules heard it, too, and J had his hands full with mules going every which way, kicking and snorting. The pack animal scraped against his leg, crowding him in her fear. The mule behind her tried to push between them; the fourth broke away, spun around, and thundered back the way they had come. J dismounted, managed to keep control of his mount and slip the lead rope in the halters of the other two.

A rank, musty scent reached his nostrils. Bear. The three mules, though spooked, allowed J to lead them back down the road where they had just been, away from the bear. He tied them to a tree. He'd look for the fourth one later.

He reached into the saddlebag for his flashlight and pulled his 30-30 out of the scabbard. His heart thudded, but he knew he couldn't coax these mules past that bear. He stepped off the road into the woods, straining to see. He quietly levered the action of his rifle to chamber a round, and, squeezing flashlight and barrel of the rifle in his left hand, he cautiously crept toward the sound. The bear remained quiet for a moment, then again resumed its thrashing, lumbering toward him.

He saw it then, a single black bear, now ghostly gray with ash. The bear raised itself on its hind feet, head held back, swaying, nostrils working, sorting out the smells of human and mule. The black bears in this region weren't especially large. On its hind legs, this bear stood a little shorter than J, roughly six feet, but it weighed perhaps 350 pounds. One front leg reached out, pawing the air, but the other hung loosely, in tatters. When the bear lowered to all fours, hide and fur hung along the injured leg.

The bear stopped and opened its mouth. J expected a loud roar and worried about the mules. Had he tied them securely? But the only sound from the bear's throat was a gurgle.

He didn't have much choice. He'd have to kill it. Years of hunting instinct took over. He drew a bead with the flashlight and rifle until he could get the shot he needed. The bear stood close, about fifteen feet away and although he couldn't see it well because of the ashy darkness, the bear's eyes reflected red from the flashlight. The light seemed to mesmerize the bear. It lurched toward J. Its good leg swung out, toed in; the injured front leg dragged.

It again opened its mouth wide and J fired one shot through the mouth to its brain. The bear dropped. J heard the mules prance and bray but he hoped they remained tied to the tree.

With caution, J made his way to the reeking bear. What had injured it? He drew near and saw it had been burned. It appeared that the leg and part of its side had been crushed by a heavy burning object, perhaps a tree. That explained why it hadn't growled, heat probably had seared its lungs.

Oh, Jesus. Where has this bear been? How far did it travel? Please, Lord, don't let something like this happen to Corrie. Don't let her get burned. Fear for her almost incapacitated him. He doubled over, unable to move. Then he drew himself up. His panic wouldn't do her any good.

Forcing his unsteady legs to move, he returned to the mules, calmed them, and then went in search of the fourth that had broken away. The mule stood a short distance down the road, and as J approached, it threw back its head, eyes rolling, but it didn't run away.

"Whoa, boy. Whoa. You're all right." J clipped a rope into the halter and led the nervous mule back to the others. He led the stock upwind from where the bear lay and then again readied them for the trail. His steady touch and murmuring voice soothed them.

He forged on. How much farther could they be? If they'd camped at Bear Meadow and were there during the eruption, he should be finding them by now. There were so many unanswered questions. What condition was the road farther up, near Bear Meadow? He knew he was on the best road, but would they know that? How far could they drive the car? Probably not far, there were so many tree branches down, to say nothing of abandoned cars blocking the road. What was the destruction at Bear Meadow? Was she all right? Was there fire? He forced himself not to dwell on that possibility. Other than with the bear, he'd seen no trace of fire.

Most of the obstructions were branches either small enough to go around or to move by hand. He'd had to use the saw a few times for larger ones, even for a couple of whole trees. The mules balked at tramping through branches, so he needed to give them clear footing.

Hours had passed. He rubbed his watch on his jeans and just barely made out the time. It was three already. He had to find them before dark. Even now it was tough to see. Night's darkness would make it impossible.

A huge limb blocked the road. Shit. He'd have to use the saw. Wearily, he dismounted and went to the pack mule for the chainsaw. He shook the saw to check the fuel level and made his way through the small branches to reach the main one. Something dangling from a branch caught his eye, a piece of cloth. He looked at it, puzzled, then continued. He leaned across the branch to clear away a spot for the cut when he spotted the body.

In slow motion he knelt down and, with a shaking hand, gingerly brushed away the ashes from the body's face. He shone his flashlight. "Al. It's Al!" He crashed through the length of the heavy limb, frantically searching for Corrie. Branches whipped his face and caught at his clothes. "Corrie! Corrie!"

Not finding her was a relief, relief that the limb hadn't fallen on her, too. But where could she be? They had to crawl through that mess to find Al, then continue down, he reasoned. He'd missed them, or they'd taken another road. What should he do? His gut told him to go back down the mountain, but he worried whether it was the right decision.

He turned the mules around on the narrow road, absently inspecting the pack animal's load and giving one of the pannier ties another hitch. All the while his mind whirled on the possibilities. He'd go back down and look for side roads they might have taken. It didn't make sense for them to go back up the mountain, and right here there were no other roads to take. He took off his hat and slapped it against his leg, then clamped it back on his head. He removed his neckerchief and shook it out. Securing it again, he mounted and began the descent down the mountain.

"By God, I'll find her if it's the last thing I do."

* * *

Corrie's parched throat ached. She remembered the water in her daypack "Let's stop for a drink of water and a candy bar."

She stood with her back to Kevin while he fumbled in her pack. They dropped the protective scarves covering their faces and took long swallows of water. Even warm, the water soothed their throats. The candy bars were soft; they split one. The sweet chocolate clogged her throat. Kevin returned the bottle and uneaten candy to the pack. They shook the ash from their scarves and tied them back on.

With supreme effort, they trudged on, their weary legs creating puffs of ash that drifted as high as their knees. Poor Kevin. Without long pants the ash was probably working its way into his socks. They were living a nightmare, the kind where it's a struggle to walk.

They stayed close to one another now that there were only the two of them. Even so, they had to walk along the road in separate, uneven ruts.

Talking was too difficult to even attempt. Anyway, what was there to say? Coming to Mount St. Helens when everyone knew it was on the verge of erupting was foolish beyond belief. Who did they think they were, trying to outsmart nature's wrath? Go through all this for a newspaper story? Had she done this to spite J? Well, look who got the worst of that.

It was several minutes before Corrie, lost in thought, heard a faint call. "Corrie!"

"Kevin!" She looked to where he had been walking beside her. He was gone.

"Corrie." She heard the faint call again.

She heard only part of Kevin's call: "...come back?" God, don't let her lose him. "Okay," she called. But it was risky. The ash quickly covered their tracks. "Keep talking."

Corrie retraced her last several steps. She heard nothing more from Kevin. A maze of trails converged here, a combination of deer trails and old logging roads. No doubt this was where they'd parted. She peered down a road he might have taken. She cupped her mouth, took a deep breath, preparing to call, but ash collected in her throat and she gagged. By the time she cleared her throat and called, there was no answer.

Fighting panic, she tried to think what to do. She knew that the banked road they had been following was the road they had traveled when they came in on Friday, the road that would lead them out. Thanks to J, she'd formed the habit of watching for landmarks, memorizing the lay of the land as she went along.

Corrie strained to see through the inky darkness in the direction Kevin might have gone. She must remember that spot. She'd find Kevin and then get back on the right road.

She bent two small branches, one above the other, as a marker.

Her heart pounded, fear crawled through every inch of her body. What if she couldn't find him? What would she do? "Kevin!" Silence surrounded her, broken only by her own raspy breathing and heavy footsteps. The world around her was padded, padded with ash. Alone. She was alone.

She had to find him. She'd walk down that road, for awhile at least, but then she'd have to turn back to get on the right road. How could he have disappeared so fast?

Corrie followed the second road for as long as she dared. It seemed the ash fell lighter than before, allowing her to see slightly greater distances. If Kevin had turned around and retraced his steps, they would have found each other by now. Should she turn around and go back to the original road or keep looking for him? She had to go back to that first, main road. There was no sense in both of them being lost. She reminded herself to look for the two broken branches, off to the right.

Fear gripped her, making breathing almost impossible. The world seemed to be closing in, yet she was lost in its vastness. Gray and lifeless, it was like walking on the moon. Alone.

She turned around to make her way back. She found a road leading off this one, but knew it wasn't the right one because there were no broken branch markers. Maybe Kevin had taken that road. She didn't dare try it, knowing she could become hopelessly lost.

She trudged on. Was it this far back? Please God, help her find the marker. When despair had almost convinced her she had somehow missed it, she found the two branches, now more heavily covered with ash. But there they were, two broken branches, one above the other.

A thrill of triumph rushed through her. She'd have to tell J. A lump clogged her throat. Would she ever see him again? Did he even know about the eruption? Anyway, would he even want to see her?

She reached up to touch the branches, to reassure herself of her small victory. Looking up, she tugged on the limbs. Ash dumped from the surrounding branches directly into her face, filling her eyes.

She shrieked a garbled scream and abruptly sat on the ground, covering her searing eyes with her hands. She didn't know how to begin to clear them, there was so much of it. She tried blinking but the sharp grit scratched her eyes. She shrugged off her pack and groped for her plastic water bottle. There it was. She shook it. Only a little bit left. She felt for the cap and opened the bottle. She held it up, aiming for her eyes. Water dribbled along the side of her face and into her ear.

Only a couple of swallows were left anyway; not enough to do any good. She needed to save it to drink.

She pressed her hands against her temples in an attempt to stop the pulsing, searing pain. Her agonized groans frightened her even more; they sounded like a stranger's.

She remained sitting, rocking in pain, under her two broken branches. She fought the urge to rub her fiery eyes; in any event, it would have been too painful.

Her entire body trembled. She would be blind. That is what she got for being so stubborn, so stupid, to come here. Her heart pounded in her ears as hot pain seared her eyes. Shaking hands tried to soothe them, but even the slightest pressure made her gasp in pain.

When Al died, she didn't think anything could be worse. Then, when she and Kevin became separated she knew raw fear, the fear of being alone in this nightmare. Now, unbelievably, the very worst thing had happened. She was all alone and blind. Her mind screamed in terror. All hope abandoned her.

Chapter Twenty-Six

*F*inally, Corrie was able to think, to rise above the consuming pain. She kept hoping that any minute she'd wake up from this terrifying nightmare. But she knew this was no dream. The searing pain in her eyes was real. Losing Kevin was real. Al died on this mountain and nothing could be more real than that. Now she was on her own, alone.

She shook her head, then shuddered with the pain. Even if she was blind, she had to get off the mountain. She had to keep going. Forming a plan cleared her head and calmed her. She still trembled, but the uncontrolled shaking stopped.

From her sitting position, she rolled to her hands and knees, and straightened to a kneeling position. Bracing herself, she stood, waiting for the light-headedness to pass. She turned to her right, groping her way with her feet, hands in front of her, expecting to fall at any minute. Sure enough, she stumbled and landed face-first in the ash. Slowly she picked herself up, but when her foot hit another rut she fell again. Sobbing, she knelt on the ground then sat back. She couldn't do it. She couldn't walk.

She began to crawl. Briars and sharp stones—probably pumice—tore at her hands and knees. The ash on the ground, though no longer hot, still retained heat.

She crawled a short distance when her right hand pressed on something sharp. She sucked in her breath with the pain and sat back to determine if it was something she could pluck out.

* * *

The mule behind J stopped and tugged on his arm. The other two mules halted behind her. J reined in and turned, trying to determine why she'd stopped. Seeing no reason, he gently urged the mule on.

"Come on, girl, it's all right."

The deep, familiar voice slowly penetrated Corrie's pain and despair. She cocked her head to listen. It was hard to hear above the sound of her heart pounding in her ears.

A soft clicking noise followed, like someone clicking his tongue inside his cheek.

J rounded a bend in the road and stopped. In the haze he could see something in the middle of the road. Was it another body? No, it was sitting upright and it moved.

Corrie strained to hear more. "H....hello?" Was she losing her mind? She tried to force her eyes open but it was useless, the ash had hardened over them.

J stood in the stirrups and leaned forward, straining to see. "Corrie? Is that you?"

"J? Thank God. J!"

He swung off the mule and ran to her, clouds of dust billowing around him. "Are you okay?"

Kneeling, he took her in his arms and held her close. She embraced him, too, but he noticed she stiffly held her head back. He gently took her shoulders and pulled her back to look at her face. It was filthy with ash. Around her closed eyes it had caked and cracked. Where her tears had oozed from the corners, the ash had set like cement. He winced. "Corrie, what happened?"

"I'm...I'm blind. I los...lost Kevin and ma.. made a marker and now..." she began to sob, fingering the mass of ash around her eyes.

"Hold on, Corrie. Hold on, now."

Both kneeling in the middle of the road, he put his arms around her, and rocked her back and forth. Stirred-up ash swirled around them. "Just try to be calm." Relief surged through him, a huge weight lifted from his heart.

"But, but, I'm bl...blind, J."

"Shhhh. What makes you think you're blind?"

"Because, I ca...can't see!"

"You sit tight. Don't move." He returned to the mules and quickly tied the lead mule to a small tree. Untying one of the panniers, he drew out the five-gallon water jug then hurried back to where she sat in the road.

He slipped off her pack. "All right. Now, Corrie, I'm going to pour a lot of water in your eyes. It won't feel very good. It'll probably hurt."

"It already hurts."

"This won't feel much better. But we need to wash that ash out."

He stooped in front of her with one knee on the ground, situating her so that her chin rested on his upright knee and her head tilted back.

He cupped his left hand around her head and balanced the jug on his right forearm. He spoke softly as he began pouring. "Okay, here goes."

She screamed and pulled back.

"Stop that," he snapped.

"Well it hurts."

"Of course it hurts." He put her head back on his knee. "Now hold still." He flushed her eyes repeatedly, gently pulling back her eyelids to further expose the eyes. She held still but clutched his leg so hard, she almost pulled him over.

"Okay, now can you see?"

She blinked. "Yes. Yes! I can see!" She looked up at him and gave him a bleary smile then burst into tears.

He let her cry, holding her close. Tears would help her eyes, and her heart. "What happened, Corrie? I know about Al, I found him, but where's Kevin?"

She told him about their separation and how she had tried to find him but then decided to return to the road. "Maybe I should have kept looking for him. I didn't know what to do," she sobbed.

"You did the right thing. You must have been on that other road when I passed by. You can tell me more later. We need to leave now. How are your eyes?"

"Gritty and sore, but not too bad." She shivered. "J...J, I need to talk to you. I'm..."

"Corrie, we have to get going. We'll talk later."
He brushed her lips with a light kiss and gave her
a gentle hug. He shook out her handkerchief and
tied it for her. He slipped his own neckerchief over
his nose and mouth.

She seemed in shock and he wanted to get
her off this mountain, but they still needed to
search for Kevin. Would this day never end? But
thank God he'd found her. Dirty, bedraggled,
exhausted, but, except for some scratched-up
eyes and hands, all right. Thank you, God, thank
you for helping me find her.

Holding her elbow and guiding her leg, he
helped her mount. "I'll lead your mule, so you can
rest your eyes." He returned the water jug and
added her pack to the pannier, then retied it to the
pack mule.

As they made their descent, J repeatedly
called out to Kevin. The effort seemed useless,
though, since the ash absorbed the calls and J
doubted if he could be heard more than a few feet.

When J dismounted to pull a fallen limb aside,
he spotted a figure staggering down the road.
"Kevin? It's J!"

The figure turned slowly and stumbled toward
them, teetering on the outside edges of his feet.

"J? Corrie? Am I glad to see you!"

J turned to Corrie. "Just stay put, Corrie. He
looks all right."

J took the few remaining steps toward Kevin.
He extended his hand and Kevin took J's in both
of his. J felt the man's exhaustion, his utter fatigue.

Kevin looked over at Corrie. "Corrie, I'm sorry. I don't know what happened. I'm sorry. I'm sorry." His voice cracked and tears flowed down his stricken face.

"That's okay, Kevin. I don't know what happened either. It wasn't your fault any more than mine. It just happened."

"Come on, we need to keep going." J helped Kevin mount. "I'll lead your mule, Kevin. You just rest. Now let's get the hell off this mountain."

They fell in line: J leading Corrie's mule, then Kevin's, followed by the pack animal.

"J, what are you doing here?" She'd finally come to the full realization that he was here, with her.

"Why, I came for you."

"All the way from Clearwater? Where did you get these mules?"

"No, I came to Randle Saturday. The mules are Rick's."

Though the ash fall continued, the world seemed a brighter place. At least in her heart. Their surroundings remained unchanged, gray and dismal. Ash coated her mule. Its ears occasionally twitched to knock it off. The dependable mules stoically trudged along. No doubt they suffered too. Their breathing seemed labored.

She turned to see how Kevin fared. He squirmed in the saddle, trying to get comfortable. "How far are we from your brother's?"

"About ten or twelve miles."

They plodded along, inky figures in thick ash-fog, the sure-footed mules picking their way over the rough road.

Although more restful than walking, riding was still hard work, sitting erect and ducking under drooping branches. Nevertheless, Corrie found it easier to breathe now that they didn't have to expend energy walking.

Despite her exhaustion, Corrie's heart warmed with joy. J had come for her. He'd rescued her. Lord, thank you, thank you. J didn't seem mad, though she might get a talking-to when they got home. Still, he'd come for her!

They encountered more fallen tree limbs and the mules walked around most of them, but J did have to cut one large limb with the chainsaw, stopping to clean its air filter half way through. They saw no other people, but came across an abandoned Jeep.

They made their way around the red Chevrolet J had passed before. But now only a small hint of red showed through. The car had inches of ash on it, piled like snow to its axle.

They reached J's truck and the stock trailer, covered with ash. Only a tiny ridge of blue showed near the top of the truck's windshield where ash had slid down. The truck was barely recognizable.

Through her bleary eyes Corrie noticed the truck and trailer pulled off the road. "J, that looks sort of like your truck."

"It is my truck. I left it here because of that car. I think we'd better stick with the mules rather than try to get the truck turned around. It's almost as slow anyway, with having to clean the air filter every few minutes. Besides, we don't know what's ahead and we might get stuck or blocked again by another car."

Corrie glanced at Kevin. He looked as though he might argue the point, but only shrugged. The decision was J's.

J swung out of the saddle. "Let's get down for a minute, have a drink of water and give the mules a break. Just for a minute or two. It's getting late."

Now that she felt safe, Corrie could joke. "Yeah, we don't want to get caught out here in the dark."

J chuckled. "This dark is weird all right. I'm looking forward to seeing daylight tomorrow."

Corrie paused. "I'm just looking forward to tomorrow."

While J checked the mules' tack, Kevin sidled up to Corrie and said softly, "I've always thought of J as some kind of hayseed cowboy, but man, I've gotta hand it to him. He's got guts. I've never been so glad to see anybody."

She nodded and started to reply, but J returned. She'd never in her life been so glad to see anybody, either. That it had been J was nothing less than a miracle. She needed to talk to him though, to tell him how she felt. Did he still feel the same toward her?

Chapter Twenty-Seven

*T*hey resumed their long trek to Rick's, mostly in silence. They came upon several more trees or large branches that J cleared. Kevin helped a time or two, but he was too exhausted to do much. Toward early evening, the ash fall subsided, making the rest of their journey more comfortable.

As they approached the ranch in the night's darkness, Rick, Barbara, and Tim ran out to meet them, wearing facemasks fashioned from coffee filters.

The weary travelers rode the mules right into the barn. Relieved to be out of the ash, Corrie breathed deeply, then coughed, her throat irritated and sensitive. Ash caked in every crevice of their bodies, nose, ears, inside their clothes. Their teeth were gritty, scratchy grime filled their eyes, their scalps were gooey from the stuff. They made futile gestures to brush off their clothing.

Barbara immediately collared Corrie. "Come on up to the house. Let me get you cleaned up."

Corrie was too tired to give more than a feeble argument. "Barbara, we'll make a mess of your house."

"Go," Rick and J ordered in unison.

J stepped over to Corrie. "Wait." With his finger under her chin, he gently tilted her face up and under the overhead light studied her red, swollen eyes. "Barb, Corrie's eyes need attention."

Barbara turned Corrie toward the light. "My word!" She pointed Corrie in the direction of the house and gave her a little push.

J introduced Kevin and briefly explained what had happened to Al. Kevin sat on a bale of hay, pale and shaken, his face lined with exhaustion and grief.

Rick nodded toward Kevin. "J, why don't you get Kevin brushed off and show him where the basement shower is? Maybe some of my clothes will fit him. I'll see to the stock."

J led Kevin to the house and took him to the basement.

Barbara helped Corrie undress on the back porch, leaving her filthy clothes in a heap. After a long, hot shower, Corrie dressed in Barbara's clothes, which were far from a perfect fit, too short in the pants, too wide in the waist, but a welcome relief from her own gritty clothes.

Barbara's nursing skills took over. "Here, lean over the kitchen sink so I can rinse your eyes." Satisfied that she had cleared them of ash, she slathered an ophthalmic ointment into them.

"You'll need to see a doctor as soon as possible, Corrie. Tomorrow I'll call Dr. Wesley. He'll be able to see if you have scratches that need treatment. You're lucky it wasn't worse."

"I thought I was blind until J rinsed them out." She shuddered and for a moment relived the terror and searing pain she'd experienced. Even now her eyes were uncomfortable and the ointment made everything blurry.

Barbara also applied an antibiotic ointment to Corrie's cuts and scratches. She examined her shoulder and found it badly bruised, but not seriously injured.

The household didn't settle down for several hours. Barbara had kept a hearty beef stew hot, waiting for them. They talked briefly, but realizing how tired they were, she suggested they rest now and talk more the next morning.

Corrie coughed again.

Barbara brought out her stethoscope and listened to both Corrie and Kevin's lungs, then talked J into sitting down to listen to his, too.

"I don't think any of you has a problem, but you should all see a doctor when you get home. I'm glad you kept your noses and mouths covered. Corrie, I think you've just irritated your throat. Let me give you cough drops."

They tried to call Chad and Gretchen and Kevin's Joanne in Clearwater. The telephones worked, but there were no trunk lines out of the area.

J hung up the receiver. "We'll try again first thing in the morning."

Barbara began to assign rooms. "Kevin, you use this room. That couch makes into a nice bed."

J broke in. "Corrie and I'll use the basement bedroom."

"All right," Barbara agreed. "Do you have everything you need? I'll get you a nightie, Corrie."

Although a little surprised at J's suggestion, Corrie merely followed him down the stairs, so tired she could barely manage the steps. J held up his hand to guide her.

As she stepped into the bathroom Corrie muttered, "I wonder how many miles I walked today." With supreme effort she changed into Barbara's old-fashioned, long flannel nightie. It was thin with age, white with faded tiny pink roses, with a lace-trimmed, stand-up collar.

J wore tee-shirt and shorts.

They climbed into bed. If she had been told even a week ago she would be climbing into bed with J, she would have scoffed. Now, with her new attitude and her exhaustion, it simply wasn't an issue. She needed his comfort, his closeness. She turned her battle-scarred face toward him. The bed stand light on his side of the bed made her tender eyes squint. He reached up and turned the lamp off. The light at her back was soft and comforting.

She reached out and put her hand on his muscular arm. "J, thank you for coming for us. I'm sorry I caused you so much worry. We never—"

"Shhhh, it's all right. I'm just glad you're safe."

"J, I love you."

His heart leapt. He tried to take her all in with his eyes. He wanted to remember this moment. She melted into his arms and he held her close.

"The night before...what day is this? It can't still be Sunday!" Her voice was muffled against his chest. "Then Saturday night, last night, I finally worked it all out."

"Honey," he interrupted, his voice rumbling in her ear against his chest, "you're tired. We'll talk in the morning." It was the first time he had used that term of endearment, yet it seemed so natural to both of them.

"No, all I thought about was telling you this. Let me finish." She pulled away to see him, so he could see her.

"J, I tried to forgive Earl but I could never seem to do it. Now I can. It's my life and now I'm in control of it. I'm not angry and I'm not afraid. I don't want to be alone. I want to be with you. When I made this decision, the anger just lifted from me."

Tears flowed down her cheeks. "J, I was afraid I wouldn't live long enough to tell you this." She nestled in his arms then and cried against his chest.

He held her tight, wanting nothing more than to bring her comfort. His heart, so recently heavy with fear, now felt light. He caressed her back and gently rocked her back and forth. The bed squeaked in response.

Her fatigue, even her soreness, faded in his tender embrace. How could she have resisted this for so long? The feel of him, his strength, his smell, his gentle touch consumed her. He raised himself on his elbow and cradled her face in his big hand as he gazed deep into her eyes. She knew she looked like a tractor had run over her, but only love radiated from his eyes, visible even through her blurriness. She felt his love, his breath on her cheek, his care to not hurt her, his tender kisses on her lips and neck, his urgent need.

She would never have to doubt this man. Every fiber of her being surrendered to him.

Chapter Twenty-Eight

*I*n her dream, Corrie walked endlessly, alone, searching for Al. She struggled for breath, could barely lift her feet to take another step. He wasn't where they had left him. She found him then, a skeleton, leaning against a tree. She screamed.

Corrie sat straight up in bed, embarrassed, and hoping the household hadn't heard.

J tried to calm her. "Don't worry about it. They'll understand. Try to go back to sleep." He spoke soothingly, holding her while he stroked her back and hair.

But every time she closed her eyes, she saw Al. She began to cry, trying to stifle the noise. She couldn't breathe; she was suffocating. Panicked, she sat up again.

J turned on the bedside lamp.

She pressed her fingers against her forehead. "I can't get Al out of my mind. It's so awful that he died. What a freakish thing to happen, having a branch fall on him. J, were we terrible to leave him? It seemed like we had to at the time." She took a shaky breath.

"Of course you weren't terrible, Corrie. You did have to leave him. You couldn't do him any good and you had to save yourselves."

"Can we go after him today?"

"Rick and I'll go up, maybe Kevin so he can get his car. But I don't want you to go."

"Why? I think I should."

"No, I want you to stay here."

"I don't understand..."

"You've been through enough. Besides, there's still a lot of ash in the air that would irritate your eyes even more. You need to see a doctor today. Other than that, stay inside and give them a rest. Anyway, you don't need to see that again, and I don't want you to."

She nodded. He was probably right, yet she should go, for Al. But J had gone through a lot of trouble and worry too. She needed to consider his feelings.

"Do you think it's safe?" She shuddered with the memory of the mountain.

"I don't know. We'll see. Let's try to get back to sleep."

The next time she woke, she was alone in bed. Fearing J had already left for the mountain, she quickly dressed in Barbara's shirt and jeans. Cinching the loose pants with a belt, she hurried upstairs. Everyone sat at the breakfast table, drinking coffee.

Barbara smiled as Corrie entered the cheery kitchen. "Good morning, Corrie. How about a cup of coffee?"

"Yes, thank you. I hope I didn't bother you early this morning. I had a bad dream."

"I heard you, but it didn't bother me. I knew you were in good hands." Barbara handed her a steaming mug of coffee.

Corrie slid into a chair next to Kevin. "How are you?"

He shrugged, his red-rimmed eyes downcast.

"Al?"

He nodded.

"I know." She felt guilty and knew Kevin did too. If they hadn't been so stupid to go up there in the first place....

Rick's sharp eyes darted between Corrie and Kevin. "Listen, you two. I don't know whose idea it was to go up there, it doesn't matter. These things happen. It wasn't your fault. It might not have been the smartest idea in the world, but it's what you guys wanted to do, you agreed to it, and you did it. You can spend the rest of your life playing `what if,' but the bottom line is that Al had an accident and didn't make it. You have no reason to feel guilty."

The tension in Corrie's shoulders relaxed as she absorbed Rick's words. She nodded and looked at Kevin.

He shrugged, "I guess."

Corrie put her hand on Kevin's. "Kevin, Al suggested we go in the first place. Not that it really matters whose idea it was, but I find some comfort in that. It was what he wanted to do, he wasn't trying to please us."

Kevin nodded. "That's true," He suddenly stood. "Excuse me. I want to find Al's camera and take that film out. Who knows, his pictures might be important, even famous."

Kevin turned in the kitchen doorway. "All right if I use the phone in your office? I want to call Joanne." He looked away, then added, "I should call the newspaper, too. I'll have to tell them about Al."

Barbara nodded. "Of course. Call anyone you need to. The camera bag is in the office, by the desk."

J looked at Corrie, his eyes warm with affection. "We were just talking about going back to the mountain to get Al's body, Kevin's car, my truck and the stock trailer."

He accepted a coffee refill from Barbara, nodding his thanks. "According to the morning news, all the highways are closed. Legally, those logging roads are probably closed too, but I'm for going up. The mountain seems to have calmed down, at least the heavy ash fall has stopped. Rescue crews will be there, too. I guess quite a few people are still up there."

Rick nodded. "Let's go right after breakfast." He glanced in the direction of the den. "Do you think Kevin is up to it?"

"I think it would do him good to get Al off the mountain. And he'll want to pick up his car. He needs to be busy."

It bothered Corrie not to be going too. "J, I think I should go."

"No." The tone of his voice closed the subject.

"I'll start breakfast," Barbara filled in the awkward silence. "Corrie, will you set the table?"

Kevin returned to the table, relieved that he'd been able to reach both Joanne and the newspaper. While Barbara poached eggs, J tried the phone again and managed to get through to Clearwater.

"Chad. J."

They all heard the explosion of Chad's voice. "Gretch! It's your dad!" His daughter squealed with delight. Then, to J Chad asked, "Are you okay? Did you find her?"

J held the phone away from his ear. They could all hear Chad's excited voice.

"Yeah, she's sitting right here at the breakfast table with me."

"Were you on the mountain when it blew?"

"No, I started out right after. Corrie and Kevin are fine, but Al didn't make it."

Chad started to ask more questions, but J cut him off. "Chad, I'll tell you all about it when we get home. How're you guys? Everything okay there?"

Chad reported that although everyone and the livestock were fine, they had to take feed out to the cattle since several inches of ash covered the ground. "It's like feeding the stock in winter, except it's not cold and this stuff doesn't melt. Weird. Tell Corrie I brought Bo over here. Moe's staying here too. We wanted everybody together."

J didn't have to tell her, she heard. "Ask how the horses are. How's Fancy?"

"Corrie wants to know how her horse is."

"She's fine. We bedded the horses down in the barn. We'll leave them there a couple of days, Moe said, then let 'em back in the corral."

"Sounds good. We can't get home today, the highways are all closed, but we'll try tomorrow. If we can't, I'll give you a call."

"Okay. Gretchen wants to talk to you."

"Dad? I knew you'd find her. She's okay?"

"A little banged up, but yeah, she's okay."

"All right. Now, Dad, hang on to her!"

He chucked. "Yes, ma'am, I intend to."

After J hung up, Barbara slipped poached eggs onto toast. "Corrie, I didn't know you had a horse."

"I don't really, but I've been using Nancy's horse, Fancy."

J's eyes sparkled. "Fancy's not Nan's horse, she's yours."

"What?" Too much had happened lately, she didn't get it.

"Fancy's your horse. I bought her from Nan for you."

Corrie's voice rose an octave. "Really?" She nearly dropped Rick's plate. He reached up and rescued it. "Whoa!"

Corrie rushed around the table and almost swept J off his chair.

"Hey, take it easy," he joked.

"Thank you." She blinked back tears, tears of joy. "I can't wait to get home and ride her."

After breakfast the men rigged Rick's truck with a homemade air filter, using the oversized filter from the tractor. J returned to the house to get a thermos of coffee and to fill an extra water jug while Rick filled gas cans from the ranch's tank.

They were alone in the kitchen. Corrie, uneasy about their going, shared her fears with J. "I'm uncomfortable with your going up there."

He gave her a wry look. "I know the feeling."

Corrie looked up at him with sad eyes.

J cradled her face in his hands. "We'll be fine. It may take us a while to do everything we need to do, but we're just going to take it easy and get it done." He kissed the tip of her nose.

"What will you do with Al?" Digging Al's body out of the ash would be a bleak job.

"I'm not sure. We'll figure it out. Corrie, don't worry.Everything will be fine. I want you to take it easy today and rest. Okay? And see a doctor about your eyes." He brushed her lips with his, then kissed her again more urgently. She returned the kisses, her blood warming to his touch.

The men loaded Rick's truck, already equipped with a winch, with every kind of tool they might need, plus spare filters, and a large tarp for Al's body.

Chapter Twenty-Nine

*A*s J, Rick and Kevin neared the mountain, a forest ranger, a hunting friend of Rick's, stopped them. Rick explained the reason for their trip, and the ranger allowed them to continue after giving them each a mask and insisting they wear them at all times while on the mountain.

After several hours of struggling with poor visibility from swirling ash, they managed to make their way to J's truck. They briefly checked it out, left it where it stood, then continued on to look for Al's body. The '78 Chevy that J had encountered before still blocked the road and Rick hooked it up to his winch and towed it to a wide spot. Then the Jeep. They cleared fallen trees and limbs off the road many times, sometimes having to cut them with the chainsaw. Because of the difficulties caused by swirling ash and foul air, each ordinary chore took longer and required more energy and skill than under normal circumstances.

As they climbed higher, driving proved even more difficult with several inches of slippery ash covering the road. It was slow going, even with Rick's rugged truck.

As they drew closer to the mountain itself, J felt as much as heard the pulsing "whump, whump" of helicopters overhead. A State Patrolman stopped them. Again, Rick explained their situation, making it sound like they had prior permission. After writing down their names, the patrolman said, "Okay, go ahead, then get out as quick as you can. Watch out for ground rescue teams and their dogs." The trooper shielded his eyes with his sleeve as a helicopter flew by, sending ash blasting down on them. "Those are National Guard helicopters up there. So far they've found more fatalities than survivors in the blast zone. You guys be careful." He waved them on.

They searched for the spot where Al lay. J dreaded seeing it again. He could only imagine how Kevin must feel. The strip of cloth that Kevin had tied to the high branch was thick with ash and nearly unrecognizable. Kevin spotted it first. "There."

J nodded, remembering his anxiety when he first saw the body and his relief that it hadn't been Corrie.

Al was buried in ash. Kevin carefully brushed away the debris from his friend's face. The body, already putrid from warm ash, had swollen. Kevin stepped aside and vomited.

Rick lifted the chainsaw out of the truck bed. "We'll have to cut away this branch." He cut two large sections of the limb and the three men hauled them off to the side of the road. Rick signaled J with his eyes and a flick of his head to get Kevin away from the body.

J indicated a bushy branch. "Kevin, how about hauling this off so we can get the truck through."

While Kevin was occupied with his task, Rick and J maneuvered themselves next to the body, lifted it onto the tarp and wrapped it, securing it with light rope.

Rick drove the truck as close as he could and the three of them gently lowered the body into the bed. They continued on to find Kevin's car. Kevin's face was set with grief, his eyes red rimmed. J prayed in thanksgiving that it wasn't Corrie's body they carried.

They continued higher up the mountain. "Are you sure we haven't passed it, Kevin?" J asked. "I didn't realize you guys had walked this far."

"Unless it's fallen down the bank, we haven't come to it yet. Everything looks different today, but I don't think we've passed it."

Finally Kevin spotted the once-white Subaru, still perched against the small tree. "I see it, but I don't know how we're going to get it out of there."

Rick let J and Kevin out. J fastened the winch to the tilting Subaru, then signaled to Rick. The car tipped precariously to one side, then righted itself with a lurch and Rick neatly pulled it out onto the narrow road.

"You guys make it look easy." Kevin walked around his car to assess the damage, grimacing at the dents and scratches.

"When you pull as many things out of ditches and mud holes as we have, it gets to be second nature." J unhooked the winch cable, again signaled Rick to reel it in.

Rick gave the car a quick inspection. "Kevin, I think we should tow it home, rather than horse around trying to fix it here. We can give it a look-over at the ranch and get it going, I think."

Kevin nodded, relieved. "I'd appreciate it. I don't think I could drive it through all this ash.

Besides, garages are probably up to their eyeballs with broken-down cars. There must not be much that you guys can't fix."

J snorted. "A rancher would go broke in a hurry if he couldn't fix his own equipment."

Rick maneuvered the truck to tow the car and they began their descent, crawling their way back down the eerie landscape. As they traveled, huge clouds of ash stirred. So far, the make-shift air filter arrangement on Rick's truck worked well, but they had to stop occasionally to clean it. No new ash fell, but a yellow sulfurous light made the scene unworldly. J couldn't wait to get home, to see Corrie and assure himself that she was all right.

They found J's truck in good enough shape, though of course they had the air filter problem. They rigged up another filter and before long had his truck operable. They cleared a spot so that J could maneuver the truck and stock trailer around.

Their little convoy continued on down the mountain. The original plan had been to take Al's body to the hospital morgue, or perhaps the sheriff's office, but they met a rescue party who told them to report to an emergency station set up nearby. At the station Kevin gave the authorities a statement and they left the body there. They were told that arrangements would be made, after an autopsy, to have Al's body taken to the morgue in Clearwater.

A paramedic offered them coffee. "From the radio reports it sounds like they're finding lots of people up there. But some didn't make it. We've had a lot of fatality reports."

He went on to tell them about a number of rescues he'd listened to on his short-wave radio, and about bodies recovered. "Some of the helicopters were disabled from that big ash cloud up there, but a few Huey pilots were able to get under the plume. Man, I'll tell you, their reports are harrowing."

He stepped over to the radio and attempted to fine-tune it to get rid of static.

"One of the pilots who knew this area really well became disoriented, the lay of the land has changed so much. 'Negative life,' they keep radioing back. So far, they've found no living thing in the blast zone. They found lots of evidence of people having been there, including a pickup truck with melted tires, but the occupants inside were dead."

J shook his head, remembering how afraid he'd been for Corrie. With good reason, apparently. His gut felt like it was weighted down with ash.

A helicopter pilot joined them and accepted a cup of coffee from the paramedic. "I'm just waiting to go up again, the mechanics are cleaning my machine now. It's clogged with ash."

Rick accepted a refill. "Pretty rough up there, I imagine."

"Oh, yeah. I've never seen anything like it. Inside the chopper it's 120 degrees. The mountain's created its own weather system with wild bolts of static electricity and bursts of hot wind. It makes flying pretty dicey. We can't fly much lower than fifty feet 'cause we kick up so much ash. We'd be flying in total blackout."

J set his coffee cup on the make-shift counter. "What kind of stuff are you seeing?" He really didn't want to know, but morbid curiosity prevailed.

"When I flew down the valley to what they're calling the blow-down zone, I could hardly believe it. Melting ice sent huge torrents of water down the slopes. The North Fork of the Toutle River is just a huge flow of mud now. Sometimes I get motion sickness from watching the mud, boulders, and hundred-foot trees crashing around down there. We've snatched folks from tree tops, or from rivers and mud flows." The pilot looked at each of them in turn, shaking his head.

J thought it probably felt good for the pilot to talk to someone about what he'd been through.

"We found some people alive in the blow-down zone, the pilot continued." You wouldn't believe how that looks, huge trees lying on the ground looking like just so many toothpicks. Thousands of 'em. All facing the same way on one side of the mountain, another way on the other side."

"How can you land in that mess?" Rick asked.

"We don't always. When we can, our crews lower lifelines to 'em. Other times we have to land a distance away so the victims aren't injured even more by being blasted with ash from the choppers' blades. Sometimes we lower a crewmember to guide the survivors to a pick-up spot. We're making it up as we go along."

"What's the spread of those blades?" Kevin's interview skills kicked in.

"Forty feet."

Another pilot joined them. "They're almost finished," he said to the first pilot as he accepted a cup of coffee.

"Are you seeing people who have been burned?" J asked, remembering the bear. He reached for his coffee cup, then decided against. If he put any more strain on his stomach, he really would be sick.

"Some," the new pilot answered. "That's how they died, burned to death or died of heat exposure. Family members of some fishermen asked us to check at Ryan Lake. I guess a party of five was up there, they rode in on horseback. We could land pretty close but there was nothing there but a few traces. People and horses, they'd all been incinerated. Even the PVC pipe used for a water system had melted." The pilot shook his head and closed his eyes at the memory.

"We met those folks," Kevin said. "They asked us to join them but we were already set up at Bear Meadow." His voice cracked. "My God. One of the guy's wife was expecting a baby in just a couple of weeks."

J put his hand on Kevin's shoulder. "Sounds like it was a good thing you didn't join 'em."

The pilot nodded. "I think we'll find a lot more like that. Some of them aren't that bad but their clothes are burned and the soles of their shoes melted. One group of four I picked up didn't have eyebrows or eyelashes, they'd been seared off."

The other pilot spoke up. "Not all of them are injured though. I picked up a family of four who hid in a cave. Nobody injured there. The family heard our helicopter and stood out in the open so we could see them. Their camp looked like a bombing range. I couldn't believe they lived through it."

The paramedic refilled the pilots' coffee cups. "One ground rescue crew found a station wagon above Camp Baker on the North Fork of the Toutle. Outside the car they found a man's body; inside the car was the body of a woman next to a satchel of cocaine and a roll of $100 dollar bills. Can you believe that? Business as usual.

"I guess a few of the scientists who were working up here died. I knew one of them, Dave Johnston. Had dinner in town with him one night. He was a geologist and a real popular fellow. He was the one that warned everybody on his radio when it blew. 'Vancouver, Vancouver, this is it.' I guess those were his last words." He shook his head. "Dave was camped about six miles northwest of the volcano at Coldwater II and now the helicopter pilots say they can't find a trace of even where his trailer was. Scary, huh?"

Kevin turned away from the others, his hand to his head.

The paramedic continued, "Remember hearing about that stubborn old codger, Harry Truman? They can't even find where his place was. It's gone. Spirit Lake is buried. There isn't a chance he survived."

Until talking with the paramedic and the pilots, J hadn't realized the utter horror of the blast, the widespread devastation.

As they talked, the paramedic kept one ear cocked to the radio. "We just had one report of a couple twenty-five miles from the blast who died, their cameras still in their hands."

Kevin shook his head. "It sounds like they were farther north than we were."

The paramedic held up his hand. "Another report is coming in now."

They listened to a helicopter pilot's static-filled radio report. The chopper crew had spotted a camping trailer and were able to land nearby. Upon investigation they found an older couple inside, both dead.

Another report faded in and out. From what they gathered, a young couple had been found in their tent, clinging to each other, dead.

They stayed awhile, listening as the reports came in.

J shook his head. "I'm glad I didn't know about this yesterday."

Rick threw his empty Styrofoam cup into a trash bin. "Let's go home." They drove on, silenced with shock.

* * *

Corrie's day dragged on interminably. The doctor's visit confirmed that her eyes were scratched, but he assured her they would heal, and gave her medication. Once home, Barbara tried to keep her occupied. They baked cookies, watched TV news of the eruption, and prepared supper, but Corrie spent much of her time squinting through light-sensitive eyes out the window overlooking the road leading to the ranch, waiting. Her eyes felt better, but were puffy and inflamed. Emotionally drained, she worried about the men and their safety on the mountain. She fought waves of guilt for having caused their dangerous trip in the first place.

J's mother, Maude, finally got through the jammed phone lines to see how everyone had fared. She had known nothing about Corrie being on the mountain nor about J going after her. "I'm glad I didn't know. I would have been worried sick." To Maude's credit and Corrie's relief, the outspoken woman didn't question why Corrie had been on the mountain.

In the late afternoon the men returned, Rick's truck towing Kevin's car and J pulling the stock trailer. Ash rose like huge rooster-tails behind them. The three men entered the house, grim and exhausted.

Corrie flew into J's arms and they gently rocked back and forth, oblivious to the others' indulgent smiles. The men told Corrie and Barbara all they had done and of the reports they'd heard.

Kevin's sad eyes settled on Corrie. "Harry Truman's gone, Corrie, they couldn't even find where his place had been. And so is that scientist, Dave Johnston. I really liked him. And those guys at Ryan Lake..." He left the room.

Although Corrie was thankful she and Kevin were alive, when she thought of Al and all the others who had lost their lives, she felt deep sadness. And regret.

As the men talked further about their day, Corrie was astounded by the high death toll. "It seemed pretty horrible to me at the time, but it could have been a lot worse for us."

Rick leveled a finger at Corrie. "You try another hare-brained stunt like that and I'll haul your ass home myself and I won't be as gentle as my brother."

Corrie's bloodshot eyes widened, but she realized Rick needed to blow off steam. Her eyes slid over to J. The corners of his mouth twitched, holding back a smile.

Barbara reached up and tenderly patted her husband's thick neck. "We have a lot to be thankful for. Let's eat. Everything's ready.

Chapter Thirty

*E*arly next morning Corrie wandered out to the equipment shed to watch J and Rick thoroughly clean Kevin's car engine. Kevin helped when he could, but the McClures knew so much more about mechanics. They got the car running and equipped it with another homemade air filter, as they had done with the trucks. The car looked like it had been in a war zone, paint blistered, dented and scratched from falling debris, but at least it ran.

"Thanks, you guys, for everything." Kevin hesitated, then looked J squarely in the eye. "J, I'm sorry about—"

J interrupted. "No need, Kevin. I'm glad you two are safe, and I'm sorry about Al, but you don't owe me an apology."

"Anyway, I appreciate your coming for us. You sure were a welcomed sight."

J nodded, then chuckled. "Yeah, you looked like you could use a ride, even on a mule."

"My first." Kevin rubbed his beard-stubbled chin ruefully. "And last, I hope."

Snowplows and heavy earth-moving equipment cleared ash from the main roads and freeways, and State Patrol opened some highways for travel. Kevin prepared to leave first, again thanking everyone for their hospitality.

Corrie was surprised and delighted when, as Kevin climbed into his car, J suggested, "Kevin, you and Joanne come out to see us. We'd be pleased to have you."

Kevin beamed. "Great, thanks. We'll take you up on that." He glanced at Corrie and nodded.

J and Corrie lingered a few more minutes, talking with Rick and Barbara.

Corrie stood in front of J, his arms around her waist. He tilted his head and looked down at her. "Well, Corrie, shall we head for home?"

Corrie leaned her head ahead against his chest and sighed with gusto. "Yes."

They packed their few things into the bed of J's truck, tucking them under a tarp to protect them from ash, knowing it was a useless effort. The ash penetrated everything.

Rick gave Corrie a hug. "I'm glad you're safe."

"Me, too." Corrie nodded, comfortable with Rick and Barbara. They were already like family. "Thanks for everything."

As they drove down the long driveway, Corrie noticed a blanket of ash already covering the tarp. Would she ever see the last of this infernal grit?

Even though ash had been cleaned from roadways, traffic kicked up clouds of it again, limiting visibility. Corrie, her nerves jittery, could hardly wait until they reached home. J stopped a few times to clean his air filter. They saw many cars stalled along the highway. At one point, J stopped and offered to tow a car to a repair shop a few miles ahead in Yakima. The driver accepted gratefully.

J had his hands full, driving under these difficult conditions. Corrie enjoyed watching him, not caring that she was staring.

At one point he said, his voice playfully gruff, "What are you looking at?"

"You. I can't get enough of you."

He took his eyes off the road for a second, glanced her way and grinned. "Well, I like the sound of that."

Corrie again gave thanks for being there, alive, and with a man she loved with a passion she'd never before felt. "J, I'd like to start going to church again. I used to go; in fact, I was really active."

"I'd like that, too. Sometimes I feel bad that Gretchen hasn't been going, either."

"Once, when I was riding, I came across that cute little white church near your property. I stopped and listened to them sing. It was wonderful."

"The people I bought the ranch from donated the property to that church, gave 'em two acres. It's right on the ranch's western boundary. It's a community church, non-denominational. We're actually members."

"Really? Let's go there."

He nodded and glanced at her. "It's a deal."

As they approached Clearwater, they found conditions similar to Randle, everything was covered with ash. Townspeople were already using heavy equipment, or hand shovels, to blow or shovel ash off streets, roofs and crops. Ash made the day overcast, unlike a usual May day in Eastern Washington.

Ash piled thickly on the ranch's entry arch, but the Circle J was still visible. As they passed under it, Corrie breathed deeply. "Oh, boy, am I glad to be home."

She glanced up at the ranch logo. "Circle J. J for James, J for joy, for jubilation—"

"How about J for Just Married?"

"Now," she leaned over to kiss him, "there's an idea."

About the Author

For a city girl, Mary E. Trimble writes about ranch life with conviction. Many *Tenderfoot* reviewers have made reference to "Trimble's obvious ranching background." One reader said it was as though she had been lurking around their ranch during spring calving. Good research pays off.

Although ranching has always been a fascination for Trimble, she knew that for her novels to ring true, she needed to know the inner workings of ranching. How many acres does it take to support "x" number of cattle in Eastern Washington? When cattle are vaccinated, from what diseases are they protected? Spring roundup? Fall roundup? What's the difference?

Before writing her earlier contemporary western, *Rosemount*, Trimble wrangled an invitation from one of the largest ranches in Washington where she saw the inner workings of a large cattle operation, participated in spring roundup and experienced first-hand the smells (lots of them), dust, noise and grueling hard work of ranching.

When researching the eruption of Mount St. Helens for *Tenderfoot*, Trimble visited the mountain and the surrounding communities, interviewing people who fought for survival after the eruption and those who were involved in search and rescue.

Trimble lives with her husband on Camano Island, Washington. Four children and six grandchildren, most of who live in the Northwest, play an important role in their lives. For more information about the author and her other books, visit www.MaryTrimbleBooks.com.

Made in the USA
Charleston, SC
15 October 2016